THE 6PM FRAZZLED MUMS' CLUB

NINA MANNING

Boldwood

First published in Great Britain in 2023 by Boldwood Books Ltd.

Copyright © Nina Manning, 2023

Cover Design by Alice Moore Design

Cover Photography: Shutterstock and iStock

The moral right of Nina Manning to be identified as the author of this work has been asserted in accordance with the Copyright, Designs and Patents Act 1988.

Every effort has been made to obtain the necessary permissions with reference to copyright material, both illustrative and quoted. We apologise for any omissions in this respect and will be pleased to make the appropriate acknowledgements in any future edition.

A CIP catalogue record for this book is available from the British Library.

Paperback ISBN 978-1-80426-578-9

Large Print ISBN 978-1-80426-579-6

Hardback ISBN 978-1-80426-580-2

Ebook ISBN 978-1-80426-576-5

Kindle ISBN 978-1-80426-577-2

Audio CD ISBN 978-1-80426-585-7

MP3 CD ISBN 978-1-80426-584-0

Digital audio download ISBN 978-1-80426-582-6

Boldwood Books Ltd
23 Bowerdean Street
London SW6 3TN
www.boldwoodbooks.com

For all the frazzled mums (and dads), go to what makes your heart sore and your stomach flip.

1

SOPHY

It was precisely three minutes past 9 a.m. on Wednesday, 7 September when Sophy finally lost all decorum outside Oak Hill Primary Academy.

A few other parents and carers who were still in the vicinity, who also couldn't bear to step outside the school gates just yet for fear of being the furthest they had ever been from their four- and five-year-old children in as many years, turned and looked on. Some with empathy for the sudden outburst, some with fear, as if just looking at Sophy's wailing would make it contagious. Those hurried away. Sophy stood and looked at the care package she had been handed by the teacher, Mrs Williams, when she walked Max into his classroom ten minutes ago. A teabag and a chocolate coin wrapped in a piece of paper. Sophy let the tears fall freely, her other hand pressed to her chest, as though that might help the pain that was searing through her and tearing her heart in two.

Max was only four years old. Saying goodbye to him wasn't the hard part, the hard part was that she wouldn't get to know everything he had done all day. The harder part was that he wasn't her baby any more. He was a 'big boy, Mummy' as he told her regularly, which hurt her heart more than she would admit to anyone.

Over the last four and a half years, Sophy had become used to saying goodbye to Max. Fortunately for her, though, it was so sporadic that she only had to put up with the crushing feeling in her chest once a week at the very most. When Sophy had first moved out when Max was a baby, her ex, Jeff, would call around all the time, trying to assert his fatherly rights as often as he could. There she was, alone in the two-bedroomed flat Aisha and Mel had helped move her into after she left Jeff, and they would dance around each other on the doorstep, her handing him a neatly packed nappy bag, him trying to avoid eye contact. Occasionally in those early days he would show up unannounced and demand to see Max. Sophy would allow him his time, but because she was still breastfeeding, he would take Max to a café and bring him home exactly an hour later, looking like a man who had just completed a triathlon. His usually slick blond hair would be ruffled and out of place, his shirt would have sick or coffee spilled on it and the once neatly packed nappy bag would have used wet wipes, bottles and sippy cups falling out of it. He would deliver Max back with relief seeping into his expression.

By the time she'd stopped breastfeeding Max, Jeff had already begun to lose interest in him and the mystery woman whose face cream had taken up residence on Sophy's side of the bed was never mentioned. Later on, a few women's names were dropped into conversation until Debbie came along and didn't leave for a while. Debbie had been good for Jeff and Sophy had even felt herself warm to her. Knowing there was a constant female presence in Jeff's house whenever Max went there to stay was a slight comfort.

'I'll get on better with him when he's walking, and I can kick a ball around with him,' Jeff said as Max began to toddle and went from a babe in arms to becoming a real handful.

'Kick a ball around?' Sophy had asked. 'Jeff, there's more to being a dad than kicking a ball around.'

The one area Jeff always came through with was financial support. She could never fault him for the generous allowance that he put in her bank account every month and never once questioned what she did with the money. Although Sophy was doing pretty well on her own. The 3 a.m. Shattered Mums' Podcast had hit the ground running with fourteen series under her belt. Sophy could never have imagined that meeting two strangers outside a cancelled mother and baby group could have led to anything, let alone a wonderful friendship between her, Aisha and Mel, which had not only helped her through the night feeds but had also given her the inspiration to create an actual 3 a.m. Shattered Mums' Club online. Sophy had almost a million followers on Instagram and she had just begun designing merchandise. She was also looking into retreats where mums could escape the madness for a few days and just 'be' with their babies. The 3 a.m. Shattered Mums' Club had become an overnight success, with Mel and Aisha occasionally popping on the socials and the podcast to support Sophy.

'Oh, God, he's really gone. My baby boy is now...' Sophy looked across the playground and felt the tears welling again and anyone might have thought she was completely bonkers and speaking to herself, but then she bent down and picked up the soft toy rabbit that was on the floor and turned and handed it to the little girl in the pushchair.

'There you go, Poppy.'

'Mama sad?'

'Yes, darling, Mama is sad. I'm going to miss Max today. Will you miss him?'

Poppy nodded fiercely. Her strawberry-blonde locks shook because Poppy always put so much emphasis on everything she did, it was the personality trait that overrode anything else about her, although there was much to love. But it was Poppy's earnestness that accompanied most things she said or did that made her stand out from other little people her age. It was a trait that Sophy believed Poppy had inherited from her father, who was dedicated, committed and the hardest-working individual she had ever known. And just at exactly the point Sophy thought she might fall to her knees next to Poppy's pushchair and cry some more, her phone rang, and she knew it would be him. She looked at the screen and her heart soared, and her stomach did a micro flip as she saw Niall's name was on the screen.

'Hi,' Sophy said, the sadness still thick in her voice.

'How'd it go?' Niall's voice came through urgently, yet the softness of his Irish accent soothed her, the way it had the very first time she had heard it that day on Jeff's doorstep when he arrived to build the extension. 'Did the little man go in okay?'

As though Sophy had been holding it all in, as if those first few tears had been a prelude to what had been brewing, Sophy now finally let rip and sobbed loudly and unapologetically. And Niall waited patiently on the other end until Sophy had calmed down.

'I take it it didn't go well,' Niall said.

'No... it... was fine... he was fine.'

'Oh, right, so you're crying happy tears?' Niall sounded confused.

'No. I'm crying because...' Sophy paused, intent on holding it together. 'Because he doesn't need me any more,' she wailed.

'Oh, Soph, no, see, you've got it wrong; he needs you more than ever. This is an exciting adventure for him, he is a very confident young man, strong, I always told you that. You should be proud. I've seen some horrors in me time, kids hanging onto the clothes of their parents, having to be physically removed to go into school. No, you'll see, he'll be aching for your arms later.'

Sophy heard the reassuring tone and words and let out a sigh.

'Now, is my little Poppy there?' Niall asked.

'I should hope so, and that she hasn't skipped off into school as well.'

'Well, won't be long, will it, couple of years—'

'Niall, stop it! You were doing so well.'

'Oh, right, sorry. Yeah. No, Pops is tiny, loads of time with her yet. Put her on.'

Sophy rolled her eyes but obliged Niall and handed the phone to Poppy, who at two and half held it very steadily and proceeded to engage in conversation with her daddy.

Sophy looked on, fascinated by the whole process, the very fact that Niall was asking after his daughter and wanted to engage in conversation with her even though she was only two, still amazed her. But the fact that Niall had called and asked after Max, who was not his son, warmed her heart so much. She knew she wouldn't hear from Jeff until much later, if at all, and that he would simply send a text. Something short and arrogant, with reference to Max being 'his son'. He still felt he needed to assert that parental authority over Niall over three years later.

Jeff's ego was well and truly bruised. He knew he couldn't be the father Max needed him to be and he was clearly missing Debbie but would never admit it. Debbie had obviously seen him for what he truly was, the way Sophy had. Sophy found it interesting that she had been with Jeff for around four years. Debbie didn't quite manage four years in the end.

Sophy had clocked Jeff's new Instagram photo, an image of him topless and tanned, wearing aviators, holding a beer, with that smile that had seduced her all those years ago. He hadn't been able to be the partner that Sophy had needed him to be, and it was only once she was well and truly out of that relationship and had begun to let Niall in that she began to see some of the gaping differences between them. With Niall, she truly knew what a real man was and what being a father to her son looked like. Max may be Jeff's biological son, but Niall had made his mark on Max's heart a long time ago. In Sophy's eyes, it was Niall who was his real daddy.

'Mama.' Poppy was holding the phone in the air at Sophy.

'Oh, thank you.' Sophy looked at the screen, but Niall was no longer on the call.

'Did you hang up on Dada?'

Sophy bashed out a text to Niall.

Think Pops hung up on you. I love you, thank you for checking up on me and for the reassuring words. I'll see you later x.

Sophy began getting her stuff together, ready to walk home, when Niall texted her back.

Oh no, she said bye and everything, and ended the call. I love you too. X

Sophy looked at Poppy, who was swinging her legs and twirling her hair around one finger.

'You're a funny little thing, aren't you?' And she began pushing the pushchair home. Home was a three-bedroom semi-detached in Putney. A house that she and Niall had chosen and bought together as soon as she'd found out she was pregnant with Poppy. The mortgage was astronomical, and they would be paying it off until they were seventy, but it was worth it. It had three nice-sized bedrooms, wooden floors throughout, an open-plan kitchen diner and a garden that was big enough for Max and Poppy to run around in, with a shaded patio area for reading and relaxing and where Sophy could sit and watch her children play. Occasionally Sophy would wonder what it would be like to live in a bigger property out in the countryside, somewhere with a utility room and a boot room, with a garden that led onto the woods. She knew Niall would love that too. When Sophy had been with Jeff, she had often daydreamed about what else she wanted; a bigger house, nicer furniture, but not once since she and Niall had bought this house had she felt she *needed* anything else. Except for maybe one thing, but she wasn't sure if she was ready to tell Niall that yet.

2

AISHA

The house felt strange without the twins in it, and it wasn't because Aisha wasn't used to having time without the boys, it was because Aisha knew they were at school. It was a milestone, something she had battled with for years. The notion that one day it would be here, not wanting time to go past but also feeling desperate for her freedom. It felt like a lifetime ago when Aisha had met Sophy and Mel outside the village hall. She had been battling depression after having her twin boys, Otis and Jude, and trying to deal with her emotions alone. Suddenly having the girls around and being instrumental in bringing to life the 3 a.m. Shattered Mums' Club had given her back the confidence she had forgotten she had.

Now, four years on, she was filled with an overbearing sense of guilt. Christ, when would it end? The twins had started school today and she was still filled with guilt. Now because they were *at* school. Their baby-hood was over and she, as well as her girlfriend Charley, was now mother to two young boys, and the guilt was there because she wondered if she had, at times, wished it all away.

She went into the kitchen and did the one thing she had been unable to do properly for so many years, she baked. Because even with Otis and Jude being slightly more independent, they were forever getting into mischief, leaving Aisha with so very little time to do anything. She had lost count of how many times she had begun a job and had to abort halfway through because one of the twins was in a predicament or was about to cause major damage. The boys had gone to pre-school two days a week but who could get anything done in two days? Aisha would spend the first day just sitting in silence, in total shock that she was alone and that the twins were being cared for. Charley had grasped the quiet time and disappeared into her recording studio in the basement. Now they would be away for five days at a time and she could almost see time stretching in front of her like a vast ocean, where Friday was a very small island on the horizon. Oh, it felt so good to have the kitchen to herself with a large amount of time to play with and to achieve multiple things, but there it was, that bloody guilt, creeping in and tapping her on the shoulder, checking in with her, drawing attention to her sudden sense of freedom. When would it end? Perhaps it never would. She had heard that as a parent, no matter how old they get, you never stop worrying; she wondered if that was the same for guilt.

She pulled out flour and sugar and baking powder and spices and began making the boys' favourite, sticky gingerbread. She had been so busy with name labels and uniforms the last few days that she hadn't had a chance to do much else. This way, she could stock up the baking tin and even pop some bits in the freezer for emergencies.

Whilst the cake was in the oven, her phone rang and her father's name flashed up on the screen. Jon. She had left his name on her phone how she had put it in there that first week after he came back into her life after twenty years. Even though now she was happy to call him her father again.

'Hey, Dad,' Aisha said as she looked in on the cake, which was rising beautifully.

'Just checking to see those boys got off to school okay?'

'Yes, they did, thank you, thanks for ringing. Is Mum with you?'

'Yes, she's in bed, though.'

'Oh.' Aisha had been wondering why she hadn't heard anything from her mum this morning, it was unusual, as Aisha had been fretting over the boys' first school day for weeks with her mother.

She thought it was sweet that her dad was trying to do the right thing and stand in for her mum. Aisha knew that he wasn't interested in how his grandsons had got on walking into school on their first day. It wasn't that he didn't care about them, Aisha had seen some very caring tendencies over the past few years since her father had been back in her life. Jon still bore the markings of a man hardened by a childhood where kids were expected to get on with things, never allowed to speak up about their feelings and there had certainly not been any such thing as mental well-being back then. Which was one of the reasons Jon had gone on to suffer as an adult before finally finding his way back into their lives. But things had been pretty good over the last four years since he'd come back.

The most surprising outcome was the way her mother and father had just picked up from where they had left off, as though the two-decade break was exactly what was required. Their relationship was healthier than it had ever been. Six months after showing back up, Jon had moved back into their home in Brixton and sometimes Aisha could believe that he had always been there. But the echoes of the last twenty years were in every nook of the old house and would often sneak back out to greet her, reminding her that Jon wasn't a part of all of their memories. Aisha would remember when Martina would creep off to her bedroom and cry silent tears, which Aisha would hear through the wall of the bedroom she shared with her two sisters.

But he was making up for lost time and here he was, letting her know her mother was unwell.

'Is she okay?'

'I'd say it's just a cold. She always used to get them after you kids went back to school after the summer holidays, do you remember? It was like she had used all her energy up with your sisters and your cousins and then she crashed. I reckon she's done the same this time with the boys.'

Oh, no, Aisha thought. Had she managed to burn her poor mother out with the twins over the summer holidays? It had been a long hot summer and Aisha had wanted to do so much as they were the last days of freedom before school and routines began. But Martina had wanted to be a part of everything and had insisted she come on a lot of the excursions Aisha had booked.

'Well, can you tell her I will pop and see her this week? And tell her to stay in bed and rest and not try and come over until she is better.'

'I will. All right, give those boys a kiss from us and we'll see you soon.'

'Bye, Dad.'

Aisha ended the call, and felt the tears that had been burning in her eyes begin to fall. It had been a tough morning already, what with dropping the boys to school, but there was a tone to her father's voice that she wasn't sure about. As though maybe he was hiding something from her, something about her mother.

It didn't matter that the boys were now at school, and she had one, or rather two less things to worry about for a few hours a day, her mother's health now played on her mind. Even though Martina was still not yet even sixty years old and was as tough as a workhorse, Aisha felt the familiar drag of worry, the one that had hounded her for years as the boys grew up fighting off every illness, follow her around for the rest of the day.

3

MEL

She could sense the mothers descending on her like a pack of wolves. Mel had that look about her, the one that drew women towards her in one of two ways: shy and slow or like a bullet. And there was something about primary school mums that made them want to form clans and bring in as many outsiders as possible. And Mel just knew they were coming for her. She had been here already back in the day when her eldest daughter, Leia, was small. But that was over a decade ago, and Mel did not remember there being nearly as much emphasis on adult participation. She had got away with keeping her head down and not really getting involved. But she could feel the atmosphere in the play-ground charging. There was an expectation brewing all around her. Everyone wanted a piece of everyone else. Mel almost wished she could go back to when Sky was a baby. She had already forgotten the roller coaster that had been having another baby in her early forties. Although she and Daz had planned Skylar, it was still a shock to her system, especially when those all-nighters kicked in around three months old. She wasn't sure she would have gotten through it if it weren't for Sophy and Aisha and their 3 a.m. Shattered Mums' Club WhatsApp group.

'Hi, you're Skylar's mummy, aren't you?' came a voice from behind her and not surprisingly. Mel had almost been on tenterhooks, waiting for someone to get their claws into her. There were two women ahead of her that Mel was sure would be the ones to reach her first, but someone had clearly intercepted them and snuck up from behind. The two women in front of her began to back off, defeated by this bolder predator.

Mel was being greeted by the most pristine-looking woman she had ever seen. She was sure she actually gasped. The shock of seeing someone so well turned out on a school run, almost distracted her from the fact that she had been addressed as 'mummy' by a grown woman – only her four-year-old daughter could be expected to refer to her as that.

Mel plastered an inane grin across her face. She had tried to prepare herself for this moment. She had hoped it would have been much like it was the first time round and she could have blended into the background. Mel knew that there had been developments in the world of the school playground mum. This she knew from mum friends who had children a few years older than Sky but not as old as Leia, her other daughter, who was older by eleven years. They had evolved. There were actual PTAs as opposed to a few mums who always ran the stall at the Christmas fete, and there was a serious expectation to bake the best cakes for the cake sales and to be part of the Facebook group. For the love of God!

'I am Skylar's mum, yes,' Mel said, asserting herself to the best of her ability, but she was tired. Mel had been feeling out of sorts last night. Maybe because it was Sky's first day at school, which was another milestone to tick off. That was it, no more babies. It wasn't that Mel was aching for another infant to cradle – although she would happily take any of her friends' babies for half an hour, knowing she could hand them back – but because she knew that was it done. She was done. That whole first part of her life: meet the man, tick. Get married, tick. Have a couple of babies, tick. What was there left to do? They had been so wrapped up in having Leia and then having Sky that knowing that raising babies was over made Mel feel bit redundant. It had come at her hard last night when she had been packing

Sky's bag; the feeling, which was a mild fear and panic, had gripped her.

Sky hadn't wanted to go to sleep last night either. First-day nerves. Sky kept going to check that she had everything in her bag and then checking that Mel had made the right sandwich for her lunchbox and Mel had to keep reminding her that she was about to go into reception, and she didn't need anything in her bag. She had chosen a fluorescent backpack from Smiggle which was half the size she was and then, of course, needed the entire bundle of lunchbox case, pencil case, and drink bottle to match. Mel had stumbled at the till when the assistant rang up the price.

'Are you f... kidding me?' Mel had almost inserted a swear but stopped herself in time. 'For a kids' rucksack?' The assistant, a young girl not much older than Leia, had looked at her and shrugged. Mel had shaken her head.

'How can you sleep at night?' Mel had added as she had reluctantly pulled out her debit card and at the same time looked down at her daughter, who was looking up at her with a sweet, coy expression that made Mel's heart almost burst out of her chest.

'Thank you, Mummy,' Sky had said as they left the shop and Mel realised that all faith in the universe was restored and despite extortionate prices of stationery, it was the love from her four-year-old daughter that she wished to add up.

Mel assessed the woman in front of her again. Mel took pride in her appearance and had even thought long and hard about her outfit for this morning – she went for her best red berry yoga pants and grey sweatshirt. But this woman was dazzling.

'I'm Saskia.' Saskia flicked her hair wildly then she leaned in closer conspiratorially. 'Me and some of the mums are thinking of starting up a WhatsApp group.' Saskia's eyes widened with intrigue, as though it were Mel who had just told her that piece of information. 'How fabulous is that?' Saskia said smugly.

Mel felt the hairs on the back of her neck go up, as though she were watching a horror movie and the lead female was about to walk into an abandoned house. *Don't do it*, came the words catapulting through her head. Mel was a contented member of two WhatsApp groups. One with her, Daz, Daz's parents Irene and Mike, and Leia, who at almost sixteen felt she was an adult and didn't want to miss out on any family gossip. Then there was her beloved 3 a.m. Shattered Mums' Club, still going strong after four years, although not so many 3 a.m. chats these days. And that was enough. That was all she needed. She'd heard stories of mums entering into what they believed was a harmless WhatsApp chat group only to be bombarded with hundreds of messages a week. And Mel was not going to join a chat group just to end up as one of the quiet ones who looked at all the messages but rarely involved herself. Because in reality that was the very opposite of who she was and so she wasn't going to display some watered-down version of herself on a messaging app.

Mel looked the woman up and down in that briefest of ways that most women would have totally clocked. Saskia seemed oblivious.

'My son is Fin,' Saskia continued when Mel didn't automatically respond to the WhatsApp group comment. Saskia cocked her head as if Mel should know who Fin was, but Mel was terrible at names at the best of times, and even more so when she was trying to match the faces to the names of boys who were all three feet with short hair.

'Yes, Fin, my little miracle baby. I wasn't sure I would ever conceive and then voila! There he was.' Saskia was offering far more information than Mel was ready to receive at this time of the morning. Then Saskia leaned in towards Mel. 'I say, us first-time geriatric mums need to stick together, don't we? We're still in the minority, after all. Need to show these whippersnappers that we have just as much energy as they do, plus twice the lifetime of experience.'

'Oh, Sky's not my first.' Mel looked over at her Sky who was playing on the bars. 'I have a fifteen-year-old daughter as well.' Mel couldn't get that piece of information across fast enough. 'And a seven-year-old Labrador, who sometimes thinks she is human.'

Saskia snapped her neck back and looked momentarily perturbed. 'Oh, well, get you, you will have to teach me a few things, let me know what I have coming.'

Fin. Where had she heard that name before? Then it hit her. Sky had gone to the nursery next door to the school for two years, two days a week, but Daz had always been the one to drop her in the morning as the start times coincided with his working hours. Mel would swoop in at round 4.30 and collect her, rarely seeing any of the other parents or carers, and Sky would rattle away in her pushchair about things she had done that day. Fin was a name Mel had heard Sky mention more than once. And never in a nice context.

'Fin bent my finger back, Fin bit me, Fin called me a poo poo head.' All the complaints suddenly came back to her at once, words she had neglected to really hear at the time because Mel had been processing her own thoughts at pre-school pick up and Sky's voice had been a background sound to them. There was always one child who was the class bully, and it seemed Fin was the one. And now his mother Saskia seemed to want to be her friend. Oh, this was not going to work; this was not going to work at all.

* * *

5.45 p.m. – Sophy – Well I was a ruddy mess. Cried like a baby in the playground, and when I got home and read the poem that came with the teabag, my God, that was it. I was a puddle on the floor. An actual puddle.

5.51 p.m. – Mel – Teabag? Bloody teabag? We at least deserve a flipping can of gin or something for the last four years we've just endured. You've got a box of teabags in your cupboard I presume, Sophy? It's quite condescending isn't it?

5.55 p.m. – Aisha – It's a token gift, Mel. I was the same as Sophy. Bit of a mess then not sure what to do with myself all day. I baked in the end and now have six loaves and traybakes. I think the teabag thing is a nice gesture, it's just their way of saying go home, put your feet up and don't worry about your little one. They will be safe with us.

6.01 p.m. – Mel – It's their way of saying we're suckers for introducing our kids into the system. She's now on her way to becoming another brick in the wall. You know I actually considered home schooling her. Well, the thoughts are still fierce. I will see how reception goes for her but already there was this mum – called me geriatric when she was clearly several years older than me – anyway, her 'Fin' is a little bully, and she is trying to bosom buddy with me. I had to feign a phone call when she tried to get my number off me. Please tell me none of you are in WhatsApp groups already?

6.02 p.m. – Aisha – No. No way. I'm not going down that road. I'm in enough with you and all my family.

6.04 p.m. – Sophy – Absolutely not, you will not be catching me signing up to any flipping WhatsApp groups.

4

SOPHY

'So that's 367 at the end.' The woman that Sophy had just come to know as Blythe was tapping her mobile number into her own phone. 'Great. I'll set the group up this afternoon and then hopefully we can think of some ideas to help the PTA out. And, well, it's just so much easier when there are lost PE kits and we want to organise a play date and my goodness, I just don't how we managed without WhatsApp before.' Blythe wittered on and Sophy felt a pang of sadness for the woman. It was her default emotion and the one that got her in trouble a lot. She ended up feeling sorry for people and saying yes to things when she really didn't mean to.

Once Max had reached about eight months old and she had begun to wean him off the boob a little, she noticed the damn trait came back into play in full force. No sooner was one person a little less reliant on her than she felt she needed to give that small part of herself away to someone else. And now Poppy was two and a half and her own little person, and Max was at school, Sophy did have a little more time to herself, in between school and nursery drop-offs and doing all the bits she did for the 3 a.m. Shattered Mums' Club. She had once heard someone say, 'If you want something doing, ask a busy person,' and that was a motto Sophy felt she lived her life by as she was usually busy but always found she got things done. As much as she complained, and longed for endless days doing nothing and not having to think about anyone but herself, she felt she needed to be busy to justify something, she wasn't sure what, her very existence maybe? Growing up with a lot of siblings in a tiny terraced house with so much going on and never really being able to get a minute's peace would do that to you, she supposed. As much as she hated to admit it and wished she could be someone who was happy doing nothing, she enjoyed a certain manicness to her life; that notion that another deadline was looming on the horizon.

'Thank you, Blythe, I'm looking forward to... hearing from you.' Sophy grinned.

'And you too, don't think I don't know all about you and your Shattered Mums' Club, I want to be a part of that. I have four kids and I think I deserve an accolade sometimes.'

'You have four kids?' To Sophy, Blythe looked about late twenties and because Sophy was never backwards in coming forwards, she just asked, 'How old are you? If you don't mind me asking?'

Blythe laughed. 'No, of course not, I get asked this a lot. In fact, I only just stopped getting asked for ID when I buy alcohol. Well, it's been six months since I was last asked so who knows, anyway, I'm thirty-four.'

'Wow! I did think you were in your twenties, though.' Sophy felt a pang of envy at this woman who was three years younger than her but looked ten years younger. Sophy had found it hard slipping towards her late thirties. She had just given birth to Poppy and the hormones, plus a bout of post-natal depression, had meant she had catastrophised over hitting thirty-six. Even though she had Niall now, even though she was a successful businesswoman, even though it appeared on the surface she had nothing to worry about, the black dog had still come to stay. Niall had been immensely supportive – he'd watched his own mother go through it with three of his siblings – whilst she tried to figure out how to feel a little bit more like herself again.

Aisha had been an absolute diamond too because she had been through it with the twins, although she admitted it wasn't as acute as Sophy's suffering. And, of course, it was up for discussion on the 3 a.m.

Shattered Mums' Club podcast and socials once she had felt ready to talk about it. 'If only we could all admit this is how we are feeling when we are actually going through this,' Sophy had said, trying to hold back the tears but failing, and before she knew what was happening, all three of them had been bawling on the recording and Mel had suggested they cut that bit, but Aisha said it sounded the most authentic thing they had ever recorded. And so it stayed and because it was talked about so much on social channels it became the most listened to episode so far. There was something to be said about speaking the absolute truth. On certain subjects.

But Sophy was always wary, no matter what the response, which was usually positive on most topics she tackled, she never wanted to cross that invisible line and end up offending people. She was acutely aware of the power she had and how she could not only abuse that power, but end up caught up in topics that she wasn't happy to discuss. Not yet, anyway, maybe in another ten years. Sophy was still in the baby zone, and as much as Mel enjoyed talking about her perimenopausal symptoms, she found she still couldn't relate to that next phase of life. She sort of hated herself for feeling that way and how she would sometimes close down whenever Mel began waxing lyrical about unwanted facial hair and a dry vagina. Maybe deep down Sophy knew she wasn't ready to give up on the idea of bringing new life into the world and becoming a mummy all over again.

Still, thirty-eight was no age. She certainly still felt young, no aches or pains to report just yet, but there was something about coming into your thirties when you suddenly started to compare yourself age-wise to other people in their thirties, Sophy found. Which was not something she had ever done in her twenties. She looked at Blythe, her youthful exuberance oozing from her in bucketloads. Four children and not one line on her skin or grey hair on her head, and she looked ruddy and pink-cheeked without a scrap of make-up, as though she belonged on a farm, her brood of young children trailing behind her in cast-offs and faded wellies.

'Anyway, can't wait to have you on board.' Blythe looked as though she were having some sort of convulsion as she spoke but then Sophy noticed a small child, a little bigger than Poppy, yanking at her mother's arm and making her jolt back and forth. An inane smile remained on Blythe's face the entire time and Sophy silently applauded her patience.

'Well, let's see how it goes—' Sophy began.

'If you could bake a cake for the autumn fete at the end of this month, that would be great.' Blythe spoke before Sophy could turn and walk away. 'Just a nice chocolate one, or chocolate cupcakes. You know, gluten free if you can but no worries if not. We have a Victoria sponge and a lemon drizzle...' Blythe looked up to her right, trying to recall what cakes were being baked by others. 'But chocolate is always the favourite, isn't it, and so easy to make. I can send you a recipe if you're stuck.' She smiled at Sophy.

So easy? She could send a recipe? Well, if it was so damn easy, why wasn't Blythe making the flaming chocolate cake herself? Sophy's face took on a look that said absolutely no bother whatsoever. 'Great!' She forced the word out through a rigid smile.

* * *

'I want a snack,' Max said as they began the ten-minute walk back home, Max's hand firmly in hers. Her whole body was tense from the Blythe interaction.

'I would like a snack,' Sophy corrected her son.

'You want a snack too, Mummy?' Max said, completely missing Sophy's point and if she hadn't been so tense from having just joined a WhatsApp group and assigned herself the role of chief chocolate cake maker then she could have laughed. In fact, she was more likely to cry because Sophy knew from experience that once you proved yourself capable of something, it became your signature, the thing that everyone would ask you to do over and over. Sophy was no Mary Berry, but she could cobble together a half-decent bake when she put her mind to it. She couldn't do a shoddy job and face the disappointed faces of the rest of the PTA – whoever they were, she was sure she would soon find out – and she couldn't do an exceptional job and become 'Sophy, the one who makes the most delicious chocolate cake that's soooo moist'.

'Max.' She looked down at her son, his little fist tight in hers. 'You must say please.'

'Please...' Max muttered.

Christ, was he his father's son, or was it just an age thing? Sophy knew she was more annoyed with herself for everything that had just happened in the playground, for allowing herself to join the WhatsApp group in the first place and then straight away sign herself up for baking duties. Her frustration did not lie with Max's lack of manners over a snack when he was clearly verging on hangry. Why hadn't she just said no to Blythe? She really didn't have the time to be in a primary school WhatsApp or make cakes and even though she had lived by the idea of asking a busy person when you wanted something done, she began to feel a surge of panic as she thought about these extra things on top of everything else she did. Mel was going to be so disappointed in her as well when she found out about the PTA group chat. She really felt as though she was about to start cheating on the girls with other mums.

'Mummy. Snack snack snack,' Max chanted and then Poppy joined in.

'Oh, for goodness' sake.' Sophy stopped abruptly and Max's arm yanked where he had begun holding onto the buggy, which was their one rule of walking to and from school where the roads were so busy, her hand or buggy. Walking anywhere with Max gave Sophy a heart attack She had always loved London but just recently she had begun to get slightly panicky whenever she was near a main road. And when she saw other people's children racing down the street metres ahead of their parents on scooters, she would have flashes of images through her head that she did not wish to see. She thought again what that life in the countryside might look like for her and Niall and Max and Poppy, but she always seemed to move away from it. Yet it hung around in the background, nudging her from time to time, especially now when she had to stop in the street, and she could feel the force of every vehicle that went past and exactly how much damage they could do.

She pulled out two packets of raisins from her bag and handed one each to Max and Poppy. She slowed down the pace and watched Max as he carefully picked out one raisin at a time and observed how Poppy did the same. Was that a trait that they had both inherited from her? She found it difficult at times to distinguish between things that her children had inherited from her and what was from their fathers. Sometimes she hated that she had two children with different dads. She didn't mind it when she saw or heard it happening with other women, in fact she was supportive and in awe that they had gone on to find happiness with someone else, but she now felt that Jeff and Niall shared an equilibrium which she wasn't entirely comfortable with. She needed the balance tipped so that she had more children with Niall than she did with Jeff. Then maybe she wouldn't feel like a label or someone who has a child with every man she gets with. Which was a terrible put-down, even to herself. But she couldn't help how she felt. But at the same time, as easy as Poppy was, she wasn't sure she or Niall were ready to have three children. There was the size of the house to think about for a start.

This was perfectly illustrated when Sophy walked through the front door of their home and the shoes were so piled up in the hallway that she struggled to get the pushchair through.

'Damn it,' Sophy cursed as one of her espadrilles became caught under the wheel of the buggy. She had meant to tidy them before she left for the school run. Max diligently bent down and pulled – with some effort – until it was free and Sophy began pushing the buggy into the kitchen. She bent down and took the slightly squashed shoe from her son and at the same time felt like she was really seeing him for the first time in days. Something in the way he had picked up the shoe and was now looking at her, her small handsome man, made her feel again as though he wasn't her baby any more. Sophy only knew she was crying when Max started wiping the tears away with both hands, his little palms cupped across her face, and she began to grin through the tears and then pulled his little body into her. He smelled like school: a mix of blue paper towels, disinfected toilets, and cooked lunches.

'Oh, Max, I love you.' She held him tight, trying to imprint this moment to her memory because she was suddenly terrified of the days rolling into one, the way they had this week, and she would miss it all.

'I love you too,' he replied, and although she had heard those words a hundred or so times, it still made her heart leap and her stomach flip.

Their loving moment was perforated by the beeps of several messages coming through one after another. Sophy reluctantly released herself from the moment to check her phone. It was coming from WhatsApp and Sophy hated that technology had invaded such a tender moment, but Max was already heading off to play with his Lego. She popped the buckle on the pram, but Poppy stayed put, still eating her raisins.

Sophy took her phone out of her pocket and saw it was the group chat that Blythe had created.

Hey ladies.

'Oh, no,' Sophy said out loud. She detested being referred to collectively as 'ladies', specifically from a woman. Sophy couldn't put her finger on why but if she had to guess she would say it was because it usually sounded so false and forced. Like in situations like this.

Here we all are then, in this group chat…
Enjoy and I'm sure I don't need to remind anyone to be kind and courteous!
I've met all of your little ones and they are all a credit to you.

Sophy did a fake vomit noise, which attracted Max's attention. Sophy grinned and he grinned back. He was at that age where involuntary bodily noises were the highlight of his day.

The beeps kept coming and Sophy inwardly groaned this time, not wanting to alert Max's attention to her emotions again. Sophy looked at the group chat, which was already filling up with messages from telephone numbers she didn't know.

Thanks for setting up this group, Blythe.

This is what primary schooling is actually about. The WhatsApp Group 😄

Oh, my actual God, I am so glad someone has set this up already or it would have been me. Well done, Blythe. I'm up for coffee soon if anyone else is.

Yes, let's get the girls together soon, Liz. Can't wait.

What was it about the tone of the other women that was leaving a sour taste in Sophy's mouth? She hadn't met them yet, and this socialising thing was what she was all about, wasn't it? Sophy now did it for a living. But perhaps this was too much, perhaps she had gotten used to her life with Niall, Max and Poppy. And her small circle of just her, Aisha and Mel.

What would they both think if she told them she was in the reception WhatsApp group? She had assured Mel that would never happen. But damn it, wasn't that what a mums' WhatsApp group was for? They were there to support each other. Sophy thought of Mel's face and the disappointment in her tone when she next saw her 3 a.m. girls and had to break the news to them. Sophy thought a minute. She was very close with her 3 a.m. Shattered Mums but that didn't mean she had to tell them everything, did it? In that moment, Sophy decided that she would keep the new WhatsApp group to herself. Sophy let out a small groan... and just as she did, the door opened and there was her husband, who still sent flutters through her.

'Hello, my darlin'.' Niall bent down and kissed Sophy first before turning to the children. Sophy's phone began bleeping furiously again, and again what had been a peaceful serene family moment of love and appreciation was now invaded by the WhatsApp group. *Damn you, Blythe.*

'Oh, no,' Sophy groaned again.

'What is it?' Ever since that day when Sophy had collapsed just after Max had been born, and had been driven to the hospital by Niall, he had never stopped being attentive if he thought she was in pain or distress of any sort. The wad of cotton that had been left inside her after her stitches had been the culprit and so she was out and back at home after a matter of days. That was when she realised her feelings for Niall. She had acknowledged some stirrings she experienced whenever he was in the same room as her, but the way he had swept her and baby Max up and stayed until she came around after the operation, was what had sealed the deal in her mind. She knew Niall was the man she was destined to be with. But she had still been with Jeff at the time. Sophy asking relentlessly to be put on the deeds to the house she had lived in with Jeff for four years was what finally made him push her away enough for her to make the move and leave him for good. Not before he tried to break up her friendships with Aisha and Mel first, the only two women who were keeping her sane at the time. It was still unbelievable to Sophy that she could be with someone who took care of her the way Niall did; he was in a different league altogether from Jeff.

'I did something really stupid.'

'Okay.' Niall sat cross-legged and waited patiently for Sophy to confess all.

'I joined a primary school mothers' WhatsApp group. Correction, I was coerced into it. I gave my number to this Blythe woman and now she has launched the group and my phone has been red hot for twenty minutes. Look.'

Sophy held the phone out to Niall as he scanned the thirty or so messages that had accumulated.

'The girls will be peeved. It's like you're cheating with other mums,' Niall said because he knew Aisha and Mel inside out.

'I know!' Sophy felt she could cry with relief that her husband totally got her and that he always referred to Aisha and Mel as 'the girls'.

'Ah, you'll be fine.' Niall stood up. 'Now, what will we be having for dinner? I'm starving.'

Sophy looked up at Niall, who had made his way into the kitchen area and had begun scouring cupboards and the fridge for food. Niall was good in emergencies but to him this was a melodrama, not worth investing his emotions in.

Sophy knew she needed to be surrounded by as many like-minded people as possible and if that meant investing time in another WhatsApp group, then she could do that. How time consuming could it be?

5

AISHA

'Come on, boys, throw it to Nana,' Aisha shouted across the field as Jude lay on the football.

'Get up, play the game!' Charley laughed as she shouted. Finally Jude got back up and kicked the ball as hard as he could towards Martina.

'He's got quite a boot on him, hasn't he?' Charley added. It landed closer to Charley, so she kicked it over to Martina. Aisha watched as Martina went stiff then looked as though she couldn't move for a moment before she finally edged towards the ball and gave it a weak kick. It landed in the middle of their circle.

'Nana!' Otis screeched.

'Hey!' Aisha jumped to her mother's rescue. 'Leave Nana alone. She's tired.'

She looked at Charley. 'I think we're all tired. Let's get these kids home.'

'I'm going to go home with Mum, are you okay with the boys?' Aisha said quietly.

Charley smiled. 'Sure. Take your time. We'll be fine.'

* * *

The bedroom smelled different from the way it had when she had been a child. That was because Aisha could never remember her mother being ill when she was a child. Her memories of the bedroom were of Impulse sprays, whatever perfumes were cheap in the pound shop and baby talc that Martina would cover herself in. Aisha remembered seeing a flurry of talc in the air after every shower or bath her mother took. Sometimes Aisha would make sure she was the first in the bathroom after her, just so she could stand amongst the floating powder and scents and pretend she was in some sort of snow-clad perfumed Narnia.

But there wasn't any scent in this room today and that was what bothered Aisha the most because wherever her mother went, smells seemed to follow, whether it was in the bedroom or the kitchen. The smells were the representation of her mother's existence and of Aisha feeling and being loved. Her mother showed love through doing, through being up and active and showing up every day. And now here she was, not yet sixty years old and clearly unwell.

'I'll get myself to the doctor this week. It's just a bit of exhaustion.'

Aisha handed her mother a cup of her favourite green tea with a slice of lemon. She thought back to the last six weeks, how she had brought the boys around to see her mum and brought her out on trips as much as possible because she wanted to make the most of the time they had before they went to school.

Aisha looked at her mum and clearly couldn't keep her worried expression at bay.

'I'm fine.' Martina slurped her tea, then Aisha heard the teacup rattling against the saucer as Martina placed it back down. Aisha tried to ignore the fretful significance of the porcelain colliding and instead was drawn to her mother's skin, which looked dry, and to her face, searching for any signs that meant it was something more than just exhaustion. Aisha was looking for a flicker in the eyes, a sign from her mother's soul that she was hiding something from her. Aisha was a worrier. She had been since she was a little girl, her mother had told her. And then when Jon had left them when she was ten, her worrying and catastrophising went into overdrive. It had subsided as she had grown older and then met Charley, who seemed to always have the exact words to soothe her irrational thoughts. There had been plenty of times when she had thought the worst with Otis and Jude. She already knew that Charley would be telling her that her worries over her mum were simply because the boys were at school now and that Aisha had nowhere to direct her angst. Maybe she was overreacting.

'Hey, whatcha thinking over there?' Martina's voice came out a little croaky. Aisha stood up from the chair next to her mother's vanity desk and took the empty teacup from her mother. She placed it down on the vanity desk.

'I can hear your brain ticking over from here, you know.'

Aisha sat back down again. 'I was thinking about the restaurant idea I had when the boys were babies.' Aisha told a half lie. She had, of course, been thinking of this as the boys had been getting closer to going to school. Aisha had been looking forward to the time at home alone. Of course, the house had felt achingly quiet without them in it. But still, she would get used to it and she needed to start focusing on herself again. Talking about it with her mum would be a good distraction from thoughts of illness. 'I don't know why it felt so urgent then to be doing it all when they were young.'

'That's how the minds of you young ones work, isn't it? You want it all at once. Life is like one big sweet shop these days. I was talking to your father about it the other day actually, how there is so much choice, so much competition and distraction, it is hard for anyone to concentrate on the thing they need to be doing.'

Aisha nodded. 'Like being a good mum to Jude and Otis when they were babies?'

'You were and still are a good mum, but you were all over the place, looking at this and that when you had the whole world right in front of you.'

Aisha remembered how it had taken her a good six months to recognise this, and then once she surrendered to her role it had become a little easier, and she'd felt she was where she needed to be right then in her life.

'No one teaches you that in the parent books, do they? They don't tell you you'll feel torn apart and pulled in all directions by life's distractions. I thought about that restaurant every day for those first six months of the boys' lives. And I'm thinking about it again now. It might be time, Mum.'

Martina let out a long sigh. 'Then it is time. Only you know, girl. Them boys are fine at school all day; you have all the time to plan the next steps. You are a wonderful cook. Learned from the best!' Martina laughed, which quickly evolved into a cough and Aisha was on her feet again, this time handing a glass of water to her mother.

'I'm fine,' Martina said after taking a sip. 'I told you, just exhaustion. What with the twins' needs and all the things me and your father have done to the place. Well, Jon did most of it, but I was a damn fine project manager.'

Aisha looked around the bedroom, which had once been a mad mix of colours and furniture but now had a calming neutral feel, with white sheets and a large rug. The sitting room and kitchen had also had work done, new kitchen units with drawers that shut quietly. 'No more slamming those drawers when you're angry, Martina!' Jon had laughed as he had fitted the last one and Martina had closed it and was suitably impressed with the muted sound. The décor may have changed but the house still had the same feel, the same vibes and loud get-togethers when the whole family were as one. It was insane sometimes and whilst it had been the very fabric of her upbringing, Aisha could barely hear herself think and she relished getting back to her own house with Charley, where it was just the four of them and they could put on a movie and relax.

'Whatcha thinking of calling it?'

'Hmmm?' Aisha said, she had been miles away thinking about when everything had felt normal just a few weeks ago. How she had taken everything for granted and how things can just turn so quickly. One minute, it had been the summer holidays and she had been running around with the twins and Martina, and now her mother was laid out in bed and her two babies were in full-time education. Aisha was worried for all of them. She wanted her mum to be okay, she couldn't face seeing her usually so active and full-of-life mother just lying there, not wanting to do anything.

'The restaurant, you got a name in mind?' Martina croaked.

'No. Not yet. I've not even found a unit yet.'

'Well, as soon as you do, you let me know. I'll come and look at it with you.'

'Only if you're feeling up to it, Mum.'

'I told you, I'm a little run down is all. I'll be back on my feet in no time.'

Aisha looked at her mum and wished more than anything for this to be true.

* * *

Aisha walked through her front door to be greeted by the usual sounds of the boys wreaking havoc. The period after dinner and before bed was the time they would always get the zoomies. Aisha was thankful they had space in the garden and the weather was still just about warm enough. She could hear Charley in the kitchen as she arrived in the hallway. One twin raced past her and straight into her knees, she quickly bent down and scooped Otis up.

'Baby boy, do you have a kiss for Mama?'

'I kissed Mummy too much today,' Otis said, wriggling out of Aisha's arms and ran towards the lounge. Next Jude ran towards her looking a little more puffed out. The smaller of the twins by an inch, he was also more slender. He approached Aisha willingly and she bent down and scooped him up as he nuzzled into her neck.

'Mummy is making pizza!' Otis shouted from the sitting room where he had just put the TV on.

'Hey, no TV until after dinner,' Aisha called. She looked down at Jude in her arms. 'Pizza, hey?' She walked into the kitchen, expecting to see empty pizza boxes and plastic wrapping, but instead she saw raw dough on the table and little pots of toppings lined up next to two small rolling pins that Aisha had bought for the boys last year for baking but had not yet managed to lure them into the kitchen to create anything. The cute women's magazine image she had conjured in her head of her and the twins rolling out pastry for biscuits and pies stayed exactly there, in her head. The boys were physical and when it came to entertaining them, Aisha had always opted for outdoor activities first. Cooking with them, the one thing she enjoyed the most, had slipped through her fingers.

'Oh, wow!' Aisha felt the same pang of jealousy she always did when she saw Charley doing something new or different with the boys. But Aisha knew this was all her own issue. Charley was doing something good, yet Aisha could only see that she was taking something away from her, something she should have done with the boys. Aisha knew she was a good mum, so why was she suddenly not feeling like one? Jude still clung to her, his light blue school polo shirt covered in stains from food from his lunchbox.

'Wanna make one?' Charley said, not looking up from the table where she was laying out the dough ready for the boys to roll.

'We get one each?' Aisha moved closer to the table, her initial defensive reaction overtaken by intrigue. Charley really seemed to have put a lot of effort into this. And Aisha was quietly impressed, despite feeling she had been relegated. This was an activity for the kids plus dinner all in one.

Aisha placed Jude down and he slid into a chair. 'Otis!' Aisha called. 'Come and make your dinner with Mummy and Mama.'

Otis came running and slipped into his seat next to Jude.

'Pizza! Yes, what do we do?' Otis started grabbing at the bowls and Charley quickly whipped them back. Jude remained still and looked at the array of toppings in front of him.

'Roll your dough first.' Charley handed Otis his dough ball and rolling pin. Otis began rolling furiously. Aisha moved behind Otis and held her hands over his little ones. 'Like this.' She guided his hands carefully and soon Otis had slowed down and was rolling at a gentler pace. 'Now we stretch it like this.' Aisha showed Otis once and let him do it himself until he had made a sort of oval shape.

'Sauce next.' Charley pushed the sauce towards Otis. Aisha had moved round the table to help Jude stretch his dough and lay it on the baking parchment. Once Aisha had shown both boys how to smudge the sauce around, leaving a gap of dough like a frame so the sauce didn't burn at the edges, she left them to it to add their own toppings, and moved over to her own dough. She quickly rolled it out, stretched it to into a nice round shape and topped it with sauce, cheese, ham and pineapple, her favourite.

Half an hour later, they were tucking into their delicious creations. The boys sipped squash and Charley opened a nice bottle of red. She held her glass out to Aisha for a toast.

'Here's to a successful first week of school runs.'

'Cheers.' Aisha took a long sip; she hadn't realised how much she had wanted a drink.

'Thanks for this, it was a great idea. The boys loved it, and it was the perfect distraction.'

'We'll get the boys to FaceTime your mum tomorrow, that will perk her up.'

'Or finish her off,' Aisha scoffed and then felt a pang of guilt at even suggesting that when all she was trying to focus on was there not being anything seriously wrong with Martina.

'Anyway,' Charley began as she stacked the plates, 'you did most of it.'

Aisha stood up and pulled a tub of ice cream out of the freezer. Charley arrived next to her with a stack of plates. 'You are so good with them, calm, collected. I was simply an observer in the end.' Charley put down the plates and put one hand on Aisha's shoulder. 'You know you're the one with all the patience.'

Aisha turned to Charley. 'Did you do this for me?'

'I want the boys to see the real you. They see me, down there in the basement doing my jingles and audio book recordings, you make them their meals, I dunno, I just thought maybe let's start injecting the passion for cooking into their lives a little more. It is in your blood so it must be in theirs too.'

'It's been hard—' Aisha began.

'I know, it's been the toughest years of our lives. You've been immense being here with them, and I get it, there is never enough time in the day, and they have short attention spans. I couldn't do this sort of crafty cooking on a regular basis, but you do because you have way more patience than me, plus all the talent. And I'm not saying things are going to suddenly be so much easier, but the fact the boys are at school gives you a few hours a day to yourself to do what you want to do. Plus I can pick them up on days when I have a little less work on or if I finish a project early. You can start to think about doing something culinary for yourself.' Charley squeezed Aisha's shoulder. 'You deserve it.'

Aisha slipped her arm around Charley's waist. 'I have been thinking about it, I'm just not sure exactly what I want to do, if I want premises or just a catering business.'

Charley looked around and screwed her mouth up. 'Well, we've kind of run out of room here, unless you're thinking of putting a unit in the garden.'

Aisha shook her head. 'I wouldn't deprive the boys of any more room; they just have enough space out there as it is.'

'So a sort of shop then?' Charley began to sound excited for Aisha and Aisha felt the fizzle of excitement begin to build the way it had when the boys were babies, when she was bursting with ideas and creativity but had nowhere to channel it. She placed bowls, spoons and the tub of ice cream in the centre of the table.

'Thanks. For believing in me,' Aisha offered quickly as the twins tussled for ice cream bowls even though they were still empty. Charley didn't say anything, but Aisha could see her smile and knew she had said the right thing at the right time. Something she knew she didn't always get right. She had the backing of the two most important women in her life for her to explore this next chapter. So, what was stopping her?

6

MEL

It was unusual for Mel's cleaner, Ksenia, to be late and so when she arrived at twenty to ten looking, if Mel had to choose a word, haggard, Mel got her to sit down immediately.

'Was it traffic?' Mel put a cold glass of water in front of her.

'No, not traffic. I always leave plenty of time for accidents and so on.' Ksenia waved her hand.

'Okay, so was it your boyfriend?' Mel said, trying to sound sympathetic. She had never seen Ksenia looking like this before and whilst Ksenia had only delivered happy news of her current relationship, she wondered if perhaps things weren't going well in paradise.

'Yes,' Ksenia began. She took a long sip of her water, looked at it as though she were going to throw up and then placed it down. Mel tried to surreptitiously inspect the glass, which wasn't up to Ksenia's standards – had she not cleaned it properly last night?

'Oh dear.' Mel sat back, unable to spot any smears on the glass. 'Was it an argument?'

Ksenia nodded. 'Very bad. We argue all night.'

'You look knackered,' Mel said. 'If you don't mind me saying so.'

'No, it's true. I look like shit.'

Mel laughed.

'And I feel like shit too.'

'So what was the argument about?' Mel asked, intrigued to know more.

'We disagree, he wants one thing, I want the other.'

'Well, that can be the case sometimes,' Mel said, thinking about her and Darren. There had been a few occasions over the years but mainly they had been on the same page.

'Yes, so he says he want children and I say I can't. I too busy, I work too much, how can I have a baby in my job, I lose all my work.'

Mel stayed silent; she wanted to speak but let Ksenia carry on.

'I come here from Russia, I build up clients, but it is only me, how can I work and keep my baby?'

Ksenia's eyes were filling up with tears. In all the years that Mel had known her, in all the time she had been coming to the house to clean, she had never seen her cry. She was clearly hurting.

Mel leaned forward and put her hand on Ksenia's. At the same time, Bess, the family Labrador, appeared and placed her head on Ksenia's knee.

'Ksenia, are you pregnant?'

Ksenia looked up at Mel, her eyes were pooling with tears. She blinked and nodded, and the tears fell down her cheeks.

Mel took in a deep breath. 'Okay.' She patted her hand. 'And you're sad because you want to keep the baby, but you don't think you can afford it?'

Ksenia nodded again.

'If I must stop working, I have to find someone to replace me, then I have no money, my boyfriend he does not earn enough to pay for both of us. He tells me, "I pay, I pay," but I know he cannot. I have worked this out and it will not work. I cannot even put my baby in a nursery, it will be the same money that I earn.' Ksenia looked down at her lap. 'I know this is not what I should do, but I have to abort the baby.'

Mel sucked in a breath, her heart pounding in her chest. She began to mull over some ideas in her head but before she spoke them out loud, she tried to decide if they would be viable. Could Ksenia start a new job so she could claim the benefits owed to her? But starting a new job could take time and before long she would start showing and, as Ksenia said, putting a baby in a nursery was too expensive and working for someone else she could earn less than what she was earning on her own. It was a messed-up system and one that Mel was well aware of. She had been in it once and thankfully not any more. Working for herself was the only way for Mel.

'Listen, Ksenia, I don't want you to worry about this because we will help you to work it out. I know you don't want to abort the baby. Do you?'

Ksenia sucked in a breath. 'No.' Then she cried very loudly and for a very long time.

The sound of Mel's phone ringing brought Ksenia to her senses and she dabbed her eyes with a tissue.

It was Mel's agent, a woman she had barely heard from in the last year. Was she actually ringing to offer her work? She took the call in the next room.

Five minutes later, Mel hung up the call, walked back into the kitchen and stared at Ksenia. She opened her mouth to speak and then closed it again.

'What is it? You win lottery? You look like goldfish,' Ksenia said.

'That was my agent. She has a job for me.' Mel picked up her mug of almost cold coffee.

'This is good, no? You said work was drier than a badger's arse.'

Mel had just taken a sip and almost spat out her coffee.

'I did say that, yes.'

The East End had been Mel's home from home for many years. Robbie had been the proprietor and a good friend. He had booked her regularly. Even after the incident with Jeff, which had knocked the wind out of her sails, Mel found the courage to get back on the East End stage a few months after Sky was born. The venue had to close its doors last year after Robbie had become ill. He recovered and then met the love of his life, sold the business, and moved to Spain with his new Spanish lover. Mel had only heard good things since he'd left and so she was certain he wasn't going to be returning any time soon. It was now a cocktail bar and Mel had offered herself up for a gig there, only to decide she was never going to return there again. It had none of the style or passion that the East End had once had; it was all new and sparkly with too much chrome and mirrors. The staff were young and awkward with nothing interesting to say and the response to Mel's performance was somewhat under-whelming.

Since then, the work had been sporadic. She had taken a job working as a yoga teacher to substitute the income, but she was missing the stage again so much, as much as she had done after she'd stopped performing when she'd become pregnant with Sky. She felt once again as though she had been forced to stop doing the one thing she loved against her will. But this was nothing to do with Jeff or any man, this was all Mel's fault. She had allowed herself to become too comfortable in her life, she had stopped pushing herself.

So this call felt like someone had just breathed oxygen into her, as though she had been semi-conscious for all this time. Of course, she loved her family with every fibre of her being, but it was necessary for her to work and not just dabble. Mel was a grafter; she always had been. She needed to be working and doing something and all she had been thinking about recently was landing something mega, a really big job, something that would consume her for a short period of time, and give her a whole ton of memories. And it had happened. Be careful what you wish for had been a motto of her upbringing and here she was getting exactly what she had asked the universe for.

'I... I got a job. On a boat.' Mel laughed.

'You drive ship now? What is this? A joke?'

Mel laughed louder. 'No, it's a cruise ship. They want me to come and sing, to fill in for someone for ten days.'

'And you leave here? Your family be okay without you?' Ksenia's voice dropped an octave. 'You want me to look after the baby?'

Mel laughed softly. Ksenia still referred to Sky as the baby, even though she was four.

'No, I have Daz and Irene and Mike. Sky loves her granny and grandpa and they'd do anything for her. Leia is almost sixteen. She's fairly independent but still needs someone checking up on her. I mean, please still come whilst I'm not here, but don't feel you need to do anything more than you already do.'

'This is a good opportunity for you. Women need time alone, away from family.'

An image of Daz was suddenly at the forefront of her mind. She would miss the kids, but Daz? She was sure he would be fine without her. She thought about the last time she had tried to talk to him about how she was feeling, how she was longing to get back to performing again, how she felt she had let a part of herself slip again. She supposed she was looking for someone to tell her she was right, that she should just start thinking of herself again. She had seen a slight flick of his head, she had heard the sigh that left his lips. And that was the end of that conversation. And that wasn't the first time Mel had noticed Daz's nonchalance when she had tried to discuss anything about herself that wasn't related to the children or the house.

Mel nodded. 'I do from time to time, that's for sure. Or I'd kill them.' She made light of the situation, even though she felt that there was a distance opening up between her and Daz.

'This happen to me, why you think I have no family?' Ksenia laughed loud and long, and Mel let out a snort. She had come to cherish these moments with Ksenia. They had been in each other's company for over four years now and had developed a close friendship. And now, she couldn't believe she was pregnant. If she was honest, she was surprised because Ksenia had not been with her boyfriend for very long.

'How are things going with Tristan? Apart from the baby, are you both happy?'

Ksenia gave a small sly smile. 'Very good. We like each other a lot. He very clean.'

'Well, that's good. You wouldn't want to share your life with someone who was messy.'

'No, I mean clean. Around here.' Ksenia motioned to her crotch area and Mel lifted her chin, dropped her mouth open and said, 'Oh.'

'Which is better than clean house,' Ksenia said and screeched out a short sharp laugh.

'Absolutely.' Mel nodded fiercely and lifted her mug. 'To my new job and your boyfriend's shiny penis.'

Ksenia cackled like a hyena for approximately three seconds, then downed her water and stood up. 'I go start work now, and clean little one bedroom.'

'Okay, Ksenia, but listen.' Ksenia stopped and looked at Mel. 'I will sort this for you, I promise. Please don't think your only option is to get rid of your baby. Promise me you won't make any decisions just yet.'

Ksenia nodded and scooted upstairs and Mel was left sitting alone, thoughts of Daz's aloofness and the prospect of ten days away sailing around the Med and singing to a full house every night filling her head. Her agent had told her an email was on the way so she opened her mail on her phone. And went through what her agent had put about the remuneration.

'How much!' she said out loud to the room.

Four thousand pounds for ten nights' work was what the cruise ship company was offering plus accommodation. But on top of that, a double room with a balcony plus two extra rooms with balconies for friends or family.

Mel thought for a moment. Three rooms plus all meals. That had to be worth a bit. And it meant she wouldn't be entirely alone when she wasn't working. All in all, it wasn't a bad deal. She'd been offered worse over the years. Plus some October sun was very much needed and she knew just the people she was going to offer the rooms to. All she needed to do now was work out how to convince them to come.

* * *

6.45 p.m. – Mel – Hey, gals. How are the school runs going?

6.50 p.m. – Sophy – The first week has flown by. I can't believe it!

6.51 p.m. – Aisha – I was just thinking how funny it is that we used to message in the middle of the night. How things have changed.

6.54 p.m. – Mel – There was that bit in between where we messaged all hours of the day when they were toddlers and slept for hours in the day, dropping naps, and then waking up at 5 in the morning!

6.56 p.m. – Sophy – Hey guys, stop talking in the past tense, I'm not out of the trenches yet!

6.59 p.m. – Mel – Soz, Soph. No offence. Also, Poppy is perfect and barely plays you up. You learned from every mistake with Max and nailed it the second time around.

7.01 p.m. – Sophy – I'd like to think so but what was the one (of many) lessons we learned in the early days?

7.03 p.m. – Aisha – I can't remember it's all a blur.

7.05 p.m. – Mel – There's no such thing as the perfect mother.

7.06 p.m. – Aisha – Damn it, I remember that conversation as well. We messaged long and hard into the night, one of the rare nights we were all awake for hours together.

7.10 p.m. – Mel – Are you okay though, Soph? You know we're always here. The 3 a.m. Shattered Mums' Club is still open for business, even now Poppy is two.

7.13 p.m. – Aisha – I was still up with the twins in the night when you'd just had Poppy, do you remember? Not for long, but there was a spell where our paths crossed.

7.15 p.m. – Sophy – I remember. And I was grateful.

7.17 p.m. – Mel – Anyway, gals, I was texting for a very specific reason. I have something to ask you…

7

SOPHY

'A cruise? Who is she now? Jane McDonald?' Niall went to wash his hands after a long day on site. Sophy laughed for a split second, she was back there with Jeff, feeling as though she needed to ask his permission to do something. But she didn't need to think like that. Niall was supportive and the relationship had been egalitarian since the day they made it official. Four years with Jeff, coupled with the fact he was still in her life as Max's father, meant she would occasionally feel triggered. But the triggers were rare, and she'd be over it before it had really begun. She hadn't realised at the time how much damage he was doing to her. But leaving him had given her a strength she had forgotten she'd had, and then Niall joined her, and their strength became one superpower.

'She's been invited to sing on the cruise ship for ten nights and she wants company. The extra cabins come as part of her payment.'

'Sounds lush. I've always wondered what a cruise might be like. I prefer me feet on solid ground, though.'

Sophy felt a pang of guilt that it wasn't her and Niall who were planning a trip away together and alone. Aside from their honeymoon to Egypt with Max in tow, and a trip to Spain last year with Max and a very hot and grumpy just toddling Poppy, they'd not actually been away much together and certainly never alone. She wondered what that would be like, just the two of them. She felt bad that they hadn't experienced it and she hated that she'd experienced it with Jeff so many times when he didn't deserve to have her.

She also knew that there were very few opportunities ahead for them to be alone for a little while but that was the choice they had made to have Poppy. It was sort of amusing that Mel, funny, sassy kick-ass Mel, was going to be a cruise ship singer. Cruise ship entertainment did bear a sort of stigma that was given as an insult by judges to fairly average singers on these reality TV shows but Sophy knew that wasn't Mel. And she would never say that to her face. Not unless Mel made a joke about it first. Sophy wished she would, as it was killing her not to have a bit of a laugh about it.

'So, you'll be leaving us for a while,' Niall said, not sounding sarcastic or the least bit needy. It was so refreshing, and she didn't think she would ever stop being grateful that she was married to an actual man and not a man-child.

'Just under two weeks. Is that too long? I can make it a week? I've already looked into a nanny coming to stay...' Sophy had messaged her sisters, but they were too full-on with their work schedules.

'Don't be daft. One of my sisters will come and stay with us.'

'What? Really? Even if I'm not here?'

Sophy had spent plenty of time with Niall's siblings and they all loved the bones of Max and Poppy but never had she expected one of them to just come to London to help when she wasn't in the country. Wendy, Jeff's mum, could barely look after Max if Sophy had had to pop to the shops. Of course Wendy saw plenty of her grandson, but it was all on her terms. Never as a favour to Sophy, but then it never had been, even when she and Jeff had been together.

''Course. I'll ask our Shannon. She's on a bit of a sabbatical at the moment and had talked about spending some time in London.'

'Oh, my God, Niall! That would be amazing. I had thought a nanny would be okay but then I panicked that Max and Poppy wouldn't know them and that Poppy would struggle with naps and then I'd be stressed—'

'Go on your cruise. You'll have a great time. And you deserve it.' He kissed her cheek. 'Just don't leave me for a handsome captain,' he added as he sat down at the kitchen table.

There it was, that sliver of insecurity dressed up as a joke. It was a comfort to her, because Sophy often felt the same, that Niall might leave her at any point for another woman. Marriage had been important to her, so they could have their day to celebrate, but it didn't mean that she had become complacent. She knew that either of them could call it quits at any time and that relationships – whether you were in a marriage or just cohabiting – needed work. Lots of work every day. But it was nice to know that Niall still had that feeling the same as she did. And no handsome captain or anyone else was going to divert her attention from the life she was building with her husband.

To celebrate the end of a first successful week at school, Sophy had cooked macaroni and cheese and chips, the children's favourite. She'd been offering green food of every description to the children all week but now she was done saying 'just one more bite of broccoli' and 'finish your cucumber'. It was a beige food night, and she didn't even feel the need to put one piece of token greenery on anyone's plate.

Niall stacked the dishwasher, as he did most nights, then scooped the children up for their baths. Max looked ready to drop and Poppy had gone very quiet, as though she was going to fall asleep any moment. Sophy did the rounds of the house, picking up discarded clothing, stray toys and tried to get it in some sort of order whilst getting the children's evening drinks ready. It was a night of opposing book choices, so Niall took Poppy to her room with *Peppa Pig* and *The Very Hungry Caterpillar* and Sophy went to Max's room with him and lay down on the bed whilst he pottered about. Sophy watched from her fully reclining position on the bed as Max put thought and time into choosing the right books. He didn't want to make the mistake of choosing one then changing his mind if it wasn't the right fit for the night. Tonight Max appeared with three *Mr Men* books and Sophy felt her insides collapse. She smiled as he approached, looking pleased with himself, and braced herself for a marathon read. Twenty minutes later, with her mouth as dry as the bottom of a budgie's cage, and unable to pronounce her s's, Sophy kissed Max goodnight and met Niall on the landing.

'Well, hello, fancy seeing you here,' Niall whispered sexily. Sophy couldn't deny he smelled so good even after a full day's work. Was he looking for some evening action? she wondered. She had some videos to edit, some posts to set up for over the weekend and she'd had a really good idea for a TikTok video. She thought if they were quick she could squeeze in sex and then crack on with her work.

'Shall I meet you in the bedroom?' she replied huskily.

'Nah, can't tonight, love. I'm meeting the lads down the pub. It's Fizz's birthday.'

Ah, yes. She'd forgotten. But she felt a pang of relief that she was off the hook for the night, she had been feeling incredibly tired these last few days, which was, she presumed, down to the sudden change in routine; getting both kids up and ready each morning for a whole week had taken its toll on Sophy as well.

Life had certainly crept up on her and with all the work she was putting into the extra 3 a.m. Shattered Mums' Club online social media whilst trying to launch events and merchandise, she wouldn't be surprised if she met herself coming back. In that moment, it occurred to Sophy that in the four years since she, Mel and Aisha had launched the 3 a.m. Shattered Mums' Club and it had taken off as a podcast and more a few months later, she had never taken a proper break. Not even when she was holidaying with the family or friends. Not even when her babies had been born and she should have taken some proper maternity time. She had continued to work and plan and do whatever she could to keep the small but lucrative brand going. But why couldn't she just take a step back for a few days, switch her phone off? She saw other influencers doing so, they would make an announcement about their intended leave and then radio silence for days, sometimes weeks on end. And when they came back, everyone, including Sophy, was pleased to see them. It would never occur to her to stop following someone because they were absent for a few weeks. The work she did via the podcast and the social channels was, as far as she was concerned, a proper job, it brought in an income, and a fairly decent one, she thought. But the thought of just stopping filled her with dread. What if she wasn't like everyone else who took cyber sabbaticals? What if her absence meant losing followers? She had felt her body asking her to slow down recently, the question was, would she be able to?

8

AISHA

'I just can't imagine myself on a cruise, Mum, not in a million years. I like solid ground.'

Aisha had the phone on loudspeaker whilst she wrapped up her mum's favourite ginger cake loaf that she planned to deliver to her later. As it was the weekend, Charley had taken the boys to the park and then the café and was now in the basement working on a piece whilst the boys watched a DVD, giving Aisha a few free units. Aisha liked to break down her day into units. Since the boys had gotten bigger, she wasn't confined to the house for hours at a time. Stripping the beds, washing the sheets and drying them was one unit, baking a cake was another. Going to the hairdresser was two units of the day and going to soft play and a café afterward was three units.

'It will do you good, my girl. Charley and me and your dad, Jon, will be there to help.' Aisha noted the way Martina always added her father's name as if he still wasn't worthy of just being Dad yet, or maybe Martina thought that Aisha needed to be reminded that she had a father. It had been over four years since they had got back together, and he had moved back into the family home, but it still felt strange sometimes.

'I can't ask you to help out, Mum, you're not well and summer was full-on.'

'I enjoy it. Them boys are my life, and they dote on their grandmama.'

It was true, the twins were nigh on obsessed with Martina and Jon. Aisha realised she had a good setup with two grandparents and occasionally her sister or cousins around to help out when she needed them.

'Listen, Mum, I'm on my way to your house now; we'll talk more then.' Aisha hung up and as she did she heard a message alert ping through, followed by another and another. It was probably the Shattered Mums' group; they were the only messages she received that came at her like a shotgun sometimes, when Mel and Sophy were chatting away before she'd had a chance to get to her phone. She finished wrapping the ginger loaf and then flicked open her phone. There were no messages on the WhatsApp group and none from anyone else. She checked her other inboxes to make sure she hadn't missed something, but everything was up to date. Then out of the corner of her eye she spotted Charley's phone. It was still bleeping, almost furiously. Aisha was intrigued, never nosy. She and Charley trusted one another, which was why they both knew the codes to one another's phones and passwords on email and social media. Not that either of them had cause to use them. If Charley was in the room, Aisha would just ask her girlfriend outright who was messaging, because really Charley was a bit of a loner; she had a few mates from uni who she still met up with, but she was an only child and was estranged from her parents.

Would a client be messaging her so frantically? Aisha hadn't seen any of the messages yet but the way in which they were still pinging through reminded her of the way an ex-girlfriend had used to text message her when they had been on the brink of splitting up. Aisha inched closer, allowing herself the notion that she wasn't prying, she was simply looking. Charley had enabled texts to appear on the front of her phone even when locked, that was how blasé she was about her privacy. Aisha wouldn't dream of leaving her texts in view of the world. But as Aisha peered at the phone, she couldn't see any texts popping up in synch with the beeping. Aisha brought the screen to life. Still nothing. Then the password option appeared. Aisha thought for a moment, Charley had obviously changed her settings so the messages were no longer showing. There were still texts coming through. Aisha's finger hovered over the screen, ready to type in the password.

Footsteps coming up from the basement. Aisha clicked the screen to blank and stepped back to the other side of the kitchen. What was she thinking? She didn't need to check Charley's messages. It was not seeing the messages on the screen that had thrown her. Charley was welcome to not display anything on her locked screen, God knows Aisha had berated her about it enough times.

The door to the basement swung open and Aisha immersed herself in finishing wrapping the cake. 'Hey.' Charley walked straight over to the kitchen counter.

Aisha could make out from her peripheral vision that she was opening her phone up and scanning through. She heard Charley let out a small sigh and then she came up behind her, tucking the phone in her back pocket.

'That for your mum?' she asked, looking at the ginger cake.

'Yep,' Aisha answered absently. She had considered asking Charley who the messages were from, but the notion soon dispersed as thoughts of heading over to see her mum took over. Even though Martina had sounded pretty upbeat on the phone, and insisted she would be helping out if Aisha decided to go on the cruise, Aisha would know more when she saw her in the flesh. 'I'm heading round there now. Are you okay to stay with the boys a while longer? I don't think Mum is up to visitors.'

'Sure. I'll do them omelette and home-made chips for dinner?'

'Sounds good. They do love their omelettes.'

There was a pause as Aisha put the cake into a tote bag.

'Okay then, I'll see you when you get back,' Charley said eventually and when Aisha turned around she saw that Charley was looking at her phone again.

'Who were all your messages from?' Aisha asked.

'Oh, no one,' Charley said quickly.

'No one?' Aisha laughed.

'I mean, no one you know. This client is being really fussy, so I agreed to let my agent put me in touch with them directly. I'm sort of regretting agreeing to it now.'

'What? The job?'

'No, just them having my number.'

'Well, I'm sure you'll sort it out,' Aisha said and left the house, she didn't want to delay getting to her mum's any longer.

Once she was on the high street in Brixton, Aisha could finally think. She turned to clock her reflection in an empty shopfront. She'd been so busy thinking about her mum and then Charley's messages coming through had distracted her, so she hadn't done her final outfit check before she'd left the house. With the encouragement of Mel and Sophy, Aisha had ditched the jeans and long-sleeved tops and begun wearing jumpsuits, three-quarter-length jeans and funky sweatshirts, colours she would never have dared experiment with when the twins were little. Today she was wearing a baby-pink jumpsuit, multi-coloured New Balance trainers and a denim jacket. She checked her hair wasn't too frizzy and as she did, she saw the shop window was empty, and there was a sign in the window.

Premises to let.

Aisha whipped out her phone and took a photo of the sign with telephone number and email address displayed. Now Otis and Jude were at school, she knew she couldn't keep putting off the inevitable. She needed to go back to work. Charley had never said anything about money being an issue, with Aisha not being in full-time work all these years, and Aisha was sure it wasn't. She had been doing the odd outside catering event over the weekend. For Aisha, it had been a way to ease herself back into the workplace and she wanted to support her family financially, but she had still needed to be there for her kids. But suddenly seeing the sign for premises to let gave Aisha a rush of hope and excitement. All those feelings from before the twins were born and during their early infancy when Aisha would dream about opening her own restaurant had returned. This was what made her heart sore and her stomach flip. This was what she was supposed to be doing. But it was just empty premises and a pipe dream at the moment. To make it anything more, Aisha would need to take the leap.

9

MEL

'I thought it was important that we met in person to discuss the ins and outs of this trip.' Sophy poured three glasses of wine and handed one each to Mel and Aisha at the kitchen table, where there was a charcuterie board with hummus, bread and olives and meats. 'I know you, out of all of us, Aisha, are the most reluctant at the moment.'

'I...' Aisha looked as though she might object. Then she sighed. 'You're right. I just have a lot going on.' Aisha went to take a breadstick and Sophy gently slapped her hand.

'Wait, I need to photograph it for Insta.'

'Of course,' Mel said. There was understanding that this was what Sophy did as her job now. As well as all the other things Sophy did with the retreats and the 3 a.m. Shattered Mums' Club merchandise, she was also quite the businesswoman now and Mel couldn't help but feel proud that she had come so far. There had been a point when Jeff had been holding her back and stopping her growing personally and professionally. It was true that the one you are with can put mental boundaries in your way. Mel had never thought that about Daz, until recently. Thinking back to the few times when she had tried to bring up her career with him and he had barely been able to lift his head to talk to her about it, she wondered if he had reached a point where he had nothing more to offer her in that department and maybe that was a normal evolution for some relationships.

Mel had always presumed it would be the opposite and that she and Daz would go on forever, being able to talk about everything. The fact that they were both in their late forties and their youngest had only just started school was playing on Mel's mind. She sometimes wondered if they had started too late and that now they were both just a bit washed up and, well, quite frankly, shattered. Had raising kids in their thirties and then into their forties meant they had lost touch with who they really were? Mel had certainly noticed Daz's advances towards her had petered off. Where she once couldn't even bend down to stack the dishwasher without him trying to mount her, she could now walk freely around the house with barely an acknowledgement she was there, let alone a cheeky bum grab.

'The fans miss you two, you've not featured for a while!' Sophy positioned her camera so that the food was central, but she could still see the hands and wine glasses of her two friends. She took a few images and then asked the girls to cheer whilst she shot a one-handed boomerang.

Then she sat down and put her phone at the end of the table. As much as Mel supported her work, she was always glad when Sophy would down tools and give her friends her full attention. She watched in wonder as Sophy hurriedly stuffed olives and a slice of meat into her mouth.

'Woah there, lady!' Mel said. 'Did someone skip lunch?'

'I don't think so.' Sophy washed the snacks down with a glug of wine. 'I ate avocado, or was that yesterday? Anyway, I have a healthy appetite. Niall loves that about me.'

'Nothing wrong with it, I just want you to breathe in between gulping down food.' Mel lifted her wine and took a long gulp.

Sophy let out a breath, took another deep breath and smiled as she exhaled. 'Yes. Okay. I'm breathing.'

'So how does it work, this cruise? We meet you on the ship?' Aisha asked, carefully putting a selection of olives and meats onto a plate in a manner completely opposing to Sophy. Mel had noted that Aisha had been fairly quiet since Mel announced the cruise and her intentions to take her two best friends with her.

'Yes, we set sail from Southampton.' Mel opened her phone and navigated back to the email with the itinerary attached. She passed it to Aisha, who studied it carefully. She and Sophy glanced at one another knowingly and gave Aisha a moment to digest the information.

'Oh, my days, our first proper holiday then,' Aisha said excitedly, as though she had suddenly just worked it out.

'Of course. Our first proper holiday. Without the babies,' Mel said.

'I'll have to leave Poppy and Max,' Sophy blurted and then looked at the other two women. Mel looked at her, she felt her mouth slightly agape and her eyes widening, not knowing what to say. Leaving their families was of course the hardest part but necessary, but Mel wondered if this was what was needed. Maybe the cruise offer had come at the right time, as Daz's attention and affection towards her were dwindling.

'I mean, I always knew I needed to leave them behind, but it just suddenly hit me.' Sophy's eyes filled with tears. The two women comforted her with arm pats, softly spoken words of empathy and a wine refill. 'I have Niall's sister coming to help look after the kids as Niall can't just take all that time off, so I am really lucky.'

'That's amazing, Sophy! He's such a sport. His family is so nice.' Aisha looked away into the distance.

'Everything okay with you, Aisha?' Mel asked, turning away from Sophy to her other friend.

'Yes, Charley is going to work 9.30 until 2.30 then catch up in the evening when the boys are in bed. I mean, my mum said she'll be back on her feet then but who knows...' Aisha's voice broke and both women's attention was now on her.

'Oh, Aisha, I'm so sorry about Martina. You must be so worried!' Sophy said.

Aisha looked at them both through watery eyes. 'I am worried. I'm not sure what is wrong with her, and I just want to make it better. But she is being so cagey and...' Aisha shook her head. 'Anyway, I don't want to bore you both with my tales of woe when we're planning such an exciting trip. Well, as we plan to gatecrash Mel's exciting trip.'

'My trip, your trip, I wouldn't go without you,' Mel said earnestly. 'Well, maybe I would, to be fair, but the point is, we love Martina, and we wish her well. But she will want you to let your hair down for a few days. Nothing will change whilst you're away. You're both lucky you have such fantastic partners with flexible jobs. I'll be hauling in the cavalry.'

'Irene and Mike?' Aisha and Sophy said in unison and Mel laughed.

'Yes. But they love it and are always happy to do it.'

'We're all lucky then,' Aisha said with a little more spirit to her voice.

'I know, so lucky,' Mel said and suddenly she was thinking of Ksenia again.

'Ksenia is pregnant,' she announced and then realised after she had said it that it wasn't her place to tell anyone.

Aisha gasped and Sophy squealed.

'That's so lovely,' Aisha said.

'It is, she hasn't been with her fella for very long but I think they are really into each other and he really wants to support her but the fact is, she is thinking about aborting,' Mel said and Aisha's brow furrowed and Sophy let out a small groan. 'She doesn't have any support here and nursery fees will cost the earth and she can't not work, Tristan doesn't earn enough to support them both.'

'That's so tragic. There must be an answer,' Aisha said.

'I'm thinking, believe me. I am going to speak to Daz and see what he can produce figures wise. Maybe they just haven't done their maths properly.'

Both women nodded their support for that idea but they all knew it was futile. The cost of living had skyrocketed and if you didn't have a support system in place, you had to pay for it. And often it could equate to the same if not more than what you earned. Mel knew this. They all knew this.

'Could she bring the baby to work with her?' Sophy suggested.

'To mine, for sure, but to all her other clients' houses? I'm not sure. How would that be practical anyway? By the time she finishes maternity, the baby will be active and need constant attention and entertainment. A crawling baby is not conducive to cleaning houses, is it?'

The girls shook their heads.

Mel's phone pinged several times in a row and Aisha, who was still holding Mel's phone, looked down at the screen. Her expression was almost questioning as she handed it back to Mel. Mel looked at Aisha and then at the screen. On the screen was a name that she had never thought she would see flashing up on her phone. But after the few messages she had already received from him over the last few days, she had finally saved his name in her contacts. The blast from the past she had never expected to hear from yet, since the first message two days ago, they had been coming in spurts.

'Someone's popular,' Aisha said, and Mel couldn't assess the tone in her voice. She was too distracted by the next in the series of messages that had been arriving on her phone since the first lot arrived some forty-eight hours ago.

'Well, what can I say, I am very popular at the moment. With this trip happening in a few weeks, there is a lot to organise.' Mel clicked the phone to blank and looked at her friends.

Should she just tell the girls? She had thought about that a lot before she arrived at Sophy's this evening. These were her closest friends. She could be completely honest with them and they would get it. But for some reason she decided to hold onto the information about the person who was texting her this evening.

'Oh, the life of a singer,' Sophy said.

'A cruise ship singer,' Aisha added, clearly not thinking about what she had said until Sophy looked at Mel, trying to gauge her reaction. Mel's mouth twitched slightly. She knew Sophy had been dying to let out some wisecrack about cruise ship singers since she'd told her about the job. She looked at Sophy's slightly contorted face, which was desperate to explode into laughter, but she was trying to hold it all in. Mel decided it was time to give Sophy what she had been waiting for. She let out a loud laugh. Aisha looked at them and laughed too.

'You're a cruise ship singer,' Aisha spluttered.

'And you're cruising for a bruising,' Mel said but couldn't hide her amusement.

'Oh, thank God,' Sophy began. 'Because honestly, if Aisha hadn't said anything, I wasn't sure I'd be able to look at you.'

'Sure, it comes with a certain amount of stigma, but it also comes with three free cabins and a half-decent wage, so I'm not complaining. But please feel free to laugh at me as much as you like. I am not going to be offended.'

'Of course not, because you're a professional,' Aisha said.

'Absolutely,' Mel said and glanced at her phone again as it pinged. She could almost feel the heat of the stare from Aisha. It would be easier to just say something, she realised, but something was making her keep it to herself, for a little while longer at least, and she was annoyed with herself, but she couldn't help one more look and when she saw Aisha reach for more nibbles, she grabbed her phone. Her face ached where she wanted to smile because of what the most recent message said. Mel looked up from her phone, ready to slip back into the conversation as if her mind had not been somewhere else, with another person, in another time.

'Well, I can't wait. I really need the break. I am going to miss the boys like mad but honestly, they are such hard work sometimes. I mean, I dream of the break and then when I'm not with them, I'm desperate to be back with them. What's wrong with me?' Aisha put her hands over her face in mock stress.

'Because kids are utter knobs sometimes. If we don't remove ourselves from their vicinity once in a while, we will go stark raving bonkers. We were never supposed to do this parenting lark alone. You know your fourth trimester business?' Mel addressed Aisha and she nodded. 'Well, when they get bigger it's like that but the opposite. We need to let other family members step in from time to time to give us a break. They bond with the babies, kids get a holiday from Mum, we all miss each other, and we come back fresh and energised, ready to parent the shit out of life again.'

Aisha nodded. 'I know, I know, you're right. I read it all the time. It's always hard when you actually do it. We've only ever done a night away before without the boys.'

'So can I take it that you are both coming?'

Mel looked between Aisha and Sophy. Sophy nodded meekly then more enthusiastically. Mel settled her gaze on Aisha.

Aisha took a deep breath then let out a sigh. 'Well, if I must and you can't possibly manage without me.' Aisha rolled her eyes theatrically.

Mel whooped loudly and raised her glass.

'Then here's to ten days of freedom!'

Glasses were raised and clinked, and amongst the chiming of the glass, Mel felt the word 'freedom' echo around her. What did that mean for her in this situation? And what did the messages on her phone mean for her? As Sophy and Aisha chatted animatedly about what outfits they were going to wear, Mel glanced down at her phone and the most recent message and felt her stomach do a happy flip.

* * *

5.43 p.m. – Mel – My God, why do I feel so shattered at this time of the day? It's worse than when they were babies.

5.50 p.m. – Aisha – I am beginning to detest the sight of the clock after 2 p.m. It's basically a countdown until the school run. I mean, I actually love them when they're home, but the thought of leaving the house and collecting them fills me with this unexplainable dread! What is that?

6.01 p.m. – Mel – I'm not sure. I have the same feeling. I think it's because we're so creative, darling.

6.03 p.m. – Sophy – It's because the school run is a right royal pain in the arse. How many years of this do we have left?

6.05 p.m. – Mel – I don't want to think about it. I'll be fifty-four by the time Sky heads off to secondary school. 😂

6.06 p.m. – Sophy – 😓

6.07 p.m. – Aisha – You only get more fabulous, Mel.

6.08 p.m. – Sophy – Okay, I'll use her words.

10

SOPHY

The primary school WhatsApp group chats were coming in fast and fierce. Sophy had thrown herself in and was giving it her absolute all, the way she did with most things. She had thought about the possibility of just being on the side-lines, maybe posting the odd smiley face and thumbs up, but that wasn't Sophy and Blythe and her crew knew that. They saw how present she was online so to them it probably didn't seem as much. And Sophy was pretty sure it wouldn't amount to much more than the odd cake sale and playdate. If she was honest, Sophy was looking forward to a new support network of mum friends who lived in Putney.

Sophy had arrived in the playground just before 3.15. She spotted Blythe watching her and gave her an enthusiastic wave. Blythe was not the sort of woman who Sophy would normally be instantly attracted to, but she was willing to give the friendship a shot. This was her first experience of playground friendships so she had nothing to compare it to. Blythe was at her side in a matter of moments.

'Sophy! Hiiiiiii!' she crooned. 'How's things?' Blythe spoke breathlessly.

'Good, thanks, Blythe. How are you?' Sophy gave a glance at the school gates, a flutter of excitement in her stomach as she anticipated them opening, her baby boy running into her arms.

Blythe began recapping the last week's worth of messages as if Sophy might not have read them, even though Blythe would have clearly seen she had by the mass of blue ticks that appeared once everyone had read them and Sophy was sure she had sent sufficient replies to the many, many messages that came through day and night. Had she missed something on one of the threads? Admittedly Sophy had speed-read a few of the posts so there may have been something vital she had overlooked. Sophy felt a strange sense of disorganisation and she hated that feeling. She vowed from now on to read each and every comment so that she was up to speed.

'Has the first week been tough for you?' Blythe finally asked and Sophy was glad to steer the conversation away from the WhatsApp messages. Blythe said it in a way that sounded so sincere that Sophy's memory of being in the playground and crying almost began replaying itself as she felt her eyes prickle with tears. Why was she so damn emotional? It was just a bloody school. She could take Max out at any point and home-school him. Jeff had threatened to enrol Max in the local private school a few times, but Sophy knew it was all bravado. Jeff did seem to be doing better for himself, but he was also a stingy bastard and would never part with thousands a year for education. He just liked everyone to know that he could afford to do it.

Sophy sucked in a breath and her nose stung with discarded tears.

'It has been an adjustment, that's for sure, but Max is fine and settled, so I'm happy. How's...' Blythe's daughter's name completely escaped her memory and Sophy began to feel her armpits prickle with sweat. This was bad, but remembering thirty-two other children's names was proving more difficult than she could have ever imagined. It was not like pre-school where Max had a few friends he connected with.

'Beatrice,' Blythe said quickly as though she weren't reminding but merely prompting.

'Yes.' Sophy finally breathed out.

'Yes, she's a doll. Settled fine. Only girl out of the four of them. It's constant chaos and there is barely a moment for me. But that is why the group is soooo important to me. It's my way of switching off at the end of the day.'

'It's not really switching off...' Sophy began quietly and then realised she wasn't speaking to either Mel or Aisha and maybe a filter would have been appropriate in this situation with someone she had just met and barely knew.

'What's that?' Blythe cocked her head to the side and gave a pained smile. She had heard her.

'I said it's not really switching off, it's more like switching on,' Sophy said a little louder and with a bit more confidence.

'Oh, do you not look at your phone in the evening?' Blythe asked. Her tone had changed and Sophy could hear a brittle edge to it. She needed to turn this around asap.

'I do and it's not good, but it's the only time I get to do my work without any interruptions. So I am very much on my device but I'm usually focusing on work stuff.'

Nice one, Sophy thought to herself, that was a double whammy. It got her off with her weird spontaneous comment and also gave her a get-out clause if she had indeed missed many comments.

'Right, right. We're both as bad as each other.' Blythe sounded more relaxed. 'Doing anything nice after school?'

'We're off to the park, this one needs exercising like a dog.' Sophy had agreed to meet with Aisha and Mel at a park that was central to them all.

But Blythe was still looking at Sophy, an inane smile plastered to her face. The school bell was a welcome sound, then the arrival of a small girl, presumably her daughter Beatrice, snapped Blythe out of her trance.

Sophy heard a small groan come from Max, who was suddenly there at her side. It was hunger. She began to frisk herself for the bags of snacks she had brought with her.

'I have some ideas for raising money for the PTA,' Blythe said, her attention back on Sophy, clearly no intention of leaving the playground just yet.

'Oh?' Sophy had never been much of a joiner when she was at

school, but that was because she had been too busy chatting up boys and touching up her make-up. Sophy looked at Blythe and couldn't imagine her as the sort of girl who would spend her breaktimes lying on the grass with the popular boys or locked in a cubicle with two other girls sampling each other's Impulse sprays. From the content she posted on the group chat, Sophy was sure Blythe was an academic and always had been and now her four offspring were consuming her time and mind, she needed somewhere for all that intelligence to go.

It was obvious to Sophy why some women were drawn to the school cause once their little ones were in the system. It wasn't all altruistic. Blythe seemed like someone who needed something else to do with her time. Sophy was almost to capacity and so she hoped she wasn't going to be overdoing things by pouring herself into projects like this WhatsApp group and helping the PTA. Maybe, Sophy thought, she could help Blythe out in return. Women from all around the world contacted her and she could quite often see this desire within them to be doing something else as well as being a mum and partner. Sophy didn't believe she had invented some sort of magical formula, but she did feel as though she were helping parents. The Mums' Club was about connection and when you connected with other women, you often became your most authentic self, and Sophy had always been an advocator of running towards what makes your heart leap and your stomach flip. She had ignored her own mantra for a few years when she was with Jeff, but she still had no regrets. That relationship had resulted in Max and he was her world.

She needed to get to the park. Aisha had mentioned she was bringing home-made brownies and she was hankering after a sweet treat as the afternoon blood sugars had well and truly slumped.

'I was going to put all the ideas on the group chat, but one of them I think we could discuss and see if we can't make a head start on it. I think it would be right up your alley.'

'Sounds great, Blythe, I will look out for that post,' Sophy said quickly, now imagining the brownie in her hand.

Blythe's face expanded and her eyes widened. 'Great, that's great, thank you, Sophy. I'll see you tomorrow.'

'Will do!' Sophy grabbed Max's hand and pressed it against the handle of the buggy and began a swift walk to the park.

It took almost fifteen minutes in total and when they arrived, Max was complaining his legs hurt. Aisha and Mel were already there, parked up on a bench complete with a table where there was an array of snacks laid out.

'My gosh, mine won't need to eat after this!' Sophy looked at the spread of cheeses and crackers and fruit and spied the brownies. She pulled out her offering, a bag of salt and vinegar kettle chips.

Mel and Aisha both eyed the kettle chips and then looked at Sophy.

'What? I was rushing.'

Mel shook her head and Aisha looked at Sophy and winked.

'Oh, for goodness' sake.' Sophy scrambled around in her backpack and found two packets of raisins and a fruit bar. She threw them with the crisps into the centre of the table.

'Gee, thanks, Soph, what would we do without you?' Mel teased. Sophy ignored her and continued unclipping Poppy out of her buggy and sitting down with her on the bench. She reckoned she had about fifteen minutes' talk time before Poppy wanted to go off exploring the park and Sophy would have to follow her around. This was something the other two didn't have to worry about any more unless they were all in a big kids' park when assistance was usually required by all parents. But this was a small park with smaller equipment which the boys and Sky would be able to navigate by themselves, which meant Sophy would be on toddler duty alone. She pulled snacks and treats in front of Poppy, so she was distracted by sights and sounds and smells for a while and then began intercepting the conversation that already seemed to be in flow between Aisha and Mel.

'So Niall and I had a spat last night, one of very few, you understand, he thinks it's not okay for Jeff to show up when he feels like it and ask to see Max, which by the way he hasn't for a long time, but I said it should really be okay as he is his son and just because we don't live together and all that, if I were Jeff I would be turning up all the time to see Max.'

'That's because you're not Jeff,' Mel said, ignoring the fact that

Sophy had completely interrupted and was talking as though she were a record playing on the wrong setting.

'And that's very noble of you, Soph, but if it were the other way round, Jeff would not be letting you just show up, out of spite may I add, and not for Max's welfare, which by the way is the reason that he can't just show up when he fancies,' Mel said and Sophy felt the passion in her voice that she always tried to hide when she spoke of Jeff. Their past was linked and Sophy would never be able to erase what had happened. Gender-based violence was the way Aisha referred to it. One night when Jeff had tried to take advantage of Mel. When she turned him down, he had tried to force himself on her. Mel had been mildly injured but it was Jeff who had come off worse with a black eye courtesy of Mel. Jeff had agreed to seek therapy; it was the one and only thing that Sophy had asked of him before they went their separate ways. Sophy couldn't bear the thought of this incident getting swept under the carpet. Mel was her friend and she needed her to know that she cared about Jeff's actions. Who knew what might have happened had Mel not given him a right hook and then managed to peg it. To Sophy's knowledge, Jeff had never done anything like that before or since.

Sophy knew that Mel was right, but Sophy had a way of always believing that others would act the same way as her, that their morals would always align with hers and she was always shocked when they were so far off. Of course she shouldn't just let Jeff show up and take Max whenever he wanted.

'Is he still with Debbie?' Aisha asked.

'No.' Sophy popped open a packet of raisins for Poppy.

'Oh, then it might be a new girlfriend, that might explain the sudden interest. He wants to show Max off.'

Sophy pulled a face of disgust. 'You think?'

'Aisha's right,' Mel piped up. 'It's a phase. He'll get bored and then Max will be left confused as to why Daddy doesn't want to see him more often. I'd stick to his every other Saturday overnight stay.'

Sophy nodded. She was already thinking of the next topic she could cover before Poppy wanted to scoot down and play.

'Should I fill the fridge and freezer with meals whilst I'm away, or will that insult Niall's sister?'

Sophy launched into the next subject. Neither of the other women batted an eyelid.

'Depends, does she cook?'

'She's her mother's daughter, isn't she?' Sophy said.

'Oh, my gosh, you sounded so Irish when you said that then!'

Sophy laughed. 'I feel so Irish sometimes, Niall's phrases have rubbed off on me.'

'So Cecilia, is it?' Aisha asked Sophy. She was good with names and faces; she could remember all of the names of all of Mel and Sophy's extended families and now Niall's family had been added, she reeled them off without having to stretch her memory too hard.

'No, Shannon,' Sophy confirmed.

'Ah, she's lovely,' Aisha said.

'I'd put three or four home-made meals in the freezer that will feed them all, lasagnes, mac and cheese, but some fresh fruit and veg and something like burgers and sausages that they can easily cook and then leave the staples like fish fingers and nuggets in the freezer for emergencies,' Mel said.

'Right. Noted,' Sophy said. Poppy began to wiggle on her lap. Sophy pulled off a piece of brownie and gave it to her. She stuffed it in her mouth and continued to wiggle off Sophy's lap.

Sophy stood up, emitting a soft sigh, and followed Poppy, who immediately homed in on the swings.

'For the love of Christ,' Sophy muttered under her breath. 'Not the swings,' as her daughter held her hands up to be lifted into the toddler swing. There Sophy stood for the next fifteen minutes, pushing her daughter, whilst she felt her brain slowly implode with boredom.

11

AISHA

There had been so much to discuss the last few days with the cruise and organising everything leading up to it that Aisha wasn't sure anyone was ready for sharing news of her business venture. Besides, she had only enquired, and although the unit came with a kitchen, who was to say that she would be allowed to run a restaurant from there? She had received a call back the very same day that she had enquired about it and had a viewing lined up for next week. She had mentioned to Charley that she was taking a look and she responded as though she had signed the contract, pure elation bursting from her.

She had almost mentioned it at the park earlier in the week but then Sophy had talked non-stop, which Aisha understood because when the twins were very young, she would cram as many sentences into a play date as possible before the babies demanded her attention. But it was probably for the best because she didn't need to be bombarded with questions from the two of them when she hadn't even drawn up a business plan. She knew it involved food, and the Jamaican twist that she had always talked about. But what else could she do to make the restaurant a success in a place where there were already so many great restaurants serving such amazing dishes? What did she have to offer that was so different, and what made her so special?

There was certainly no guarantee that it would work and be a success. All she had was the fire in her belly that had reignited the moment she saw the 'for let' sign in the window. It had been a low energy that whirred away when the boys were very young and she knew she was unable to be anywhere but with them. But every now and then she would see or feel a glimpse of it like when she saw a recipe or some crockery that she thought would be perfect for the brand she was hoping to create. Then she would think to herself, *There you are. Don't worry, I'll get to you soon.* But not all dreams became a reality and Aisha needed to decide if it was the right thing to do for her family. It was a big commitment; she would be at the restaurant a lot and then there was the admin. Could she be a mum and a businesswoman?

When her phone buzzed and snapped her from her daydream, she was catapulted into another area of worry. Her mother. But at least Martina was texting, which was a step up from last week.

It was Saturday and usually Aisha would go meet up with her mum or they would take the boys bowling and then for a milkshake. Charley would often be with them, and it would be a dinner cooked at home with both Jon and Martina there and then they would bathe the boys and put them to bed. But the text from Martina was brief and short.

I won't make it out today. Give them boys a kiss.

Aisha felt her gut lurch again. She felt as if she had been living on the edge the last few weeks, every time her phone pinged with a reply from her mum. Martina was not what Aisha or any of her family members would describe as jolly and she always held a degree of seriousness about her, the authoritarian parent to five children that she had been unable to fully shake. But over the years it had softened and from that hard chrysalis, a more content and less stressed Martina had evolved. But these recent messages definitely lacked any spark or emotion of any kind and Aisha knew she had cause for concern. But Martina continued batting away conversations on the matter of her health and because Aisha knew her mother had never been ill in her entire life, and she still hadn't seen any signs apart from this exhaustion and cold, she couldn't decide if she was overreacting.

And the cruise was a matter of weeks away and Aisha knew she would be worried the whole time she was away. She needed to somehow extract the information out of Martina before she went. At least that way she could process it before she left the country rather than trying to work it all out whilst she was away.

It was a rainy morning and Aisha had suggested pancakes in Brixton, near the unit that she was viewing on Monday. It was the ideal location for two reasons: one, Martina didn't need to walk too far from her house and two, they could all casually walk past the unit after, and Aisha could mention that she was viewing the property. She was sure there would be an outpouring of questions but she couldn't keep this to herself. If she was going to do this, she needed the support of her entire family. But now Martina couldn't come, so it would just be the four of them. Which was also fine. Aisha bashed out a message to Martina – much longer than the message she had received – telling her not to worry and that they would FaceTime her later.

They chose tables near the window because if the boys became bored with their food, they struck up a game of 'I spy' before pulling out the colouring books and then the iPad as a final resort if they wouldn't settle and Aisha and Charley just wanted that extra twenty minutes to order another drink and get to finish it whilst it was hot. Taking the boys out was often a like a monkey's tea party, with drinks getting spilled, dishes not to their exact taste, and food that required cutting up. But as Charley said, it was all part of their learning journey. Learning to be little twats, Aisha had muttered under her breath after one particularly distressing café time which involved Otis requesting quite clearly to a packed café that his whole apple be peeled. When Aisha had finished peeling the apple – which remained in one perfect piece – Otis had demanded the skin be put back on. When Aisha tried to calmly explain to the then three-year-old that the apple skin would not go back on, all hell had broken loose. Otis fell to the floor like a rag doll, refusing to get back up again. Jude, thinking it was a game that he needed to be involved in, joined his brother under the table, only for Otis to scream blue murder until she and Charley had each picked up a twin and left. Just as they reached the door, a well-dressed lady in her seventies held out an apple and offered it to Aisha with a smile and a few kind words of encouragement.

Aisha had managed to snatch the apple on her way out as Otis threatened to catapult from her arms. She'd barely had time to thank the woman and she certainly wasn't going to reward either of the boys with the food that had got them into this situation in the first place. Instead she and Charley had marched down the high street looking like two lunatics carrying two smaller lunatics.

Once at home, the boys had behaved like perfect angels, all that angst and frustration had been left behind on the café floor.

But here they were, over a year since such incidents, and the boys had come on in leaps and bounds. Their table manners specifically. And Aisha had learned not to pander to their needs and give in to silly requests the way she had in the past. It only led to a massive aggravation.

'I think I'll have the chocolate pancakes with blueberries and a flat white.' Charley laid her menu down then unexpectedly took her phone out of her bag. Aisha eyed her as Charley scrolled quickly then put her phone away. She looked out of the window and not at Aisha. Did Charley know Aisha was staring at her, willing her to explain the slightly uncharacteristic behaviour?

Aisha noted how surreptitiously Charley took her phone out and flicked through it, just for a second. She had been looking for something. She had been checking her phone, something that Charley rarely, if ever, did. She used her phone for business and calls, checked her emails twice a day and occasionally caught up with social media at the end of the day to 'keep her foot in the door' with her uni mates, as she put it. This was not like Charley at all.

The waitress took their orders and they kept two hungry boys entertained until their food arrived in just under ten minutes, which was a relief all round.

'Is everything okay?' Aisha asked as Charley took another surreptitious glance at her phone. It didn't suit Charley to look so tetchy.

Charley looked like a rabbit caught in the headlights as she pushed her phone to the side of the table.

'Are *you* okay?' Aisha put her hand over Charley's.

Charley's face softened. 'Yes. I'm fine. Just thinking about work. Sorry.'

'That's okay,' Aisha said, screwing her face up. 'It's not like you, that's all.' Aisha leaned over, cut up a piece of pancake and nudged it towards the edge of the plate for Otis, who had suddenly become distracted with a sugar sachet.

'You should be feeling excited, though? With the viewing on Monday? Do you want me to come?'

'Well, only if you can, I don't want to drag you away from all your work. You seem pretty busy. I can show you pictures.'

Charley shook her head. 'It should be fine.' She popped a blueberry in her mouth.

Charley chatted about what she fancied for dinner that night and they drew up a shopping list for the way home. The boys were still very well behaved, both finding relaxation in colouring. This was unusual but Aisha tried to take in the moment, savouring the cinnamon and apple pancakes with whipped cream and caramel sauce. It was a bit of an indulgent treat, but it had been two weeks of school for the boys, and she was proud of them, and happy they had settled so well.

Charley popped to the toilet and Aisha found herself scanning the table to see if she had left her phone, then when she realised it wasn't there, she began timing how long she was in the toilet for.

When Charley came back, Aisha scanned her face for any more signs of frustration. Aisha began to feel the importance of properly getting back to work bearing down on her. Charley may not have mentioned that she needed Aisha's support now, but based on how much time Charley was spending on her phone for work, she made the decision there and then. After the viewing on Monday, if she was able to run a restaurant from the venue, she would scribble up a business plan.

They paid up in the café and left, each holding a twin's hand, and headed out onto the street.

'I've just realised I need to send off an audio sample today for that chocolate commercial. Will you be okay grabbing those bits from the supermarket without me? I'll cook.' Charley planted a kiss on Aisha's cheek and waved as she went ahead, not giving Aisha any time to protest. It was fine, except it wasn't. Her gut was flipping and not in a good way. The boys had been at school for a mere few days and suddenly she felt as though it had been forever, the way she saw Charley working so hard in comparison. Her days were still long and full with the boys and she wasn't sure how they would juggle her running a restaurant and Charley working as well, but she was sure it would all work out if it was meant to be.

She felt flustered and pulled at the boys to hurry to the supermarket. Once inside, she took a small trolley and tried to concentrate on what they had agreed for dinner. She opened her bag to pull out the list. Where was Jude? She spotted Otis picking up tomatoes and looking as though he were threatening to throw one at his brother and then she saw Jude, on the floor, having just completed a sliding knee skid and looking very pleased with himself.

Oh, shit.

She had just filled her four-year-old boys with sugar and brought them into a supermarket, alone. If Charley were here, they may have survived this. But alone, she was just a sitting duck. She had been so busy worrying about Charley that she had forgotten to read the riot act to the twins before they entered the supermarket, or at least offer incentives for good behaviour. Now it was too late. They had crossed the boundary into no man's land, and she was about to get annihilated. All that time sitting quietly in the café was a prelude to the carnage that was about to unfold before her.

Aisha wasn't about to walk out of this supermarket a failure, not when Charley was working so hard and over the weekend as well, which was rare.

She looked at the boys, looked at her list, gripped the trolley and walked towards them both.

Twenty-five minutes later, Aisha emerged from Sainsbury's on the high street in Clapham with two boys on a sugar come-down, a bruised knee from where one of them had rammed the trolley into her leg and a handful of punishments to deliver when they arrived home. None of which she could remember. She had no recollection of which twin did what and what punishment she had dealt out to whom. It wasn't their fault; she knew that she had been unprepared, and the boys had been high as kites. They'd go home, the boys' blood sugar levels would even out, and she would go back to worrying about everything else that was on her mind.

12

MEL

There were six messages on Mel's phone by Sunday morning. After the few she had read at Sophy's house, she had replied to two, not wanting to encourage things too much.

She stared at the name on the screen in bewilderment, his profile picture, and a snippet of the latest message.

So looking forward to seeing you.

Mel felt her stomach lurch.

It was some sort of weird coincidence. It had to be.

Mel had met Leo Monroe when she had first lost her mum and she had begun to apply to work in the pubs and clubs when she discovered her passion for singing and dancing. He had been the proprietor of a bar and had offered her instant work. She would sing on a Saturday night and for the other three nights she would work behind the bar. It was great hours, leaving her time in the day to exercise and sleep – one of her favourite things to do at the time – and the busy night shifts helped her forget about her grief over her mum for those hours she was at work. She and Leo had become close and eventually they were an item. He was about six years older than her, had gambled all his money into businesses but somehow got lucky. He dressed well and smelled even better. It was the security and companionship she had been craving.

Then she'd met Daz. Daz was everything Leo wasn't. He was sensible, educated, and incredibly cautious of Leo. Leo was busy with work and had little time for Mel but the spark was still there and so when she began casually dating Daz, who hinted at his dislike for Leo, Mel had put it down to ego. But as time went on, it was clear that Daz was feeling more and more uncomfortable and that if their relationship was going to last then she needed to cool things with Leo. He wasn't so much forbidding her to see him, but he made it clear that he wasn't going to share her or put himself at risk later on down the line. Mel had been smitten with Daz, but Leo had always been there in the background, reminding her of what could have been. But Mel knew she had made the right choice. Leo had never had a serious girlfriend when she had known him and he had showed no signs of wanting to slow down. Daz had offered her a home, a chance at a real life. Something she never thought she would get after her mum died because she thought it was all over for her.

But she did love Daz and had fallen for him. But there was always the notion for Mel of 'what if?' She loved her life, her home, and her girls. But how would her life have turned out if she had made a go of things with Leo?

And now here he was, over fifteen years since the last time she saw him. When her agent had asked if she minded if the head of entertainment call her to discuss plans, she had been fine with that, as it was something she had come to expect from venues. But when she'd seen Leo's face on his WhatsApp profile, she'd felt her stomach do a small flip – a sensation she had felt a lot when she had been with him. There had always been a sense of excitement when she had been with Leo. But she knew deep down it was superficial, that that feeling couldn't possibly last. Which was why she had been drawn to Daz in the end. Of course, the passion was there, but it went deeper with the two of them, when she looked at Daz, she had seen a future she could never imagine with Leo. Yet here they were, their two girls growing up and this vast space had opened up between them. How on earth were they supposed to fill it? By getting a couples hobby? Mel couldn't see Daz at a Zumba class and Mel wasn't about to tag along on one of his annual *Star Wars* conferences.

Leo said he would be on board the cruise ship and if she felt like seeing him, that would be great. A few drinks for old times' sake. That's all it had to be, Mel told herself and tried not to overthink it. Although it hadn't passed her by that perhaps there was some element of closure needed here. Maybe from both parties. She just needed to accept she was going to see Leo, it would be a nice element to the trip, she would still have plenty of time to spend with the girls. Besides, there was only so much hiding you could do on a boat and before long, she was sure she would bump into him anyway.

So why every time her phone pinged did she get a toned-down version of that stomach flip that she'd had with Leo all those years ago?

'Mel?' Daz's voice rang through the hallway into the kitchen. Mel spun around, shame and guilt flooding her body, which she was sure was evident on her face. Daz came into the kitchen and stood in the doorway.

'I called you like four times?' Daz was rummaging through the drawer of doom. The drawer that contained everything that didn't have a home.

Mel clicked her phone to blank, but the last message from Leo had engrained itself in her brain.

Still Sassy as ever.

Sassy. That had been his nickname for her. She had been in her early twenties, her grief manifesting itself as a bit of an attitude that Leo had found so endearing and which had become her default personality for a while. And then it became their thing. She was his Sassy.

'I was sure there were some triple As in here,' Daz said into the drawer.

Mel could feel her heart returning to a normal rate. This was not what she needed. Work had never made her feel this wound up before.

If she could just compartmentalise this as seeing an old friend whilst working then she would be okay. But she knew it wasn't as simple as that. She had yet to mention any of this to Daz. He was completely supportive of her going away – a little too supportive, if she were being honest. She wondered if she felt him pushing her away because of how he had been towards her lately. But she had yet to tell Daz that Leo was running the entertainment for the ship and that he would be on board for the duration of her trip. She couldn't cancel the gig, she didn't want to let the girls down and yet at the same time she was holding back from being completely honest with Daz. Yet he had been so busy lately, always with his head in one of his accounts, bringing more and more work home and then, when he wasn't working, he was falling asleep. She would have to find a way of telling him, maybe she would cook a meal and then they could have an early night.

Mel opened the drawer next to the drawer of doom, a place she kept a selection of household essentials that from time to time would be needed. Yet Daz never thought to look in there. She handed him an unopened packet of batteries, mulling over his expression, wondering if she could slip in the words, 'My ex Leo will be on the ship.'

But he already seemed so engrossed in whatever he was doing.

'Thanks.' He ripped them open, leaving the cardboard and plastic on the kitchen counter, and went back into the front room. Mel followed behind and found the pair of them with a toy microphone, the one they had bought Leia for her third birthday.

'I'm going to be like Mummy!' Sky announced as Mel walked through the room. 'I'm going to siiiing.' Sky twirled around and Mel felt her gut jolt with love for her daughter. She was so free, so unaware of the strains and obstacles that lay ahead for her. And there she was now wanting to emulate her mother. And that was when the guilt began to seep through. She wants to be like me, Mel thought. Why? Mel did not feel like a good person, nor did she feel like a good role model for her daughter right now. Mel should tell Daz that Leo was going to be on the boat. He would tell her how unhappy he was, but that there was nothing he could do about it. And if Mel knew what her husband would say, quite possibly, verbatim, then why didn't she just tell him?

'Mummy, look!' Sky did a quick cartwheel followed by another. She was about to do a third when Daz held his hand out. 'No more room, darlin'. Cartwheel outside.'

'Wow, Sky, you've got really good with your cartwheels. We'll have to get her to acrobatics or something.'

'Or something...' Daz said absently as he pushed the batteries into the microphone and the device came to life with colours and a jingle.

'Yeeheee!' Sky shrieked and grabbed it from Daz. He shook his head and looked at Mel.

'You okay? You seem a bit... dreamy.'

Mel looked at Daz and wanted to tell him that she could say the same about him, how he had been somewhere else every time she had tried to speak to him recently. Maybe this was the time to mention Leo.

'I have a lot on at the moment.'

'Oh, what's that then?' Daz stood up then sat down on the sofa. His whole attention was on Mel. What was this? He had barely been able to look at her the last few weeks and now this?

This was her chance, she thought. Sky was consumed with her new, old toy and Leia was out.

But even though the words were teetering at the edge of her mouth, ready to fall out into the room, to shift the atmosphere, to change the expression on Daz's face from bright to dark, she wouldn't let them out. She couldn't face whatever drama would unfold, however short-lived, however much she wanted to be 100 per cent honest, she guessed it was because she didn't want to feel his disappointment. She knew that having any interaction with Leo was going to bring back memories of those months that Daz had felt he needed to fight for Mel. And Mel wasn't sure he was up for a fight. She wasn't sure he had anything left in him any more.

'I was just thinking about Ksenia,' Mel said eventually.

'Ah,' Daz said.

'I just think there must be something we can do.'

Daz sighed. Mel felt her body go tense.

'What can we do?' he said eventually. 'We aren't responsible for everyone. We have our own lives to worry about,' he said and he sounded solemn. Mel wanted to ask if there was any more meaning to that and if indeed they should be worrying about their own lives more than she currently was.

'She's such a good cleaner. She should just set up on her own. She could sit back and take some proper maternity leave then.'

'Businesses take time to set up, and is Ksenia even that business minded? I know she is straight talking. I mean, so I have heard. You know I barely get a grunt out of her.'

'That's because she is cautious of men. I still don't know why.'

'I've never been alone in a room with her.'

'That's because she usually comes when you're at work.'

'I just know she hates me.'

'She doesn't hate you, Daz.'

Daz went quiet.

'I really want to help her, I just don't know how,' Mel said, more to herself.

Daz stood up and walked away, leaving Mel standing there watching her daughter spinning around in the centre of the room.

13

SOPHY

'I haven't done a thing. I need to make some pies or something for the freezer.' Sophy pulled out another skirt from the wardrobe and threw it on the bed. She was going through outfits that needed washing ready for the trip for which, even though it was still over a week away, she knew she needed to get super organised. Not just for herself but for everyone else she was leaving behind. Despite Shannon coming to help, she wouldn't know her way around the house.

'Ah, Soph, me and me sis will be grand, you don't need to go getting yourself all het up the week before you travel, you'll be stressed by the time you get there.'

Sophy looked over to the other side of the bed, where Niall was flimsily folding clean clothes and placing them onto already teetering piles. He always offered to help with laundry but his folding skills were so bad the piles were like the leaning tower of Pisa.

Sophy whipped one of Max's T-shirts from the pile.

'It's much easier if you do it like this.' She expertly folded it in mid-air then laid it on the bed and finished the fold in one swift movement. Niall looked at her as if she had just performed a magic trick then continued in his own shoddy style. It meant that Sophy would need to re-fold everything again before it went in the drawers anyway as they wouldn't fit, but it seemed it was what she had become accustomed to.

Her phone beeped. She looked at it and threw it back on the bed. The autumn fayre was being held in the school hall tomorrow and she had yet to make the chocolate cake she had promised Blythe she would make.

'I bet you make a beautiful celebratory cake what with all those gorgeous photos on Instagram,' Blythe had said and somehow Sophy had not been able to correct her and tell her that her culinary skills stretched to a couple of recipes that she had nailed; lasagne (although she always used the Dolmio white sauce), a chilli con carne that she added dark chocolate to because it made Niall say, 'Wow, that chocolate really brings out all the flavours,' every time and home-made jelly because she had loved watching her mum make it when she was a kid and she was so impatient for it to set she would usually end up sneaking some sips of the liquid, which tasted like a really strong flavoured squash.

'Who's that?' He looked at the bed with the messages open on the phone. 'I thought you had notifications muted on that group?'

Niall had suggested that Sophy mute the group after twenty-four hours of relentless messages. Sophy had agreed with his idea but then decided not to go with it because it made her feel like a failure. What sort of working woman with two children couldn't handle receiving a few WhatsApp messages from the school mums?

'Damn it, I was going to schedule posts for when I was away today.'

'Ahh, your Instagram and Twitter and what not will be fine whilst you're gone.' Niall picked up a shirt of Sophy's and Sophy watched as Niall attempted a fold but it ended up being rolled into a sausage shape.

Sophy took a deep breath, trying to contain her frustration, but ended up leaning over the bed and snatching the shirt out of Niall's hand and folding it herself.

'Would you take a breath for a minute?' Niall said.

She looked at Niall, who was now stretching out on the bed next to Poppy, who had fallen asleep an hour ago with a high temperature.

'And look at her! How can I go away when she is ill? What if she gets worse?' Sophy fell to her knees and leaned over the bed, looking at her daughter, her soft wispy hair, her small lips and rosy cheeks.

'I told you to take a breath,' Niall said in a stage whisper as Poppy gave a slight shudder and a long sigh. 'Is she sleeping in with us?' He stroked his daughter's head.

'I think so.' Sophy picked up the rest of the unfolded clothes and threw them into the corner of the room, having completely given up for the day. What she would do for a utility room. She put the folded clothes on top of the chest of drawers and then went into their en suite and brushed her teeth. Poppy was in the middle of the bed and Sophy gently climbed in, grateful yet again that they had opted for the super king instead of the king mattress and frame even though the room was only just big enough to take it. 'Who needs to see the carpet anyway?' Sophy had said after the bed delivery company had been and gone.

Sophy let out a huge sigh as she plumped up her pillow to get comfy. She leaned on her side, looking at her daughter sleeping. She was a perfect angel when she was asleep.

Niall reached his hand around the tops of the pillows and stroked his wife's head. He knew all the right things to do. He could read her signs of stress and respond to her in the right way. Always. So she forgave him for his shocking inability to fold the simplest of fabric into a neat square flat package. It was insane. Was she lucky or was this how it was supposed to be? She knew the answer, but she would still from time to time be struck with wonder that there was a man on this earth that fitted with her so perfectly.

When Sophy woke the next morning, Niall and Poppy were not in the bed. Sophy gasped herself awake, threw her dressing gown on and padded downstairs. She could hear the sounds of her family before she reached the final step. Poppy was in her highchair, Max was at the table and a pile of pancakes was in the centre of the table.

'What's this?' Sophy asked.

'I made pancakes,' Niall said.

Sophy lifted one up to her nose and smelled it. It was definitely real and home-made. She kissed Max on the lips, tasting the maple syrup he had slathered over his breakfast, and then Poppy threw her arms in the air to be lifted out.

'She had three,' Niall said.

'Three? But my poorly girl?'

'Just a sniffle.' Niall lifted her out and she flung herself into the waiting arms of her mother.

'I can't believe you made pancakes, though,' Sophy said. And Niall looked at her with his head tilted down slightly. If he were wearing glasses, he would look just like her old English teacher, and she'd fancied him a little bit as well.

'What on earth are you talking about? You make it sound as though I have never made a decent breakfast before. I will survive here without you, Sophy. I'm just reminding you of that.' Niall had a cloth and was wiping the highchair. 'Don't you remember the times when you were so sick when you were pregnant with Poppy and Max and me would get up and make the wholemeal banana muffins before you came down because that was all you could stomach all day?' Niall threw the cloth at the sink, and it landed on the draining board.

'Of course I do.' Sophy sat down at the table with Poppy on her lap. Poppy turned into her and cuddled her. 'But then you stopped once I was back up on my feet.'

'I know,' Niall admitted.

'Why?'

'Because I had... I have a full-time job. I managed a bit of time away then I had to get back to it.'

'So muffins can't be made when you're focusing on your job?' Sophy said absently, not looking at Niall. She knew Niall was a great man, but it always intrigued her how women were able to function on so many levels.

Niall looked at Sophy.

'What do you want me to tell you, Soph? I can't multitask to the level you can. It's muffins or cement mixers.'

Sophy smiled and shook her head, then nuzzled into Poppy's neck, inhaling the sweet scent of her morning skin. She felt her eyes prickle with tears. Ten whole days where she couldn't do this. It was actually going to kill her. The kids were her oxygen. She would die without them, surely.

Why the hell was she feeling so emotional about this? She'd left them for days and even a night before and she knew they would be absolutely fine with Niall and his sister and that time away from them was what she needed.

And in the long run, she would probably be glad that she had taken this time away now because there was a small vibration whirring away within her telling her to go. Sophy just needed to fight against her conscience and remember that she deserved this.

Sophy thought about the cake in the fridge, the one she had bought yesterday as a back-up. She was feeling completely overwhelmed by everything and this morning wasn't any better. Just as she had thought. So she had bought two Belgian sponge cakes from Waitrose, a tub of chocolate frosting, some chocolate hundreds and thousands and a packet of giant buttons.

She put Poppy down on the floor, where she began scooting around on her bum as though she were a baby again, and set everything out on the kitchen counter. Niall looked on, intrigued, as he began clearing up breakfast.

'What's that, Mummy?' Max was by her side. Always ready to get involved when there was baking going on, even it was fake baking.

She picked him up and popped him on the counter.

'You want to help me?'

Max nodded eagerly. 'Yes, yes, yes.'

'Okay. Let's do this.'

Twenty minutes later, Max was just finishing off sticking the last chocolate button to the side of the cake. They had pushed two cakes together on top of one another and then slathered them all over with more fondant. The extra icing gave it more of a rustic feel as well. She stood back and admired her handiwork. Very little work required for a cake that would easily pass as home-made and she and Max had had fun doing it too. Blythe and the PTA mums would be none the wiser and she would look like the Mary Berry of Putney.

'It's a shame it will get eaten,' Sophy said as she snapped an image of the cake, wondering if she would put it up on the 3 a.m. Shattered Mums' Club page (#homemade #cake #ptamumsrock).

She would see how she felt later. She hadn't branched out with anything to do with her life as a primary school mum yet. It felt too different to the 3 a.m. Shattered Mums, she was almost still there with Poppy, who even at two and a half would still wake her up at silly o'clock from time to time.

Sophy looked at the time.

'Max, it's gone ten! We need to be at the fayre before eleven. Let's get our skates on.' Max looked confused by Sophy's comment for a second and made a big show of looking around for a pair of skates before Sophy hauled him upstairs to get dressed.

They arrived at the school at 11.15. Sophy tried hard not to look flustered as they burst through the hallway doors with the cake balanced in one hand, her handbag slipping from her shoulder and a mardy Poppy clutching her skirt. Poppy had decided she was going to use the toilet for a number two, three minutes before they were about to leave. Whilst Sophy had been pleased that Poppy was keen to use the big toilet and not the potty or her pullups, she couldn't believe it was happening on such an important day. She knew they would be late and she knew everyone would be looking at her. They were late when they entered an already buzzing and hot packed hall and Sophy clocked Blythe at the end of the hall, where the cake stand was. Niall trudged behind her with an excited Max, who was already talking about having a go on every stall.

'Blythe, I'm here!' Sophy announced breathlessly to the small crowd that Blythe was with. They all looked and smiled meekly.

'Sophy!' Blythe exclaimed. 'This is Sophy, everyone, the fantastic social media guru and now an amazing baker by the looks of it!' Blythe addressed the group and then looked down at the cake.

'I... well, it was nothing.' Sophy moved from foot to foot, her arm ached to put the cake down.

'No, Sophy, it's really special,' Blythe said.

'It looks so... edible!' one of the women said.

Sophy laughed. 'Well, that's the best compliment I could hope for.'

'You know you're now the official chocolate cake maker for any future events,' Blythe said.

'Mummy got the cakes from the shop, I helped stick them together and I helped put the icing and chocolate buttons on,' Max announced, clear as day, so that all the women looked down at him.

Sophy felt her heart begin to speed up even more than it already was and she felt sweat prickling down her back.

'Sweetie, where's Daddy?' Sophy looked anxiously around.

'I want some of the fake cake, Mummy!' Max began to jump up and down on the spot.

Sophy made a funny face that implied she thought her own son was mad and not talking any sense.

'Oh, is it not home-made?' Blythe asked.

The group of women she had been talking to dispersed.

'Okay, I am just going to put this here.' Sophy slid the cake off her sticky palm on to the table into the centre. She let out a deep breath and smiled awkwardly at Blythe. 'So, I'm just going to...' Sophy bent down to Poppy. 'What was that, sweetie, we need to find Daddy? Come on, then,' Sophy said to a totally mute Poppy, took Max with her other hand and led them away from the cake stall. As she walked away, she took a sly look back and as she did, she saw Blythe moving her cake to the side and to the back of the cake table and putting a tray of scary-looking but very obviously home-made green and blue Cookie Monster cupcakes in its place. She felt a pinch in her heart as she strode over to the chocolate tombola and handed over twenty pounds for tickets. She had her eye on a giant Toblerone and she was ready to panic eat the entire tube.

14

AISHA

Aisha couldn't believe it was the end of September and that they would be going on the cruise in a few days' time. The weekend came to a close with Aisha's head a whirl of thoughts about her mother and the unit she had viewed. Her phone had been red hot for a week with the agent calling her, leaving messages about whether Aisha was interested. It seemed there wasn't anyone brave enough to just take the plunge and start a business. She and Charley had discussed it thoroughly and they both understood the risks, of which there were many. But the agent had not hinted at this, her job was to lease it and she had told Aisha, unable to hide the excitement in her voice, that the unit could become a food outlet. Aisha had felt her insides flip over as images soared through her mind of what the place might become.

She had spent the day beginning her packing, filling the freezer with a home delivery order of things the boys would love whilst she was gone and making their favourite lasagne to eat together the night before she left. Charley was competent in the kitchen, so she wasn't about to undermine her, but the thought of the kids eating a few bits that she had cooked left her with a great sense of satisfaction.

The boys were exhausted. Today had been a day scootering at the park followed by board games and a family film, during which Aisha had managed a sit down for half an hour while she cuddled both boys, trying to imprint the experience to memory, exactly as it was happening, each smell and sound they made, so she could relive it over when she needed to when she was away.

Otis and Jude shared a room, because they were obsessed with one another, in every sense, good and bad. Despite any fights that had occurred that day, they needed to be in the same room by night-time. It was one of Aisha's favourite times of the day. She would pile the boys onto hers and Charley's bed, get a handful of books, usually four, and each twin would choose two books each. Sometimes bedtime reading went on for half an hour, but that was fine. She and Charley took it in turns and when it wasn't her turn, Aisha would often hover near the door just so she could listen to the animated cries of delight from the boys or watch their little bodies slowing down and becoming sleepy in the arms of their mummy.

Now they were sleeping, and it was just her and Charley. Aisha was running through a list in her head, mentally ticking things off and adding extra things she needed to do before going away. She really needed to put together some sort of business plan and then get back to Rachel at the estate agents'. Aisha pulled open the drawer under the coffee table and took out a pad of paper and a pen. Charley had settled in for the night at the other end of the sofa, she had turned the TV on and began scrolling. Watching Netflix series and documentaries was how she switched off. Aisha's brain was not going to let her rest this evening. She opened the pad and looked at the blank page. Her mind started to whir with thoughts of her mum and then the trip and she had these ideas just brewing on the edge of her mind to do with the restaurant. She wanted to keep it small and exclusive. It was only a small unit anyway, which was why she chose it. She drew a large circle in the middle of the page. That would contain the name of the restaurant, she thought. But what would it be called? She had nothing.

'Shall I get us a glass of wine?' Aisha stood up and headed to the kitchen. Aisha heard Charley searching through the quiz shows or looking for a period drama then she heard the familiar sounds of the characters from her recent favourite, an American family saga/drama.

Aisha had been watching bits of it with her recently. Charley had already settled on that programme but would still half-heartedly ask Aisha if there was something she wanted to watch when she returned. But Aisha wasn't much into TV and preferred to listen to an audiobook or read some non-fiction on her Kindle. She had put a pile of cookery books on the sofa and wanted to refresh her mind with some of the recipes, partly for some family cooking, partly for some work ideas, but despite everything she could be doing, she couldn't make herself focus on just one thing.

Aisha bent down to the wine rack, spotted the red she fancied and when she stood up, she clocked Charley's phone on the kitchen counter next to the fruit bowl. Charley had made the boys' lunch boxes this evening and had left it there when she had finished. Aisha edged her way to the device. She could hear the TV in the sitting room. For no other reason than because she was frustrated and unable to settle, Aisha brought the screen to life. She wasn't looking for anything in particular. Charley had been a little more into her phone recently than was absolutely normal for her, but still, Aisha really didn't have any reason to go snooping except as a way to distract herself.

The black screen asked her to enter the passcode.

The date of birth of the twins had been Charley's passcode for years. She heard Charley shout out something at the screen because Charley always got heavily involved in her shows. Aisha's fingers lingered over the phone screen for a second, then she typed in the digits.

The phone gave a shudder, the four circles popped back up. It had rejected it. She must have gone too fast and hit the wrong digit. This time she typed the numbers in slowly. When she had hit the last one and the phone responded in the same way, she knew that she wasn't going to be opening Charley's phone today. Because the passcode had been changed.

* * *

5.40 p.m. – Mel – Hope you're all packed and no last-minute wobbles, not from the adults anyway. I just wanted to say I am truly excited, and I can't wait for you all to join me on this wonderful experience. Thanks for agreeing to come along. If I forget to tell you later, I had a really great time tonight.

5.45 p.m. – Sophy – Aww, I just watched *Pretty Woman* the other night. Love that movie so much.

6.01 p.m. – Aisha – I haven't seen it for years. Great line. Cute. I'm really looking forward to it. Can't wait to see you both.

6.09 p.m. – Sophy – I'm stressed to the hills, but I think I'll be okay once I step on that boat.

15

MEL

The first step onto the boat felt like Mel's heart had just shot into her throat. A completely unexpected reaction to the beginning of the next ten days on board the *Audacious*. It could just be nerves, the likelihood was she was nervous for the next few nights of back-to-back singing with no support, just her. The reality was something entirely different. She could almost sense Leo around every corner as she walked through the ship with her carry-on bag.

She kept thinking back to last night before she left. She had promised herself that she would tell Daz about Leo being onboard. She had made a vat of lamb stew and mash. It was one of Daz's favourites, but she had been being practical and knew it would last them all another two days eaten with jacket potatoes or rice. She then cleared down the kitchen, insisting that Daz go to bed and wait for her there. Her message couldn't have been any clearer. Or at least she had thought. When she arrived upstairs twenty minutes later, having let Bess out for her final wee of the night, stacked the dishwasher and locked up, she discovered Daz in bed snoring. It was only nine o'clock. He knew that this was their last night together for ten days and so Mel had gone back downstairs and put on a film to watch. It had helped distract her from how nervous she was feeling about being on board the *Audacious* in a few hours' time. This morning, Daz had cuddled her and then kissed her on the lips – nothing sensual, just a normal peck – before he headed off to work. Mel had dropped Leia and Sky to school and then headed back home to grab the last bits before she drove to Southampton. She was allowed to board early as one of the staff and would see the girls later when they drove down together about teatime.

For now, it was just her and her handbag. Her cases and dress bags would arrive at her room at some point – she hoped – there were so many of her best outfits in there and a few more that she had treated herself to especially for the gig. She needed a fresh outfit each night and also spares in case of tears or spillage. It was handy that she could walk about a bit and get her bearings, then report to the girls anything they were unsure about. She was certain there would be plenty of questions from both women, from Wi-Fi to how many lifeboats were on board. Mel would make sure she was armed with as much information as possible so the two of them could feel totally relaxed whilst they were here.

Mel knew that Aisha was worried about her mum and that Sophy was worried about dumping so much responsibility onto Niall's sister. But this was going to be a chance for them all to be together for ten days, to sit and relax and read and drink and talk – in the day, at least. In the evenings, Mel would be performing to hundreds of guests, which would leave little time for socialising. And that she was nervous about. She had been gigging but not as much since Robbie left the East End. She just couldn't find anywhere where she felt as at home as she had there. She had only felt at home with one employer and that was Robbie. Except... maybe with one other person. Leo was probably here, right now, somewhere on this ship. Maybe he had an office or some sort of barracks. He had been a night owl, when she really knew him. He would rarely go to bed before 4 a.m. She wondered if time had changed him. She had waited way over a decade, so what was a few more hours' wait to see what had become of the man she had cared so much about for such a significant part of her life?

She walked along behind the porter who was showing her to her room. He swiftly opened the door with the card and left two of them on the dressing table.

'Thank you.' Mel stood awkwardly for a few seconds. Should she tip? She didn't have any cash; she was sure there would be something in the manual which would tell her everything she needed to know. She thanked the porter, and he left. Mel stood and looked around. She was standing in a very bright and spacious area. Had Leo sorted this out for her? Made sure she got some decent digs? She took a quick selfie of her with the window and sea view in the background and sent it to Daz. She was going to keep him involved with the trip the whole time. She didn't want to feel for a minute that she wasn't posting messages to him regularly enough over the ten days. She needed Daz to know that he was as much a part of this trip as she was. Even though he had barely showed any interest in her going or seemed to be sad that they would be apart for almost two weeks.

She knew she was omitting a piece of information about the trip and might put a spanner in their relationship. But somehow, with the way Daz had been of late, she was not allowing herself to feel any guilt for being here with someone who just happened to have been the love of her life once. She didn't need to feel guilty because this was all purely professional. She had been hired to do a job and she was here to do it. But even after all the time they had spent together, she felt a tremor of fear over coming face to face with him again soon. Time apart from people did make her nervous. She was never quite sure how to act. And surely they couldn't just fall back into the roles they had assigned to themselves all those years ago: him calling her Sassy and acting all cool and sophisticated, her a little bit young and naive and unsure of herself but thrilled to have found this worldly man. Things like this made her so nervous. She was a changed woman, she had two children, she had different thoughts and ideas about life. She was not the same woman he had known back then and she was a far cry from that young woman who was desperately seeking something and had found Leo. She couldn't help but feel conscious of what he would see in her after all these years. Mel was trying hard not to overthink it. She wanted to see Leo, that she was pretty certain about, but she couldn't quite work out how the whole interaction would pan out – would he want to spend a lot of time with her and how would that impact her trip? Would the girls hate her for it? Berate her, even?

There was a loud knock on the door and Mel jumped at the sound. Christ, she was tense, she really needed a drink. It was only just after lunch. She shouldn't be thinking like that already, otherwise this whole trip could end up being very messy. It crossed her mind that it might be Leo at the door.

Mel touched the top of her hair, which was packed into her signature messy bun, and glanced at herself in the long mirror on the wall just by the door before she opened it, her heart pounding hard in her chest.

There was a woman dressed in a similar smart uniform as the man who had just escorted her to her room. She was just about visible behind a huge bouquet of flowers.

'Good morning, Mrs Fortuna. I have these flowers for you.'

The steward pushed the large bouquet forwards and already Mel was worrying about how to keep the things alive for the duration of the trip.

'Thank you.' Mel accepted the flowers awkwardly due to the size, so at no point did she seem to get a good look at the girl, who had now turned and was walking back along the corridor.

Mel turned back into her room, giving the door a little kick with her foot so it closed, and went over to the dressing table, where she put down the bouquet. Then she took a few steps back to admire it. It was really something else, not like any bouquet of flowers she had seen for some time. She spotted the card poking out of the green foliage that encased the blooms. She stepped over, slid it out, and then perched on the bed. She held it for a moment, looking at her name scrawled on the front. She couldn't tell if it was Leo's writing or not. She wasn't sure she would recognise it after all these years anyway. The pounding in her chest continued and she was already convinced that they were from him.

She slipped the card from the tiny envelope and read out loud. 'Dear

Mel. We're so thrilled to have you aboard the *Audacious*, from the entertainment crew.'

That was it. No mention of Leo anywhere. Did he even know she
was here yet? Maybe he had that information and had organised for the
flowers to be delivered. Mel looked up and caught a glimpse of herself
in the mirror.

'Get a ruddy grip,' she said to herself.

Next her phone let out a dual ping.

'Double whammy.' She opened the WhatsApp messages and saw a
reply from Daz. A thumbs up and two words.

Looks great.

Daz had never been much of a texter, preferring emojis to actual
words. But even that was sparse for him.

Then there was a string of messages on the 3 a.m. Shattered Mums'
Club group that Mel had missed as she had been making her way onto
the boat. There was the expected flurry of questions from the girls, but
overall a very excited tone. Mel texted:

Can't wait to see you this evening, girls! We'll have an early supper as I'm on
stage at 8 p.m.! Just familiarising myself with everything now.

Time was getting on, Mel was hungry. She had been advised that
she could grab some lunch from the crew mess, but after that, all her
meals were included, and she could eat at any of the vendors around the
ship.

She headed towards the main dining area, hoping that she would be
able to spot someone who could show her the way to the mess. It was
quite eerie walking around a ship that was deserted of cruisers. She
would come across pockets of staff finishing up their last-minute jobs
but would walk for minutes at a time before she might see someone.

Eventually she reached the main foyer and approached a steward
and asked him the way to the mess. He looked her up and down briefly
as if she might be a stowaway, so she flashed him her staff card. He

nodded and she followed him up a flight of stairs, along a long corridor then down some stairs, then they swung a right into a door that said 'private' and headed down a corridor before going down another door and further down some stairs. Finally they burst through a door where Mel could hear the sweet sound of loud conversations being had. She felt a wave of relief as she saw long grey tables and orange chairs filled with people laughing and talking loudly. She made her way to the buffet and looked at the array of foods of all different textures and colours, it was amazing and to think this was the staff quarters. What a treat she was in for the next ten days. But she would have to make a conscious effort to be in the gym for an hour each day to burn off the excess calories she was about to consume.

'Hi!' Mel sat down next to a young African woman who had been deep in conversation with a middle-aged man with an American accent and had just paused to take a bite of her lunch.

'Hello.' She smiled kindly with her eyes. Mel ate the Moroccan stew, intermittently chatting with her fellow diners, as new ones arrived, and others left. She finished her lunch feeling satisfied, full of food and conversation. She made her way back up the stairs, remembering the route she had memorised on the way in. She was at the end of the first corridor that would take her to a set of stairs when she heard her name being called. Initially, as she began to spin around, she thought it was probably one of the staff she had just been sitting with, many of whom had promised to see her perform tonight, but that voice, low and gravelly, earned from decades of working in pubs and clubs, was recognisable just before she saw his face. And when she did, she couldn't control the emotion that overcame her. She began walking back and then, before she knew it, she was running into Leo's open arms.

16

SOPHY

'You're squeezing my hand too hard!' Sophy whispered to Aisha. They were gathered in the entrance to the foyer along with thirty or so other cruisers, listening to a steward go through the muster list for their safety. Aisha and Sophy had been swept into the space so quickly that they had grabbed each other's hands and Aisha hadn't let go since. Aisha was concentrating hard. She didn't want to miss one piece of information about what to do in an emergency. She had always been a listener, and a doer. Now here she was, showing Sophy up. Sophy had tried to stay in the cabin, she had just started unpacking and wanted to finish it.

'No one will know,' Sophy had said.

'They will know, and we will be evicted from the ship.' Aisha had grabbed her hand and pulled her to the meeting point.

'You're squeezing my hand,' Sophy said, a little louder this time. Aisha looked at her and let go.

'Sorry,' she whispered then carried on focusing forward where the demonstration for putting on life jackets was about to commence.

'You'll need both hands for the life jacket anyway.' Aisha pulled hers over her head and gestured with her head and neck for Sophy to do the same. Sophy reluctantly pulled hers over her head and stood like a grumpy teenager.

Twenty or so minutes later, after what felt like three days, the muster list was coming to an end and Sophy could practically taste the food from the smells that were wafting into her nostrils from the dining room a little way away.

They had arrived on board about ninety minutes ago and they had both texted Mel and tried to call her, but there had been no response.

'Do you think Mel has messaged back yet?' Aisha looked at her phone that was across her body on a shoestring. 'Uh uh.' Aisha answered her own question ten seconds later. 'She's not even read them? What do you suppose she is doing?'

'Sound checking or something gig-like.' Sophy looked at her own phone, waiting for the message she had sent to Niall twenty minutes ago to get two blue ticks. It was Tuesday, just after 5 p.m. It was the children's dinner time and all she could think about was if Niall and his sister had everything under control. She tutted loudly and hit the dial button and put the phone to her ear.

'No, you're not!' Aisha tried to grab the phone off Sophy, but Sophy dodged and collied with a fellow passenger who was coming in the opposite direction.

'So sorry,' Sophy called after them, but they didn't seem to care, they were too busy laughing with someone walking with them. 'Everyone is so jolly here,' Sophy commented as she listened to the sound of Niall's phone ringing out.

'He'll be feeding the kids. He'll be up to his eyeballs.'

'But he has his sister there, they can't both be up to their eyeballs. It's two kids, not a pack of wild hyenas.'

'Well, I don't know, I've seen Poppy when she's hangry. It's not a pretty sight.' Aisha spoke but Sophy noted she looked distracted with her own phone. Was it Mel she was still trying to contact or was she checking in on Charley or Martina? Sophy knew that Martina was ill and wasn't being very transparent about it. Sophy had been the height of optimism and told her there were a million possibilities for her being reticent about her health and if Martina was telling her not to worry, she should listen to her mother.

'I'm going to call her again.' Aisha put the phone to her ear as they reached their cabins, which were conveniently situated next door to one another.

'Who?' Sophy wasn't sure.

'Mel. She wanted an early dinner; she'll be on stage in a few hours. We are supposed to meet her. Where is she?'

Sophy noted a tinge of panic in Aisha's voice and hung up the call to Niall.

'Okay, I'll call her, leave her a message, we'll get changed and go for an early dinner. If we don't see her, at least we'll be fed and ready to see her in the show. She's obviously just got caught up in something.'

Aisha nodded.

'So I'll knock you in forty minutes? Is that long enough for a shower and change?'

'I'm a mum of twins, my PB is three minutes, fifteen seconds.'

Sophy's mouth fell open. 'Shower, dried and dressed?'

'Shower, hair wash, body dried, dressed and base make-up.'

'Shut up.'

Aisha nodded. 'Uh huh. Good, right?'

'I knew you were super woman but, my God, that's impressive. How did I not know this about you?'

Aisha looked smug.

'But hey, take your time tonight. Don't rush.'

'I will. I might even do a face mask.'

'Ooh! Now there's an idea. We should have a girls' night in one night.'

'Absolutely. We're here for ten nights.'

'I can't believe it.' Sophy grabbed Aisha's hand as though it had just suddenly hit her, the freedom, the possibilities. 'Ten whole nights!'

'I know. I feel so guilty yet so liberated.'

Sophy clung onto Aisha's hand for a moment longer before pulling out her cruise card, the one that did absolutely everything on the ship, and let herself into her room.

'Forty minutes!' Sophy called as she shut the door.

* * *

Sophy sat bolt upright...

Bang bang bang!

One of the children had hurt themselves, it was an Amazon delivery at the door.

'Coming, hold on.' Sophy shot out of bed and collided with the wall. She groaned loudly. That wasn't there this morning. She looked around. She wasn't at home, and this wasn't her room.

The cruise. She was on a cruise. The door. Someone was knocking.

'Sophy, it's me, are you okay?' Aisha's voice came through from the other side of the door.

'I'm okay,' Sophy called out. 'I think,' she said quietly to herself. She felt a little dizzy but that was because she had just hit her head and barely woken up. She had fallen into a really deep sleep and very quickly too. It was the sudden sense that she didn't have to be anywhere or do anything that had drawn her to the bed and then saw her pull the crisp sheets back, slip her trousers off and crawl in. She looked at her phone quickly and saw that it was after 6 p.m. Shit. She had slept for almost an hour. She had said she would knock on Aisha's door and now she was outside, probably worrying herself stupid that something had happened to her as well as Mel.

'I'm coming.' Sophy pulled her T-shirt back on and threw the door open. Aisha stood there in pink flared trousers and a bright blue body suit. Her hair looked great, and she'd done something different with her make-up. She had clearly made excellent use of her hour, whereas Sophy was still standing in the clothes she had arrived in, which were as crinkled as her right cheek.

'What happened?'

Sophy looked down at herself. 'I fell asleep.'

Aisha rolled her eyes, marched over to the wardrobe that Sophy had half unpacked in and pulled out a green Karen Millen dress.

'This.' She laid it on the bed. Then she went into the shower and turned it on. 'In you get,' she said to a still startled Sophy when she returned. 'You've got three minutes and fifteen seconds. I'm timing you.'

Aisha took out her phone with a smirk across her face and Sophy let out a loud yelp and ran to the bathroom.

Fifteen minutes later, which was still a record for Sophy, both women were headed for the main formal dining room, where they had arranged to meet Mel. Aisha had spoken with her when Sophy had been sleeping.

They heard the scream before they saw her and within seconds, all three women were standing in the dining room, hugging one another so hard but trying not to topple out of heels and off wedges.

When they had composed themselves and Aisha had dried her tears, they sat down at Mel's table, and all let out a collective sigh. Then they were in fits of giggles again.

'So here we are, girls. All aboard the *Audacious*.' Mel looked around.

'It's amazing, Mel. It's a great ship. Thanks so much for all of this,' Aisha said.

'It was part of the package. Bring some mates. I'm sure it bumped my fee down a smidge but hey, I'd rather have you gals here than make a fortune by myself.'

'I didn't know that.' Aisha sounded forlorn. 'You should have said!'

'I'm joking! I'm very happy with the remuneration. I would have done it for free just for the experience and to have you two here. So what are we having?' Mel lifted her hand politely to a passing waiter and all three women chorused, 'Cocktails!'

* * *

Sophy took a sip of her second cocktail and felt her stomach gurgle. She looked at Aisha and Mel, who were happily slurping away. The announcement had just come over the Tannoy that the *Audacious* was now leaving the port and there had been a loud resounding cheer which echoed and reverberated through the entire ship. Perhaps that was what it was, Sophy didn't have her sea legs yet. She had never been on a cruise in her life. What if she couldn't drink, what if she was throwing up overboard whilst the other two were throwing back cocktails? This was a disaster. She had not accounted for this dilemma. She had been so focused on packing clothes, making sure Niall and the kids had everything they needed, right down to finishing the last wash and rolling up all their socks into pairs just before she left, bringing the cans of baked beans to the front of the cupboard so they were easily identifiable and buying Earl Grey tea for Niall's sister because she knew that was what she preferred. They would have survived without any of these final touches, but Sophy knew that she would feel more content on her trip knowing that Niall wasn't on his knees scouring the back of the cupboard for a can of beans, muttering Irish expletives to himself whilst the kids wailed for their dinner.

'Are you okay, Soph?' Aisha asked, which attracted Mel's attention and soon both women were sidling up to her. Tears had sprung to Sophy's eyes, and before she could stop them, she was weeping openly in the formal dining room.

'Oh, no, what is it? Is it the kids? Niall? Are you missing them? That's okay. I miss the twins and Charley.' Aisha rubbed Sophy's arm quite vigorously, she detected a slight slur to her voice. Aisha could get drunk on two drinks, which was endearing and something she and Mel had come to love about her. But Sophy wasn't missing the children. She was still at the stage of bewilderment, as though she was still at home. She felt as though she should be doing *something*, not falling asleep in a cabin alone then dressing for dinner with her girlfriends. Tomorrow she would miss them, when she had begun sailing away from them and she could see the vastness of the ocean between her and her babies. But now, she was crying, and she wasn't sure why. The sudden bout of sickness had brought it on, surely. Maybe she was still tired.

Mel waited patiently for Sophy's sobs to end whilst Aisha continued the vigorous strokes. They were distracting her from the sickness, but they were pretty rough, even by Aisha's standards. Perhaps Aisha was hiding behind her own fears and anxieties tonight and Sophy's arm was now taking the brunt of it.

'I'm sorry, I don't actually know what's wrong. Except I felt a bit sick and then I started to catastrophise that I wouldn't be able to drink and you two would be necking them back and I wouldn't be able to join in and the whole holiday was going to be a disaster because I am obviously sea sick and can't handle being on the ocean and I'll be the annoying one out of the three of us who needs to be constantly up on deck to be able to see the horizon so I'm not vomiting every five minutes.'

'Okay, Soph, that is a lot of catastrophising,' Mel said as a matter of fact and raised her hand to a passing waiter. She said something to him, he nodded his head and walked quickly away. Sophy watched the interaction but barely had the strength to ask Mel what she was up to. Besides, she trusted her, whatever she had asked him for was probably going to do her good.

'We haven't eaten!' Aisha said. 'We had those snacks before we boarded, but we haven't had a proper lunch.'

'But we had a big brunch,' Sophy said.

'You did eat a lot, to be fair.' Aisha looked at Mel. 'She had three hashbrowns. And they weren't even small.'

Mel nodded knowingly as though she had been there. Then she looked at Sophy and smiled a soft and caring smile, but one that really seemed to be aimed at just her, as though Mel wanted to say something but without words. Sophy slightly furrowed her brow in question but let the frown evolve into a smile.

'I don't think you have anything to worry about. It's a little sickness which will pass. I suggest more food. Pronto. And we wouldn't disown you if you were a bad traveller. We would simply adapt to suit and drinking isn't everything. We're here for each other, not necessarily to get bladdered.' Mel looked at Aisha. 'Are we, Aish?'

Aisha had her glass to her mouth and was downing the last dregs of her second cocktail. She put her glass on the table and shook her head.

'No, of course not.' So sincerely that both Mel and Sophy erupted into fits of laughter.

The same waiter that Mel had spoken to earlier arrived back at the table and placed a mug in front of Mel.

'Thank you,' Mel said and pushed the mug towards Sophy.

'Peppermint tea. It will help with the sickness.'

'Thank you.' Sophy's eyes pooled with tears again.

'Oh, for the love of God.' There was a hint of joviality to Mel's tone and Sophy laughed her way out of a good cry.

'There we go. All is well. Right, drink that up and we'll order. Lots of carbs for you.' Mel picked up her menu and began scanning.

'More drinks and carbs!' Aisha said loudly, and then looked around. 'Sorry,' she whispered. 'I didn't mean for that to come out that loud.'

'Let's get you another drink!' Mel whooped. 'You're fun on cruises.'

'You're fun all the time.' Sophy grabbed Aisha's hand. She suddenly felt as though she wanted a group hug there and then in the middle of the dining room, but she felt that would be peaking too soon, they had only just left the port. There were ten more days to go and Sophy was certain that there would be a lot more tears to come, not just from her but from all three of them.

Sophy sipped her peppermint tea and perused the menu. She liked the sound of the southern fried chicken, corn bread and cob, Aisha wanted to try the jerk pork chop with rice and peas, and Mel went for the herb-crusted salmon with a side salad.

'Nothing too heavy or spicy on the first night – apart from the fact I'm a bag of nerves, I have an absolute killer dress.'

'I can't wait to see you in it and up on that stage.' Sophy felt cheered by the prospect of seeing Mel perform. 'I haven't seen you do a gig since the festival in the summer.'

'That was months ago. Not a lot has changed.'

'I know. But I love seeing you sing. What are you doing tonight?'

'There's something for everyone, some Toni Braxton, a bit of Whitney, that one from *The Greatest Showman*.'

'Not that one?'

'"Never Enough",' Mel said smugly.

'You added it?' Aisha squealed into her napkin.

'I've been practising for a month.'

'Oh my God.' Aisha was beside herself.

'Initially my heart said yes but my vocal range said no, but there is something to be said for getting older, my range has changed, adapted maybe. Or maybe I just have more confidence than I had before.'

'You're a woman in her prime.' Aisha grinned. 'I am on the edge of my seat for this already.'

'You'll hear Aisha applauding, right?' Sophy laughed.

'Oh, yeah.' Mel laughed.

'Are you ready to order?' All three women looked up to see the waiter standing next to their table.

'Yes,' they all said in unison then burst out laughing.

'Oh, my goodness, it's going be like this for ten days,' Mel laughed after they had reeled off their choices.

'And one more of these.' Aisha held up her glass.

'It was a Cherry Bakewell,' Mel told the waiter. 'And two bottles of mineral water, one sparkling, please.'

'Oh, yes, must drink water in between.' Aisha tapped her head. Sophy smiled but inside she could feel her stomach gurgling again. She glanced out of the window and could see the lights of the outside deck had come on and that there was barely any light left outside. Tomorrow they would be cruising at sea, and she would be miles away from her loved ones. She would deal with that heartache tomorrow. The peppermint tea had helped her sickness, but she was sure there was nothing on board for a bout of heartache.

17

AISHA

She was sure that she was swaying and not the boat because she had been told that the boat came equipped with... she wasn't sure what exactly, she had heard someone discussing it, but where? Who had told her? Basically, she wasn't to worry about sea sickness, the boat wasn't going to rock on waves like cruise ships did years ago, this was advanced technology. It was definitely her then. Aisha had drunk four, or was it five Cherry Bakewells? She had never tasted anything like it in her life. She was going to have to find out the recipe because when she opened her restaurant, she was going to sell them by the bucket load.

Hold on, did she just say to herself when she opened her restaurant? Aisha had been keeping it to herself, but she was sure that she was going to pop if she didn't speak about it soon. She had viewed the premises and oh, my goodness, it was perfect. She had known from the second she had walked through the door. She could feel the energy of the business she had in mind already taking hold of the place. It was madness. She had never run a business before, had never had the confidence to go beyond that level, but owning your own business was the only option that Aisha could see for herself. She was so good at her job, and she didn't want to be making money for other people any more. She needed to be a proprietor. She would be a good one, she knew it, and she had felt it as she was walking around with the agent. And the ideas had been flowing ever since, non-stop. It had almost been enough of a distraction from her mum – for a while, at least.

'Are you okay in there?' Sophy's voice came through the door, bringing Aisha back to the present. Yes, she was on a cruise ship with her two buddies. They were headed out to sea. Then on to Spain. This was all very exciting. But she was very drunk. When she opened the cubicle door, Sophy was looking at herself in the mirror and then at Aisha from the same position. She swung around.

'You good?'

Aisha gave a thumbs up.

'Oh, God, what a pair, me seasick, you drunk.'

'Let's go and see our girl,' Aisha said, just slurring a little. She would focus on water for the next hour or so and then a nice nightcap, that was what you did on a cruise, a nice night cap.

It was just coming up to 8 p.m. and Mel was going to be on stage at any minute. They had seats reserved at the front, where else? Not that they needed it as Aisha would make sure that Mel would hear her from anywhere in the auditorium.

'This is so exciting.' Aisha linked arms with Sophy. 'Are you feeling a bit better now?'

'I am a little, yes. I'll keep off the alcohol for tonight until my tummy properly settles.'

They opened the door to the auditorium and were shown to their seats.

'Oh, this is nice,' Aisha commented about the small table with a screen for ordering drinks on it. 'I mean, I get it, it's so the staff aren't walking across in front of people and ruining the show.' Aisha began swiping and tapping the iPad.

'I'll order us some water.' And just as she had finished typing in their request and hitting send, the lights began to go down and there were some whistles and whoops, and Aisha felt her skin go all goosebumpy with anticipation at seeing her friend appear on the stage. Then a voice rang out around the room, announcing the evening's entertainment. They didn't mention Mel at first because she was about to come on, once they had listed the line-up for the evening, then came the 'But first...' and Aisha couldn't contain herself, she let out a loud whoop and looked at Sophy for backup. Sophy gave her the thumbs up and then the drinks arrived.

'Wow, that was fast,' Aisha said to Sophy, then she caught sight of something from the corner of her eye. From where they were sitting, they could see the wings quite clearly, and Mel was hovering at the edge. Not looking out at the stage, but at a man next to her, tall and well kempt, in his late forties, early fifties. He was in a good suit, all of this was normal except the fact that his hand was around Mel's waist and the next moment he was bending to kiss her, on the cheek. Mel looked perfectly fine with this, she looked relaxed and ready to perform. But as the man turned to leave, she looked back at him and watched him go, then Aisha tried to read the expression on her friend's face, was it sadness, despondency? But in a flash, her expression had changed as she pushed her shoulders back, shook her hair and began walking onto the stage because she was being properly announced. Sophy shoved Aisha.

'Why aren't you doing your whoop thing?' Sophy was clapping loudly. Aisha let out a quick whoop and joined Sophy with her clapping. Mel was now on the stage and the applause was dying down.

Aisha suddenly felt quite sober as she watched Mel compose herself, ready for her first number. She looked stunning in a red lace dress, fitted around the bust, with straps that lay across her shoulders rather than sat on them.

Aisha felt as though she couldn't move or speak for a few seconds, then Mel came out of her trance and just before she hit the first note, she turned to Aisha and winked.

Aisha felt a wave of relief flood through her. For a moment there, Aisha had been focused on the small act she had seen between that man and Mel. Aisha didn't know that Mel knew someone on this trip, let alone a good-looking man like that. Not that Daz wasn't good looking, because he was, but that man had been like someone out of an after-shave commercial. Maybe Aisha had overthought it, seen it wrong. Mel was in showbiz, and it was all very hands on and kisses flying here, there and everywhere. Of course Mel knew so many people. They would rock up in Vigo tomorrow and Mel would bump into someone she knew right there in the town. That's how she rolled, and she didn't even bat an eyelid. Once she had been in Bali and she'd bumped into her grandad's neighbour's daughter, on the beach. They had played with one another as kids in the paddling pool in her grandad's garden and there they were, both on a beach in Bali. Madness. Aisha was sure it was that scenario, there were plenty of other 'loveys' – was that what they called them? – on board and the entertainment team was vast.

Mel finished her first song, and the crowd went wild. They were all fresh out of the port and ready for a party it seemed, as Mel ramped the tempo up for the next few numbers, which encouraged quite a few passengers to stand up and start dancing. Mel ended the show with Shirley Bassey's 'I Am What I Am', which had the crowd roaring. Even Sophy, it seemed, had managed to cast aside any thoughts of sickness to show willing and stood up and clapped. And Aisha put her worries to one side. For now.

Aisha and Sophy were chatting to some fellow cruisers when Mel joined them. She had changed from the stage dress and was wearing a floatier dress.

'I can smell the Spanish sun already,' Mel said as she sipped on the cocktail Aisha had thought to order for her when she was singing her final number, so it arrived just in time.

The first thing Aisha wanted to ask was who the man was in the wings, but already it sounded nuts in her head. Mel was on a high, just like she always was after a gig. Sometimes it was hard to bring her down, it was handy then that they were stuck on a moving vessel surrounded by water and hundreds of litres of alcohol. Plus there were enough cruisers who were all approaching Mel to congratulate her on her performance and ask her if she had ever thought about going on *Britain's Got Talent*. Mel always waved her hand away and would try not to laugh, especially the time when someone added that they were sure there was an 'older' category.

'No, you're thinking of *X Factor*, when they used to have the over-thirty-fives,' Mel had said to a woman twice that age. But it had fallen on deaf ears. The woman requested a selfie 'just in case'.

'Just in case what?' Mel had asked.

'You get famous.'

'Okay,' Mel agreed.

'Did you enjoy that?' Aisha asked after the fifth person had stopped by to tell her what an amazing voice she had, and she was wasted on this ship.

'Not wasted enough,' Mel had whispered to Aisha as she readied herself for another selfie and Aisha had snorted loudly.

'I did and you know why? Because we're moving. I know it sounds weird, but I realised, I've never done a gig in motion before. Except the Clapham carnival 1986, I was a cat. As in the musical. I sang "Memories", none of the mics worked and no one heard me, but the idea was there. But yeah, it just felt surreal, and I don't know, I was full of adrenaline.'

'It was awesome, Mel.' Sophy was hugging her. 'I actually went when you sang "My Heart Will Go On". I just thought of Jack and Rose, and I was actually gone. Wasn't I, Aish?'

'She was, I was about to throw a glass of ice at her so she could have the full immersive *Titanic* experience.' Aisha laughed.

'*Draw me like one of your French girls,*' Mel said in a soft American accent and Aisha and Sophy squealed with laughter.

'I'm sorry, I don't mean to disturb,' said a male voice.

'It's okay,' Aisha said through tears of laughter She looked up at the man. Then she recognised him as the man who had been behind the stage with Mel, and she composed herself.

'Sorry... I...' She wasn't sure what to say because she hadn't relayed to either Sophy or Mel what she had witnessed or that she thought it was a strange, yet intimately brief encounter, between a man and a woman.

Mel looked up and seemed to flush slightly. She breathed in, almost a gasp, as she rose to greet the handsome stranger.

'Hi,' she whispered.

'Hi,' he said in low, hushed tone.

Aisha flicked a look at Sophy, who was looking up at the man as though she were a five-year-old girl and Santa had just stepped into the room.

Aisha looked at Mel and gave her a look that said, *Well?*

'Oh, this is Leo Monroe. Leo, this is Sophy.' Mel pointed to Sophy, who stayed sitting and gawping but managed to hold her hand out for Leo to shake it. 'And this is Aisha. My actual biggest fan.' Mel laughed and Aisha thought it sounded odd, higher than usual.

Aisha held her hand out but stood up. She wasn't short but somehow, she felt some sort of primal instinct, as though she needed to protect Mel from this... oh, my days, was she really thinking... predator? Stop it, Aisha. He's just a nice man.

'Hello, Leo.' She held her hand out to Leo. My God, his hands were smooth, Aisha thought as she sat down afterwards.

'Leo and I...' Mel began.

Jeez, why couldn't Mel get her words out, Aisha thought, as she watched her usually unflappable friend become coy and lost for words.

'Sass and I worked together back in the day. She rescued my business,' Leo said in a voice that was gravelly with a low tone. Damn it, he seemed nice.

'Sass?' Sophy laughed and looked at Mel with wide eyes. 'Is that a nickname?'

'Oh, yeah, sorry, Mel was pretty sassy back in the day, gave me all the attitude, but it worked a treat on me. I was captivated.' Leo looked longingly at Mel.

Oh, Christ, what was going on here, Aisha thought. Her instincts had been right.

'She still is sassy, aren't you, Mel?' Sophy said, sipping her drink.

'She's lost a bit of that young lady attitude, all bravado and pure defence, of course – who can blame her – but she still has an edge and what a performance. I wanted to shout out to everyone to grab their life jackets, I thought you were going to blow them overboard.' Leo's eyes were glimmering as he looked between the women but finally rested his gaze back on Mel. Sophy was still staring at him, agog. And Christ, what was that line, Aisha thought, had he rehearsed that before he came out? Yes, her friend was good, but come on, life jackets?

'We think she is pretty amazing,' Aisha said, feeling as though she needed to claim a bit of her friend back before this stranger clawed her to pieces. 'So you know each other... well.'

Leo stopped smiling at Mel and looked at Aisha, his charming demeanour dropped for a split second. Was it the way she'd asked the question? It was obvious to everyone on this boat that the two of them had history.

'We do,' Leo said earnestly and in a way that presented the words as a full stop. There was no more information to be offered but he was making his position very clear. 'I've not seen her for a few years. I run the entertainment on this cruise. There could be a few more gigs in it for you, girl!' He looked back at Mel again, clearly not wanting to look anywhere else right now.

'How about a photo?' Leo looked primed and ready to pose. Oh, my goodness, this man was everything that Daz wasn't. She wondered if she could bring Mel's husband's name into the conversation or if that would make things awkward. She decided against it.

'Do you want me to take a photo of you two?' Aisha went to pick up her phone.

'Take one with mine.' Leo scrolled to the camera on his phone and handed it to Aisha.

Aisha watched as Leo slipped his arm around Mel's waist casually yet as though he had done it a thousand times and it required zero effort, and when Aisha was looking at them through the lens of Leo's ginormous phone camera, it was clear that the pair of them looked good together. Mel said something that made Leo laugh and Mel looked up at him at the exact moment that Aisha took the photo and damn it, when she saw the image, she couldn't deny that the pair of them looked like some sort of glamorous Hollywood couple.

She handed the phone back to Leo.

'Now one of you girls.' Leo held out his hand for Aisha's phone. She swiped to the camera and handed it to him. Sophy slipped into the middle as she was the shortest and the three of them had perfected their photo pose order, with Mel always on the left, Sophy centre and Aisha right, the way Ant and Dec always appeared on stage in the same places. It worked for them for their 'best sides'.

'He's nice,' Sophy said too loudly to Mel, and Aisha was sure Leo had heard. He snapped away, asking for various poses and phrases to be shouted out, until finally handing Aisha back her phone. Aisha began swiping with Sophy hot at her heels, ready to pick out the one she looked terrible in, but there wasn't one bad image. All three women looked amazing in every photo and Aisha was never keen on having her photo taken. But there she was, looking glamorous and happy with her three friends.

'He is nice,' Mel said after the photos before she went back to Leo's side, and they began sniggering like teenagers.

'Drinks, girls? What can I get you?' he asked.

'I think I can manage a gin and tonic,' Sophy said, sounding rather pleased with herself.

'Double Archers and lemonade, please,' Aisha asked, deciding to stick with the sweet spirits.

Leo headed off to the bar, leaving all three women standing looking at one another. None of them knowing what to say, as if suddenly they were stuck for words, there was a flutter of awkwardness between them. The energy felt fragile – to Aisha, anyway. But Sophy soon perked up.

'He's very nice, where have you been hiding him all these years?'

'That's just it, I haven't seen him for years. It's so strange.'

'Did you know he was going to be here?' Aisha said quickly and Mel shot her a look that read she did not want to be asked that, but she was going to have to answer it.

'Yes, well, I only found out he was in charge of the entertainment here after I'd been booked. He texted me, told me he'd be on board and did I want to meet. It was nice to hear from him. Anyway, how are you both? Are you tired or do you have a few more drinks in you?'

'I fancy a walk to the top deck, to look at the lights and see the view,' Sophy said. 'We could pop back to my room and get my coat.'

Sophy spoke absently but Mel wasn't really listening, Aisha could tell, she was somewhere else. She kept flicking her eyes to the bar where Leo was collecting their drinks.

18

MEL

'I had a great night; I just want to say thank you so much for bringing
me on board. Literally.' Mel laughed.

Leo smiled, dropped his head to the side, as he leaned against the
wall. They were somewhere between both of their cabins. Aisha and
Sophy had gone to bed half an hour ago and Mel wanted to have one
more drink. Leo had insisted on walking her back to her cabin, which
was a couple of corridors down from the girls, but she had said no, she
would be fine. So there they found themselves. There was a happy
atmosphere on board and people were milling about, not ready to go to
bed yet on their first night, staying up like excited children. But Aisha
had drunk quite a bit and Sophy, well, Sophy just wasn't herself and
needed a day or two to acclimatise. Mel had thought that Aisha seemed
a little unlike herself at the end of the evening and wondered if it was
something Mel had or hadn't done. She had tried to be as accommo-
dating as possible, but her mind had been on her first gig and of course
there was the added distraction of Leo. She had spent a few hours lost in
a world of nostalgia with him. From the moment he called her name to
the second the girls found her at dinner. And then of course there was
now, this last half an hour, as Mel had tried to bring the evening to an
end and finally had to stand up and leave.

'Such a shame we couldn't go all night like we used to.' Leo smirked and Mel was sure he was aware of his own double entendre, but she didn't bring attention to it. So far, the day and evening had been nice. Mel had caught a glimpse of the woman she had been all those years ago and it felt fantastic.

'I am forty-seven now, Leo. I can't party all night the way we used to.'

'Shame that things change. I liked them how they were.'

Mel felt the weight of his words and there was a part of her that was lost in the past that felt the same way. Why did things have to change? She had been such a fun person when she had met Leo. She used to take chance after chance, not a care for the next day, she simply lived in the moment. Now her and Daz were quite the image of domesticity with his nine to five, roasts on a Sunday, dropping one child to gymnastics, the other to ballet. What about them? What did they do as a couple or as individuals? Mel was a shadow of the person she was when she had started working at Leo's bar in her twenties. She had a sudden surge of nostalgia, an aching desire to reclaim some of the person she used to be.

'They were great days,' Mel sighed and Leo smiled and stood back up straight.

'Anyway, we have plenty of time left on this trip to make sure we reminisce about all the fun times.' Mel was genuinely tired. The gig had taken it out of her, her first big one like that in a while. Plus being somewhere new, and all the lights and people. And seeing Leo, of course. It was all quite overwhelming.

Leo nodded. 'Okay, Sassy. Goodnight.'

He leaned in slowly and brushed his lips against her cheek. It was the softest gesture and whether it was tiredness or the sudden influx of memories that were triggering emotions, Mel suddenly felt as though she wanted to weep.

'Goodnight, Leo.' Mel turned and headed down the corridor towards her cabin. She felt her eyes fill with tears and she didn't need to turn around to know that Leo was still watching her as she walked away.

* * *

Mel woke up to the sound of her neighbours leaving their cabin excitedly and remembered she had promised the girls they would meet for breakfast. She checked the time, it was almost 8.30 a.m. Damn, she had meant to set her alarm and had clean forgotten. She had taken a quick shower before getting to bed and fallen into a sleep full of wild and colourful dreams featuring Leo and all the characters from her past who they had talked about last night.

She woke feeling a little hungover and decided she would keep to her schedule of training and eating breakfast later. She would pop to the restaurant and meet Sophy and Aisha for a juice before hitting the gym.

She saw them hovering around the breakfast buffet queue and joined them whilst smiling at the passengers she had essentially queue jumped in front of.

'Morning,' Mel sang.

'Oh, my, you're gym bound?' Aisha looked Mel up and down.

'I am, and I cannot wait. Care to join?'

Sophy spun around, her plate was already piled high with waffles, watermelon, yoghurt.

'Someone's peckish?' Mel said to the plate.

'I don't think I ate enough yesterday and besides, have you ever seen such a spread? I love a breakfast buffet, it's my absolute favourite.'

'I am partial to a Travelodge brekkie. But yes, this is so much better.' Mel was impressed. 'I think I have time to do a quick workout then get back here before ten, what do you think?'

'I'd say go for it,' Aisha said. Mel was glad Aisha seemed herself this morning.

'I was going to get a juice, but I'll just dash and then have one later with my breakfast.'

'Okay, we may still be here when you get back.' Aisha gestured to Sophy's plate with her eyes. Mel and Aisha caught each other's eyes and smirked at each other.

'Okay, well, I hope so, but no worries if not. Let's have a coffee about eleven? Have you been up top this morning? There's nothing but sea.'

'I know, but I'm kind of trying not to think about it. It's quite disconcerting.' Sophy grimaced.

'Ahh, you'll be fine. We'll all go up later,' Aisha said.

'Umm, I don't know. I feel like that chicken from *Moana*, I might lose the plot if I can't see land.' Sophy pulled her mouth down.

'Right, I'd better dash. I'll see you in a bit.' Mel was off.

Mel speed-walked her way out of the restaurant to the fading sounds of Aisha convincing Sophy that coffee on the top of the deck later would be a great plan. Already Mel could feel the endorphins beginning to kick in just thinking about a good workout to start the day.

She found her way into the gym and began with a gentle warm-up on the treadmill which she eventually took up to a light run and twenty minutes later she was sweating buckets. She worked her shoulders and arms and then finished up with fifteen minutes on the cross trainer.

She had forgotten her water bottle and was taking another drink from the fountain when she heard his voice.

'Well, there is a sight for sore eyes.'

Mel spun around, water dripping from her mouth. Leo was standing just behind her in a white T-shirt and neon-green shorts.

Mel felt instantly out of her comfort zone. She was wearing no make-up and was sweating profusely.

Mel dabbed at her face with the towel she had remembered to bring, thank God, for the workout and she could hide her embarrassment behind a genuinely red face. 'Wow, now that is a pair of shorts, I really wish I'd packed my neon pinks now. Damn it.'

'Well, I did like you in pink, but then you never did wear it much. Now how about finding you down here on the first day at sea. Keen, aren't we?'

'I'd say the same about you.' Mel kept dabbing at her red face that was raging even more from the mortification of Leo finding her here dressed this way. Why the hell she cared, she didn't quite know.

'Well, I'll have you know that I am an avid gym goer these days. Not something that I could ever have said a few years ago, but there we have it. What can I say, I am a changed man, sometimes I barely recognise myself.'

'That's not too hard in those shorts,' Mel quipped, skirting past the seriousness to Leo's tone. She knew he was trying to make quite a statement over having changed, but the words were making her feel as though she needed to say something back, which would lead to more conversations about the man he was now compared to then.

'Fancy spotting me?' He gestured to the benches.

Mel pulled her lips in. 'Can't. I'm meeting the girls for coffee, and I haven't had any breakfast yet. But I'll see you tonight.'

'Maybe a drink before the show?'

'I can't, I'll be having dinner with the girls.'

Leo held his hands up. 'I get it, I get it. I'll just pick up the scraps of you where I can. You're here with your girls, I was a surprise to the whole trip.' He smiled and his eyes shimmered, even in the hazy morning light after what could only have been a few hours of sleep. Leo had always been such a night owl. Mel presumed that still ran fiercely through him.

'I'll take the scraps,' he said softly, which caused Mel to take a deep breath.

'So, tonight?' She tried to cobble together a sentence, but her words came out breathy and laboured.

'Tonight is perfect. Have a great day with the girls. Sophy and Aisha, isn't it?'

Mel smiled warmly and felt her heart do the same. 'Yes, it is.'

'See you later.' Leo headed off into the gym and Mel felt an obligation to turn. She saw him approach a group of young men who seemed to know him and were all chatting animatedly. It seemed as if he was a regular here after all. Mel had initially thought he was there because she was certain she had mentioned she would be in the gym this morning.

Perhaps this was the new Leo, the gym, the early mornings, remembering her friends' names. But what did it matter? The man she had known then had been there physically but in time he had not been enough. He hadn't wanted to commit to her, he had never said as much but when Daz came along, the difference between the two had been stark. And what Mel had never admitted to Leo or any girlfriend since was that when she fell in love with Daz, she had also had to get over Leo, because he had let her walk away, because she knew that he couldn't be what she wanted him to be for her. And now, twenty-five years since she first met him, here he was, kind and attentive, available and financially stable. And he was here. This man that seemed to be everything that she had wanted. Just two decades too late.

19

SOPHY

Why did she have to be seasick? This was a big deal, a time to be with her friends, to find a little sliver of herself and ease her way back into that shell until it fitted her again, so she could look in the mirror and say, 'Oh, hey, I remember you!'

But no, instead here she was sitting upright on the bed, trying to find a comfortable position where she didn't feel a spurt of sickness. She had been fine over breakfast but now she could feel it creeping up on her again. She knew she needed to be on the top deck so she could see the horizon and that would probably help but she had to be honest with herself and the girls, she was a teeny bit terrified of seeing all that ocean and no land. She wasn't sure what this strange phobia was, but it had definitely come on since having kids. She would be afraid of things that she had never been afraid of before, like roads and oh, my... trains. Like her mum! She was fine on them until she started thinking about the speed and she had stopped taking the tube unless she really had to.

Beside all of that, she was suffering today. And it was beginning to make her feel sad. She really just wanted to feel normal. She was jealous of Aisha, who was able to knock a load of cocktails back last night and not feel a thing this morning. Sophy had managed one and a half. When Leo came back with the drinks from the bar, she had thought she was going to be okay, but she just felt rough again. She had swapped her drink for a lemonade at the bar and then carried on drinking, unbeknownst to her friends and guest.

So far this morning she had read a very long thread on the school mums' WhatsApp group.

It had been started by Blythe, obviously, telling everyone how much money had been raised at the autumn school fayre. They had raised over £365.55, which was a massive achievement for their first event and everyone should be proud of themselves. Then she had added something that had gotten under Sophy's skin.

I want to say a special thank you to those of you who took time to make a home-made cake. It was really so very special and made such an impact on the cake stand, which alone raised over £50!

Sophy had felt sick as she was catapulted back to the mortifying morning when Max had outed her over her fake bake. Blythe had hardly been able to look at her for the rest of the fayre. She was sure she wouldn't be asked to make a cake again. Which Sophy should have taken as a blessing but instead it just made her feel like a failure. It was important to her that she made a positive impact at Max's school, that she made a few friends and that women liked her. She wasn't sure why she craved that affirmation from other women, it was just in her. Maybe that was why she had turned to Instagram, because it gave her that buzz when women congratulated her or asked her for advice or simply wanted to follow her. She was trying to emulate that same experience in real life and in the playground. So far she didn't feel as though she were doing very well. Just don't give up, she told herself. Sophy West was not a quitter. She had bashed out a reply to Blythe's message.

That's amazing Blythe, thanks for organising. Can't wait to see how the money will be spent and what the next event will be.

But instantly her comment was lost in sea of other responses, ones that received thumbs ups and hearts and were even requoted with responses from Blythe. No one said anything to Sophy's comment, no one responded. She thought about where she was, sailing on the ocean, and had never felt so far out and away from her comfort zone amongst this group of women on the WhatsApp group. But as she had told Max on his first day, don't worry if he didn't make any friends to start with, it would happen in time. As it happened, Max made a ton of friends on his first day and seemed fairly popular and happy.

Sophy then FaceTimed the children and choked back the tears when she saw all of their faces squashed into the little screen. Poppy especially made her heart pound, she was still her little baby and she had left her. She felt the guilt hit her hard. She wouldn't disturb them again today, besides, it was painful to see them when she was so far away. She knew she needed to create some content for her social media, so she spruced herself up, brushed her teeth – which usually made her feel better – and took her selfie stick, and headed out of her cabin. She could smell the fresh air coming through the corridors where she walked. She took long deep breaths. She had about half an hour before she would need to meet Aisha and Mel for coffee.

She set the camera to video and slowly made her way up to the top deck.

Once at the top, Sophy took herself over to a railing that was far enough away from people so they wouldn't get in her shot. Sophy was no longer bothered about looking like an idiot as she walked around talking to herself or posing outside fancy doorways or graffiti-clad walls. She did, however, feel a sense of unease that she might make a fool of herself by falling or throwing up. So she just dived straight in before she could think about what she was saying and started monologuing. It felt like a secret diary entry and all the while, she knew she would not be posting this particular footage anywhere for anyone to see.

'Well, here I am on the top deck of a boat, and I feel absolutely terrified like I'm about to fall off the edge of the world and there's no one to catch me. I'm not sure what's happened to me lately, but I am so scared of... well, everything. Maybe it's hormones, maybe it's being a mum of two, I don't know. Anyway, I don't really want to be up here, but I am... so that's something.'

Sophy stopped recording. It felt good to get it off her chest. She went to press delete when a man raced over to the railing where she stood, leaned over and threw up.

Goodness! thought Sophy, if she had kept the camera running for a few seconds longer she could have caught that on camera.

Sophy wished she could easily change from sick to fine the way that man had in a nanosecond. Perhaps being sick was what she needed to do. Her phone pinged and it was a message on the group chat from Aisha.

I'm hungry again, is it the sea air? See you in the café shortly.

Sophy needed to hurry up if she wanted to make it for coffee on time. She had been away from Niall and the kids for almost twenty-four hours, and she thought she might have a lot more content by now. She needed to keep up with the regular posts, especially as she was on board such a great ship experiencing a wonderful holiday with her original 3 a.m. Shattered Mums, but she was feeling rather lazy, the holiday mood had kicked in straight away and she felt as though she could sleep for England.

'Well, here I am on the top deck of the *Audacious*. We boarded late yesterday afternoon and today we are fully at sea.' Sophy tried a slight glimpse behind her, an attempt to look longingly at the sea, but it ended up as more of an awkward flick of her head. She felt side-tracked as she wondered if she would be able to delete that bit of the post. Probably not, she thought.

'Aisha and I were lucky enough to be Mel's guests on board this spectacular cruise ship. Mel is a guest performer here for the next nine nights and we couldn't be prouder of her, and we bet you will feel the same. I am going to film loads of stuff each day and then pop a montage together of all the best bits, so it feels like you are all here with us. What we've all found during the last twenty-four hours is that being away from our kids is hard, yes, but it's also necessary. The original 3 a.m. Shattered Mums' Club hasn't been away together ever, so it's a really special time for us all right now.'

Sophy paused as she felt her stomach gurgle. She needed to eat again, then she would be fine. Hopefully, the girls wouldn't rib her too much when she treated herself to an almond croissant with her coffee. Sophy tried to pull herself back to the present, what had she been saying?

'So keep checking for updates, and hey, maybe we should start making this a thing, the 3 a.m. Shattered Mums' Club cruise! Love you all and wish you were here.'

She felt proud of that last bit, she had always wanted to say it and she felt like a proper travel presenter, like the ones her parents used to watch when she was a kid.

She slid her phone out of the selfie stick and slotted the stick down, so it was now quarter of the size and able to slot into her crossbody bag. She hurried through the ship and made her way to the café. She was surprised to see she had arrived before anyone else.

Great, the perfect opportunity to upload the video to Instagram and TikTok. She turned the volume on her phone right down, opened Instagram and tapped on the video.

'Hi, love, is anyone using this chair?' a woman asked.

'No, it's yours, take it.' Sophy waved her hand, already pressing 'next' on the screen to take her to the section where she could write the text and add her hashtags. She began bashing out the usual spiel and then hashtagged all the important ones, like #the3ammumsclub and #shatteredmums, then she tagged the cruise ship company as well as Aisha and Mel. Then she repeated the same for TikTok, working on autopilot now as she kept one eye out for the girls and then sat back, feeling satisfied that she had completed some content and she could relax for the rest of the day.

'Hey!' Aisha arrived first, sitting down in front of Sophy and putting a large paper bag on the table between them.

'I bought these for Otis and Jude.' She pulled out a massive cuddly dolphin. 'I got them one each. The same so they don't argue. Aren't they cute?'

'They are cute!' Sophy stroked the fin. 'Are they into dolphins?'

'They will be when I get back and we tell them about the dolphin excursion we're going on in Tenerife. Honestly, I can't wait to see their faces when they watch the footage. That's why I got them the dolphins, I'll give them to them after. Oh, it's going to be awesome, are you excited?'

'Yes, totally excited.' Sophy didn't want to say that she was excited to get her feet on solid ground and that by this time tomorrow they would be in Spain, and she could do just that. Hopefully, by then she would have found her sea legs and be ready to take on the rest of the trip.

'Sorry I'm late.' Mel wandered over to the table. She was out of her gym gear and in white linen trousers and a blue and white striped T-shirt with scooped arms accentuating her fabulous biceps and the edges of her shoulders.

'My, look at you, you look so good.' Sophy admired her friend. 'Well done for doing the workout. I should join you tomorrow.'

'I feel really good. Better than if I exercised at home. Is it the sea air?'

Aisha laughed. 'I feel like everything is the sea air. Can you actually believe we are floating in the middle of the ocean right now? I mean it's nuts.'

Sophy felt her gut tighten as she thought about the miles of water all around them and below them. It was nuts that she ever agreed to get on the damn thing in the first place. Her body had been trying to tell her something since she set foot on the ship yesterday. She only hoped she would start to relax and then the bouts of sickness and panic might end.

'Coffee?' Mel asked.

'I'll take a peppermint tea,' Sophy said. She didn't want to risk feeling ill if she ate the croissant as well as the coffee.

'Oh, no, still feeling rough?' Mel grimaced.

'No, I just want a croissant, the two together might be too much.'

'Ah, gotcha. I'll get them in. Aish?'

'Latte, please.'

Mel wandered off to the bar. Aisha stayed fixated on her dolphin, smiling to herself and imaging the boys' faces when they saw them, no doubt.

'Have you heard from Martina?' Sophy asked, keen to talk to keep her mind off her gurgling stomach. Suddenly an image of the man throwing up overboard was fresh in her mind and Sophy felt her mouth fill with saliva. She pulled out a bottle of water from her bag and took a few sips.

Aisha's face dropped and Sophy felt a tug at her heart.

'I'm FaceTiming her tonight. She's been busy.' The gap between the two sentences sounded as if Aisha wasn't entirely sure that she believed Martina. But why would Aisha's mother lie to her? They had an honest and open relationship about most things. Sophy looked at Aisha, she was squeezing the fin of the dolphin and making a slight humming sound under her breath.

'I'm sure it will be fine. Martina is a strong woman, whatever she is fighting off won't be serious.'

Aisha looked up at Sophy, locked eyes for a second and then picked up her phone. She watched as Aisha began scrolling emails and then swapped to her socials.

It was a welcome break when Mel showed up with a tray of beverages and her croissant.

'There was this sweet couple in the queue and they remembered me from last night,' Mel began as she got settled and began handing out the drinks. 'Can you believe that? I haven't a scrap of make-up on and they just started talking to me as if I had just stepped off the stage and—'

Aisha let out a loud gasp.

'What is it?' Mel said. 'Are the kids okay?'

'Is it Martina?' Sophy said, feeling terrible for not giving Aisha more of her time just now.

Aisha looked up, first at Mel and then at Sophy.

'It's you, Sophy. Your post.'

20

AISHA

Aisha held her phone out to Sophy so she could see the post she had just put up a few minutes ago. Already it had received over a thousand likes and there were a load of comments. That was pretty good going for any 3 a.m. Shattered Mums' Club post. They usually gained traction quickly, but this was good going for any post. Sophy knew the ins and outs of things better than she did, but it wasn't the blue sky or sea they were commenting on, or even Sophy's hair and make-up which did look pretty good even by Sophy's immaculate daily standard, they were commenting on what Sophy had been talking about.

'I had no idea.' Aisha looked at Mel. 'We had no idea.'

'What are you talking about?' Mel took the phone from Aisha and took the video back to the beginning and began playing it. She turned up the volume so Sophy could hear too.

'Well, here I am on the top deck of a boat, and I feel absolutely terrified like I'm about to fall off the edge of the world and there's no one to catch me. I'm not sure what's happened to me lately, but I am so scared of... well, everything. Maybe it's hormones, maybe it's being a mum of two, I don't know. Anyway, I don't really want to be up here, but I am... so that's something.'

Aisha watched as Sophy's face went from confused to horrified.

'Oh my God, oh my God, oh my God!' There was a heightened panic in Sophy's voice that Aisha hadn't heard before. She squirmed in her seat and darted her gaze back and forth between Mel and Sophy. What the hell was the right thing to say here? Sophy had been suffering on board the last twenty-four hours or so and not just here. This was an anxiety that had been going on for some time, something separate from the post-natal depression she had after Poppy. And neither she nor Mel had noticed it. Aisha felt a heat rush through her body and suddenly her eyes were prickling with tears.

Sophy had her face in her hands and looked like she was shaking. Mel was leaning down by her side.

'Sophy.' Mel was using her deepest, most calm voice. 'Take a moment then take some deep breaths, please. In for four, out for four.'

But Sophy wasn't listening. She had grabbed her phone and was desperately pressing and sliding her finger, presumably to get to the post. She finally had it and pressed the drop-down menu, that could only mean one thing. She was about to delete it.

'Sophy, no!' Aisha stood up and swiped the phone from Sophy's hand, it went flying across the table and landed a few feet away from them on the floor.

All three women looked at it, all equally shocked, and said nothing for a few seconds. Aisha's heart was beating so fast she was terrified she might have broken Sophy's phone, but she didn't have time to react. She could see out of the corner of her eye that Sophy was coming out of her state of shock and looked as though she were about to make her way to the phone. Aisha leaped from behind the table and was next to the phone in less than a second. She picked it up and held it tightly to her chest the way she had done with objects of hers when she was a child and hadn't wanted either of her sisters or cousins to have it.

'Aisha, what the hell are you doing?' Sophy sounded exasperated. Aisha clung to the phone.

'The comments on that video, Sophy, are all supportive.' Aisha felt her body convulse with the terror. She didn't want to keep Sophy's phone from her, God knows it was her lifeline, but she needed to tell her, and she needed her to understand.

'They love you, Sophy, so do we.' Aisha looked at Mel again. Mel's eyes were glistening with tears. Aisha felt her throat tightening with the tears that longed to come out. She was aware there were a few eyes on her now, but she stood her ground and kept holding on to the phone.

'We didn't know, Sophy,' Aisha said.

'We couldn't have known.' Mel shook her head at Aisha and then Sophy. 'You're always so... jolly!'

Sophy let out a small sound that could have been a laugh or a cry.

'It was a mistake, I meant to upload the other one. That was just me...getting stuff off my chest, I meant to delete it but...'

'Please consider leaving the post up.' Aisha moved closer to Sophy. She couldn't stop her, if that was what she wanted to do. It was her post, her business. But Aisha saw Sophy's face soften, and her shoulders drop slightly. Aisha edged closer again.

'Everyone is being so supportive. Please just read the comments before you make any rash decisions. I think it's important to keep showing the harder times as well as all the positive stuff.' Aisha held the phone out and Sophy looked at it for a second before taking it.

'I'm going to need a bit of time on my own.'

'But your tea and croissant.' Mel pointed to them as if Sophy would forget.

'I'm going to go to the other side of the restaurant, you stay here.'

'No,' Mel said firmly. 'You stay here. Come on, Aisha, I have somewhere we can go.'

She put the coffees back on the tray and began walking away. Aisha followed with a slight tip of her head, looking backwards to check on Sophy. She was sitting down and was looking at her phone. Aisha hoped she would heed her advice and keep the post.

Mel took them to a quiet little foyer between the dining room and a set of steps that led up to the next deck. Aisha felt they were close enough if Sophy needed them but far away enough to give her some space and time to make the right decision. Aisha hoped it was to keep the post.

'I can't believe we missed that. I feel like such a knob.' Mel glugged hard on her coffee. 'I've been so immersed in my own world and getting here and doing the first gig which was terrifying and exhilarating all at once. And all the while... poor Soph.'

'Don't.' Aisha could barely take it. With all the worry in her heart over her mother, she hadn't had room to see that Sophy hadn't been a 100 per cent on the trip. Of course Sophy wasn't herself. There was the sickness, which could have stemmed from anxiety from being away from Max and Poppy

'Do you think that explains the sickness?' Aisha asked, having just sussed it all out in her head.

'Possibly.' Mel drained her coffee. 'I imagine it's a bit of both, but the stress is egging on the sickness.'

'Don't say egging and sickness in the same sentence,' Aisha said, po-faced. Mel put her empty coffee cup on the small table between them and looked at Aisha. Aisha turned to look at her.

'What?'

'You're so funny.' Mel looked back ahead at the glimpse of sea and sky through one of the windows.

'It just sounds so wrong. The word egging, followed by sickness, the very words make me want to vomit.'

Mel laughed and shook her head. 'Okay, well, we need to think of a way to help our Soph. Nine more days here and she needs to be able to enjoy the trip, otherwise what a waste for her. She's clearly anxious about being surrounded by sea, she said the *Moana* thing and I thought it was just that, a joke. But it's not uncommon for people to hide their anxieties behind a joke. We should have been in tune. I guess I've been a little distracted.' Mel looked away in the distance and Aisha wanted to ask if her distraction was a certain six foot silver-fox male who happened to be aboard this ship at the same time as Mel. But she didn't say anything, she was as much to blame for not seeing beyond what Sophy was perhaps subtly trying to tell them both.

'Okay. So what about mindfulness stuff? Get her meditating in the evening, loads of deep breathing visualising positive things.'

'Sounds good to me.' Mel stood up. 'I have to dash off for an hour. The ents team has decided they want me included in the opening number tonight so I'm going to run through the track with them.

Shouldn't take long. Then we can have a game of tennis or something. Maybe book us a court. I'll see if I can get Sophy something for the sickness on the way back from the pharmacy.'

'Sure.' Aisha smiled then cradled her coffee as she watched Mel wandering off.

But just before she turned the corner, she saw the familiar figure that was Leo approaching. The pair of them stopped and appeared to greet one another, then they disappeared around the corner out of sight. Aisha's mind raced with ideas about what this relationship with Leo meant and had Mel been entirely honest with them? He was an old friend/lover from back in the day before Daz and they were just friends now. If there was anything more going on, Mel would surely tell them both.

Aisha vowed to stop overthinking it, it was her holiday as well. She needed to relax. She closed her eyes, trying not to think about Sophy or Mel. Her phone began ringing. She grappled to answer it, not recognising the number.

'Hello,' she answered breathlessly, having been thrust out of a relaxed state. Her heart was thumping in her chest, images of Martina sprang to mind. Maybe her mum had taken a turn.

'Hello, is that Aisha?' came a woman's voice.

'Speaking?' Aisha answered too quickly, needing to get to the part where this person told her why she was calling.

'It's Rachel from Duke and Cambridge.'

Aisha stayed quiet, trying to work out why she recognised that name. Was it a pub? Oh, no, it wasn't Jon, was it? Had he had some sort of relapse?

'The estate agents,' Rachel prompted.

'Ahhhh!' Aisha said and felt her stomach lift and her heart soar at the mere mention of the place. She had been ignoring the calls, because she hadn't had a chance to make a final decision before she left. Wow, it felt like an eternity ago that she had viewed the premises and it felt as though she had been on this cruise for a week already.

'Ahhhh!' Rachel mimicked.

'Sorry, you lost me with the name there for a second.'

'Not to worry, it happens a lot after only one viewing.' Rachel laughed a little and Aisha did too. There was some kind of nervous energy fizzing between the two of them on the line. 'You already know that the unit can be used as a restaurant and now I've had to properly speak to the landlord and they are very happy for you to proceed. If you're still interested, we'd like to process your application fully, more forms to fill out I'm afraid, but he was thrilled about your vision for the place and yes, they'd love to offer it to you. All being well.'

Aisha felt something rise in her chest and she had to supress the need to shout out loud. She knew this would be the case when Rachel had told her there wouldn't be a problem with her using the unit to trade as a restaurant. But she had never got round to finishing that business plan, she hadn't spoken to Mel and Sophy and she'd barely said anything to either of her sisters or Martina and Jon. Aisha had yet to make any of this real in her head and yet here was the agent giving her the go-ahead, telling her it *was* real and that it could happen. She had not expected this. All the while, as she had been pursuing what was essentially her life's dream, not once did she actually envisage this sort of phone call.

'I don't know what to say.'

'Shall I give you some time to absorb the news and maybe call you back tomorrow?'

'Tomorrow,' Aisha said absently. She would be in Spain tomorrow. 'Yes, please call about midday, that would be great.'

'Okay, Aisha, speak then.'

Rachel hung up and Aisha looked at her phone. She had that tingling, excited feeling all over her body. The one she had often had when the twins had been young and she'd been unable to do anything with it. Now she had the money, the spare time and was oozing with creativity. She could hardly believe it was happening.

21

MEL

Mel sat in a café on the street, waiting. She had been waiting for half an hour. He said he was going to be here and so far he was not. He was late. And it had been Leo's idea.

'Let's meet at a café when we dock in Vigo. Have a conversation on dry land.'

It had felt like a good idea, because being on a boat and constantly moving felt slightly jarring at times, as though time and everything else wasn't real. And Mel didn't want to feel that way. She needed to feel in control of herself.

Yet here she was, feeling like the same young woman she had been when she and Leo had been a thing. That deep feeling of worry that started in her stomach and went right up her throat and she felt it seize up, making it hard to swallow. She was reminded of the way she would wait for him to show after an evening at the bar and it would sometimes be 5 a.m. before he would roll into his flat, where she would have gone home to some four hours before.

The temperature was a balmy 23 degrees as she sat watching the flurry of tourists and workers and locals. Sophy and Aisha had insisted on sightseeing and were currently hot-footing their way to Castelo Do

Castro, a local historical site, so they could then cram in lunch and shopping before re-boarding the ship. Sophy had been overjoyed to see land and was feeling a little less anxious now she knew that there would only be two more days cruising at sea and the rest would be destinations where she could get off and explore.

They were all looking forward to Tenerife in a few days, where they could snorkel and swim with dolphins and turtles. For now, Mel was satisfied with sitting and doing very little. She was not one for wanting to look at old ruins and castles. She had hated history when she was in school, and the class trips were an excuse for her to find a quiet place away from the teachers where she could smoke and drink.

Mel swallowed down the lump in her throat that had caught there as old memories of her and Leo flooded back. Finally she caught a glimpse of him, shimmying his way through the crowds, aiming confidently for the café where they said they would meet.

Mel shifted in her seat, arranging herself more comfortably to greet him. She had already decided she wasn't going to stand up to receive him. She would stay put and already that air of nonchalance was brewing.

'Sorry, sorry, sorry,' Leo called as he approached. He bent down and kissed her on the cheek.

'The meeting ran over, then part of the stage collapsed, then my phone has been ringing off the hook all morning.'

Mel listened. It was all so familiar, the Leo she had known then had always been part of some drama or another, always in demand, always needed. Often never where he said he would be when she needed him.

'Well, it's a good job I didn't order you a coffee. It would have been stone cold now,' Mel said breezily; she didn't feel malice towards Leo. She was a woman with her own mind and had managed perfectly well without him for all these years but there was still this small part of her that wondered how it would feel if she had been put first, if he had given her all of his attention. Leo had shown a different side on the boat yesterday at the gym, the way he was with Aisha and Sophy. She had presumed that behaviour would have stretched to more traits. Mel had needed attention as a younger woman, but so had Leo. It hadn't always worked. But now Mel didn't need it as much. She knew she was the centre of Daz's, Leia's and Sky's world. And her job gave her plenty of attention. As a more mature woman now, she knew what was relevant and what wasn't. But here was Leo, asking to meet her, and arriving half an hour late.

Mel knew she was damaged; like many she was scarred by her past, meaning sometimes she would return to the things that didn't necessarily help her grow as a person but gave her the buzz that she needed there and then to exist in that moment. Trashy TV shows like *Love Island*, reading arguments between strangers on Mumsnet, drinking too much alcohol and then not exercising when she knew she should. Leo had been that one thing back then. There was never anything beyond the moment that they spent together, in that sense, Mel knew their whole relationship had been all about sex, and bigging one another up, she felt good next to him and vice versa. But with someone like Leo, when he did finally give you his full attention, it was like the sun was shining just for you. And as he sat down next to her, edging his chair along the pavement to get a little closer to her, the clouds that had been stubbornly sitting above her head suddenly passed and the sun was free and warming her skin as he sat within clutching distance of her.

'Beautiful spot.' Leo smiled. He was dressed casually in a white short-sleeved shirt and grey slacks, the buttons to his shirt were open, exposing a flash of tanned chest and light grey and blond hairs.

'Do you come here often?' Mel said, smiling at the cliché and feeling that familiar sense of euphoria when she had Leo all to herself, when it was just the two of them. Right then, she could only see him, like a light that was so dazzling it blocked out everyone and everything else, even her family, who were almost a thousand miles away.

'I don't, actually. I'm usually so busy by the first dock, I rarely get chance to get off and relax. Usually by Madeira I'm ready to get off and take some time for me. There's this great spa there I go to, beautiful views. Delicious beer and amazing seafood. I just stay there for a few hours, then head back. Hey, maybe you could come with me?'

Mel breathed in, the sound alerted Leo.

'Okay, I get it, too intimate, the pair of us splashing around in our swimwear. Plus you'll want to see the girls.'

Mel breathed in again and glanced away from Leo as she spoke. Leo looked so good after all these years. He had always been insanely good looking, but the years that had passed had only made him look better. Mel let the thought of her and Leo in a jacuzzi slide slowly through her mind before she tuned back into herself and answered.

'Well, I dragged them out here, it was supposed to be our trip. I had no idea about you being here until afterwards.'

'Good surprise or bad surprise?' Leo probed.

Mel looked at him. 'It was a surprise.'

Leo laughed through his nose and fell sideways a little, a boyish gesture as though he were having bants with one of his male friends. 'I love it. Keeping it real. Always the cool one,' Leo said. 'Even when things were raging hot,' he added more quietly, only for her ears. Mel felt a burst of heat in her chest. She put her sunglasses on and alerted the waiter with a flick of her hand.

'You need a drink to cool down,' Mel said and when the waiter arrived, Leo ordered an iced coffee and Mel a sparkling water. Once the waiter had left and Mel was settling back in her chair, Leo spoke. Soft and hurried.

'Look, I'm just going to say it, I've missed you, Mel. I didn't say it initially because I didn't want to freak you out, but I've thought of you often, how could I not, you're unforgettable. When your name cropped up on the list, I knew I couldn't miss the opportunity to see you.'

Mel swung her head around and looked at Leo. 'You're the reason I'm here? I thought my agent got me the job and you running the ents side of things was a pure coincidence.'

Leo smiled coyly. 'No. I was sent a bunch of bios by agents and when I saw your face and name... Look, I'm sorry if that is a shock, if you were led to believe some other force was responsible for you being here. But I own the business that looks after all the entertainment. I make all the decisions.'

Mel's mouth felt open. 'You own the business?'

'I didn't say that?' Leo said coyly with a hint of sarcasm.

Mel wasn't sure how she felt any more, it was all down to Leo that she was here. He was the one still pulling the strings. Over two decades later, she felt like the girl in her early twenties again, lost and looking to the cheeky chappy bar manager to help her.

Mel shook her head. 'Well, well, who knew. Leo Monroe, after all these years, you actually own a business that is doing well and looks fairly kosher from the outside. What's really going on behind the scenes? Fiddling the books, dodging the tax man?' Mel felt her body go tense. Where she had been turned slightly into Leo before, she now moved her legs away.

Leo shook his head. 'I know that's what you think of me, because that's the guy I was. I've grown up a lot, Mel. I've achieved success that I had never thought I was capable of. I just don't have anyone special to share it with.' He added the last bit as an afterthought but it impacted Mel harder than any other of his words. How could he be saying that to her now? Those were the words she had longed to hear all those years ago.

'It's just all I've known of you, Leo. It's hard to suddenly see you in this light. And I am grateful for the invite and for you picking me as the entertainment act. I just wish you had been more honest. I wish you had told me you were responsible for me being here.'

'You wouldn't have come if I had. And I didn't want you to miss out on such a great experience. You're a spectacular singer, performer and so much better than you think you are. But you don't seem to have been up to much recently. I checked out your social pages. I felt like you needed this. You deserve this, more than anyone I know.'

'I've been having a baby, Leo. I had to put the career on hold for a few years.'

'And now you're back!'

'So it seems,' Mel said.

'I know you don't need me, but I think after this, you won't be short on offers for a while. This will do you good. Please don't look at me like that, Mel.'

'I'm wearing sunglasses!'

'I can tell by the way your lips purse up. You're cross.'

Mel folded her arms.

'And now the defence barrier.'

'Oh, for the love of God.' Mel uncrossed her arms and thankfully the waiter arrived with their drinks.

'Cheers.' Mel lifted her glass up to Leo.

Leo watched her for a second, unsure whether to join in her half-hearted toast.

'Cheers,' he said after a while and lifted his glass.

He took a long sip and sat back in his chair. Mel glanced at him through the side of her glasses. He would know she was watching him; he had a sixth sense for stuff like this. She had been sparse with her words these past few days, she hadn't wanted to give the wrong impression, to give Leo even a scrap of a thread that he could pull at. But there was no doubt what was going on here. Leo had always been there in the background, murmuring away like one of those quiet central heating systems that would kick in sporadically through the year. She couldn't have forgotten about him; he had been a significant part of her life for so long. And she had been so very in love with him. Even though she didn't know how to show it back then, even though she had been reserved and defensive, unable to articulate her feelings.

But now, now he was telling her that he had so much more to offer her and not just in terms of financial stability. Now he didn't need to worry about dodging his taxes and hiding from the bailiffs, he was a fully-fledged businessman with a successful company that was clearly doing well. And he was living the absolute high life. He probably didn't need to even be on every ship himself, but if as Leo had said he had no one to share his life with, being on board was less lonely. It clearly massaged that part of his ego that obviously still needed massaging. But success wouldn't necessarily change everything about a person. Leo would always be Leo.

So what had this all been about? It wasn't a trap, because he had made himself known to her way in advance of her boarding the ship. She could have changed her mind, not accepted the gig. But she needed this, and she had been longing for a break away with her girlfriends. Away from Daz.

But Leo had put his feelers out and made the connection with her. He knew she was married with kids, but it hadn't stopped him. To offer Mel a chance to perform on a prestigious cruise ship, Leo had spread his peacock wings, displaying everything he had, everything he was, and everything he could be to Mel. This was not just business. This was personal. This was a proposal.

22

SOPHY

Back at sea after a wonderful day in Spain, Sophy didn't feel as pathetic and wretched as she had done two days ago. They would be in Madeira when she woke tomorrow. Tonight, she, Mel and Aisha were having an early dinner in the grand dining hall where they would be dressing up and making their plans for the trip into Madeira.

Sophy's gut hadn't completely calmed down, she was still suffering slightly with the sea sickness, but she had been thankful that she had faced up to her fears, even if it had not been in the manner in which she would have liked to have done. But the good thing was the followers on her 3 a.m. Shattered Mums' Club site had not known that she had mistakenly posted; they saw her as an honest and authentic person. The comments had not stopped coming in from parents who had lost all of their confidence since having kids. Mums and dads who had suddenly begun to experience debilitating mental health symptoms.

There had been a message on the primary mums' WhatsApp group. There was no name, just a number.

Loved your honesty on your latest post. Hope you're feeling more settled and enjoying your trip.

The comment had received a handful of cuddle emojis and hearts. No one else commented. Not even Blythe. And there was a full house of blue ticks, so she knew everyone had at least seen the message. Sophy wasn't sure how to reply and she was put out that Blythe, the very person who had set up the WhatsApp group, couldn't even bring herself to reply. Maybe she hadn't seen the post. But Blythe had said that she followed her. Even if she hadn't seen the post, surely she would have asked. Sophy didn't know who the person was who had sent the message and so she felt uncomfortable sending a message back to a nameless faceless person.

Sophy realised she needed to post something else as a response to the hundreds of comments the Instagram post had attracted.

She was sitting in her cabin and began typing out a post, accompanied by a picture of her looking a little fresher faced after a bit of sun she had got on her face after she managed twenty minutes on the top deck today, with the assistance of Aisha and Mel.

Bringing small people into the world has brought with it an unhealthy portion of anxiety for many parents, in a world where everything was supposed to be quicker and easier, we are all juggling too many balls and have stress levels that are unhealthily high. Thank you for understanding and for helping me come to terms with the psychological changes. You are always all so supportive and that's what makes us such a special group of humans. Please continue to post your comments, they have been helpful as I try to find ways to alleviate the symptoms. Thanks so much for all your suggestions and sign posting. I will be checking some of these organisations out soon and giving myself the help I deserve. Lots of love, Soph x

The sickness was there again, brought on by focusing on her phone, no doubt, it made her spin out at the best of times, let alone when she was bobbing about in the Med. There were some tea- and coffee-making facilities in the cabin and they had just been replenished. She was sure she had seen some biscuits. She wandered over to the nook and picked up the tiny packet. Ginger flavour. Perfect. They were renowned for easing sickness. She had nibbled them by the bucket load when she was pregnant with Max and Poppy.

Then she popped a note on the 3 a.m. WhatsApp group.

Having a rest, won't fall asleep this time, I promise.

Immediately Aisha messaged back.

I wouldn't mind if you did. I'm enjoying these late afternoon rests before dinner. I feel like I'm in *Downton Abbey*. What will I do when I get home? At the boys' teatime I'll be disappearing upstairs for a lie-down.

Mel piped up next.

I'll get you a little bell you can ring to summon Charley.

The banter continued for a few more comments and then Sophy turned her phone to silent.

* * *

Bang bang bang. Sophy leaped off the bed, her heart thumping in her chest, her body slick with sweat. She couldn't work out where she was. She stood up and looked around the room, searching for where the sound was coming from.

'Pops!' she called out. 'Where are you?'

'Sophy!' A voice from somewhere, then a rattle to accompany another short sharp bang. Sophy turned and the door leaped out to her, she felt like she was in a dream.

'Sophy, it's Aisha. Are you okay?'

Shit shit shit. The time. What was the time? Sophy had fallen asleep again and had clearly been in a deep sleep for some time. They were supposed to be having drinks before the meal and she wasn't even dressed. She grappled for her phone, read the time from the screen. It was 6.33. They had a table booked for 7 p.m. Mel was on stage at 9 p.m. This was a disaster. She was hot and sweaty and disorientated.

She went to the door but didn't open it.

'Aish, can I meet you there, sorry, wardrobe malfunction.'

It was quiet on the other side for a second then Aisha's voice was calm and steady.

'Are you sure, Sophy, is there anything I can help with?'

'Nope! All good. Go and grab yourself a drink, I'll be ready soon.'

'Okay. Call if you need anything. Shall I get you a sparkling apple?'

Sophy felt her stomach drop and her mouth filled with saliva at the mention of the fruit drink. It was usually one of her favourites.

'Umm, yes, please.' Sophy's voice was shaky. She heard Aisha mutter something but had to ignore her as the sensation became overwhelming. She needed to get to the toilet. She flung open the bathroom door, still feeling completely out of it, and managed to shut it behind her. She flushed the toilet to block out the sound that she knew was coming as she leaned over the toilet and watched her lunch rush out of her.

Sophy ran down the stairs and through the corridors until she reached the dining hall, twenty minutes after Aisha had knocked. She slowed down before she approached the entrance and took two big deep breaths. She had showered with a shower cap, applied minimal make-up and put on a floaty back dress which pinched in at the waist and bunched up just after the elbows. She had bought it for this trip. She had thrown on some chunky jewellery but no perfume. She couldn't bear anything upsetting her stomach before dinner.

'Can I firstly start by apologising, I couldn't decide what to wear, I was down to my underwear when Aisha called by, and I didn't want to hold you up. Please forgive me,' Sophy said, gasping for air despite the deep breaths. 'I ran here as well.'

'Jesus, Soph, you didn't need to kill yourself, it's just a dinner,' Mel said.

A waitress arrived at Sophy's side and held the chair out for her as she sat down before placing a napkin on her lap. Sophy looked up and thanked her and admired her uniform and neat hair.

'It's so nice here,' she whispered as the waitress poured water into a glass and handed her a menu.

'It is. This dinner is complementary, so we can't eat here every night.'

'From Leo?' Aisha asked and Mel shot her a questioning look.

'It's from the ents team.'

'Oh, that's nice.' Aisha picked up her menu and began perusing. Sophy watched a wry smile form on Mel's face as she looked away from Aisha and at her own menu.

'Well, I'm having the crab,' Mel announced.

'Just that?' Aisha asked.

'With a salad. I can't eat too much before a performance. I get too burpy.'

Sophy felt her stomach gurgle and her mouth fill with saliva again. She gulped and felt her body start to shiver and then she felt her armpits prickle with sweat. She was panicking. What if she were sick here in the dinner hall? It was strange because she couldn't actually feel the motion of the boat, but it was definitely affecting her, and she hated her body right now for doing this on such an important trip. When would she get the chance to do this again? She couldn't make this an annual thing – it was far too much to ask of Niall and any member of his family who decided to pop along and help. She wondered if it was the guilt that was making her sick.

She decided lots of salt and carbs were the way forward, so she ordered truffle and parmesan chips and a starter portion of risotto. She sipped the sparkling apple juice and was thrilled when the food arrived without too much of a delay.

But as much as she felt she wanted to eat, she could barely manage a morsel. And it did not go unnoticed.

'You're usually stuffing it down you.' Mel leaned over and helped herself to the truffle fries.

'I think I just ate a lot today. I scoffed too many biscuits in the cabin when I was resting.'

'They are good biscuits.' Mel shoved another fry into her mouth then stopped herself. 'What am I doing? I'm on stage soon, I'll be bloated and burping.'

'Maybe that could be your new act, burping out the songs,' Aisha quipped.

'Yeah and the audience has to guess what they are.' Mel went to take another fry then pushed them away.

'Prize for the right answers.'

Sophy tried to laugh along but the constant talk of burping was causing her mouth to fill with saliva again, and this time she felt a wave of nausea rush from her gut to her head. Before she knew it, she had let out a small sound that could have been misheard as a burp, but Sophy knew it was a retch. She was going to be sick, there was no doubt about it, in the next thirty seconds, it would be coming out of her mouth. She stood up and tried to push her chair back, but it was upholstered and therefore heavy, so she remained stuck between the table and the chair. Another retch slipped out of her mouth and both women were staring at her now.

'I need to go to the toilet.' Sophy clambered out from behind her chair and made a dash for the door. She could hear the calls of the women from behind her, but she could only think about getting out of that room and to the bathroom. She scanned the walls for the signs and realised the toilets were there right in front of her where she stood in the foyer. She dashed through the door and burst into a cubicle. She only just managed to throw the toilet seat up and fall to her knees before she emptied the final contents of her stomach into the pan.

23

AISHA

'And you're sure you're feeling a bit better?' Aisha held her hand to Sophy's head the way she would with the boys when they would suddenly slump and complain of sore throats and tummies. Sophy was stretched out on her bed and Aisha propped on the edge.

'I told you I'm totally fine. I needed to throw up whatever has been sloshing around in my stomach for days. I actually feel hungry now.'

'Well, why don't I order you some room service, some toast and fruit or something light on your stomach? I'll explain you've been feeling rough the last few days, I'm sure they will accommodate.'

'Thanks. That would be nice.'

'How about I make you a nice cuppa?'

'Oooo, lovely,' Sophy said in a northern accent.

'Cups of tea always make everything better.' Aisha got up off the bed and made her way to the tea corner. 'I love the tea- and coffee-making facilities.'

'That's so funny.' Sophy managed a small laugh.

'Why?' Aisha asked.

'The way you say it. It sounds so formal. Yet so cutesy.'

Aisha sniggered. 'I know. But I look forward to seeing that whenever I'm in a hotel. It's like my own little café. It reminds me of being a kid when I used to play shops or restaurants.' Suddenly Aisha was filled with thoughts of potentially having her very own restaurant – that childhood fantasy would finally be played out in real life.

'I wish we could be that age again, and just play and feel free from all the constraints of modern-day society,' Sophy said wistfully.

'I know.' Aisha did know, because she understood Sophy and appreciated the friendship she had with her. She wished Sophy had felt she could have been more honest about the fears and anxiety she was experiencing. Aisha filled the small kettle halfway with some of the bottled water next to it and then began preparing two cups with teabags. As she worked, she thought about the unit that was waiting for her back home. In a few months' time, she could be cooking her own food and serving customers. It was just about imaginable but still so very hard to believe that this was something she was planning to do and she had still not really spoken to anyone about it except for Charley. She decided there and then as she poured boiling water into the cups and dribbled in milk that she would get the keys and then invite all her friends and family there and surprise them all with her good news. Something fun like that, anyway. It had been a while since Aisha had done anything fun and spontaneous. Aside from heading off on a ten day cruise, she almost chuckled to herself.

She took the tea over to Sophy and put it on the bedside table.

Aisha entered the cruise ship app on her phone and ordered bread and butter and a platter of fruit.

'It's quite something, this app, how we can do so much.' Aisha's brain was already firing with ideas of how she could get up to date and utilise modern technology in all its glory to assist her in running a functioning restaurant.

Aisha sipped her tea, and although she was bursting to tell Sophy about her plans for the unit, she decided to go as far away from that topic as possible and so said the first thing that popped into her mind.

'So what do you think about this Leo then?' Aisha perched on the bed and sipped her tea.

'Well, there's a loaded question if ever I heard one.' Sophy eyed Aisha over her teacup. 'I'm guessing you're suspicious?'

Aisha twisted her mouth and squinted her eyes. 'I just think he sort of popped up out of nowhere; like who even is he?'

'He's her Mr Big, by the sounds of things.'

Aisha held her palm out. 'I know, right, Mel seems totally smitten, as though time just stood still or they went back in time or something.'

'It's sweet, I suppose.'

'Sweet?' Aisha said.

'Yeah.' Sophy edged herself up the bed, so she was sitting straighter. 'It's sweet. We all have our Bigs out there, the one who could have been, or even should have been.'

Aisha gulped and her hand went to her throat as she thought about girls from her past. There had been some that she had been too scared to be open with when she was in her early twenties; she had not been confident enough about who she was, who she wanted to be and what she had to offer. What if one of those girls – and as she thought about it, one in particular sprang to mind – was supposed to have been the one? What if she had been a bit more forward and spoken up, might things be different? She loved Charley but watching Mel reunited with her ex was making her feel flustered. What if things weren't as simple as meeting someone and settling? What if you were supposed to go back and reassess people who had passed you but weren't meant to? Was that what Mel was doing? It exhausted Aisha just thinking about it.

'I don't believe there is one person for all of us,' Sophy continued. 'I mean look at me; I thought Jeff was the one and now I have Niall, but I could have met anyone, and I am sure with the world population of, what is it? Seven, eight billion?' Sophy continued to witter on, and Aisha began to think she had preferred her when she was sick. At least she spoke less then. Where was all this suddenly coming from? All these revelations? Why did Aisha feel like the dunce in the class who couldn't work out the sum when everyone else was talking about it like it was second nature?

There was Mel gallivanting off with Leo and now Sophy was suddenly waxing lyrical about multiple 'the ones'. Was this why Charley had changed her password on her phone and seemed a little more active with her mobile? She had heard of the seven-year itch, but they had just had the twins then. Was this a delayed reaction? Was Charley hooking up with one of her own lost soulmates? Aisha felt a sweat sweep across her whole body. And she had left her for days on end and come away on a cruise. Sophy was still talking, but all Aisha could hear was the rushing sound of blood in her ears. She needed to get to the top deck; she needed to call Charley.

She distracted herself by tidying up after the tea making.

A knock at the door made Aisha spin round and she could hear Sophy's voice again.

She opened the door and there stood a porter with a tray.

'My God, that was quick.' Aisha took the tray and the porter left. She set the food down next to Sophy.

'I am going to get some air before bed, so will you be okay?'

'I'll be fine. You go get your air.' Sophy opened the plastic lid on the fruit platter. Aisha thought it a terrible waste of packaging and made a mental note to add this to the review she would be writing after their trip.

She left Sophy and headed for the upper deck. When she got there, she sucked in great big gulps of air. Then she turned and saw the sun was setting across the water. The horizon was a blur of blues, pinks and oranges and she felt a rush of calm. Suddenly she felt a pining for home, for Jude and Otis and Charley, and wished they were all here with her to witness this amazing display. She had been so worried about Martina and then Sophy that she had barely had a chance to appreciate really being on the boat. But now she decided to take a moment, several moments, to appreciate the beauty and vast waters of the Mediterranean. She might not ever experience this length of time on a boat again. She leaned against the railing and looked down at the water, at the white streaks trailing behind them.

She took out her phone and snapped a few pictures of the sunset. She looked at the images. Damn, they didn't do the real thing any justice. She sent them through to Charley anyway and was surprised to see they were read straight away. Charley was on her phone at night? This was unheard of.

Looks amazing. I'm so jealous.

Aisha couldn't help herself; despite the perfect surroundings and the calm tranquil hiss of the waves and the sounds of guests milling above deck and clearly just enjoying life, she felt the urge to just say something to Charley.

I didn't expect a response, you don't usually look at your phone in the evening.

She watched the dots appear, which indicated that Charley was responding.

Well, I was hoping I'd hear from you. You've been a bit quiet today. The boys have missed you too.

Aisha felt her heart pound with want and lust and happiness. It was true, absence did make the heart grow fonder. This was exactly what all relationships needed from time to time, a little space. Although Aisha had put quite a lot of space between her and her girlfriend, fifteen hundred miles or so.

I really miss you and I wish you were here.

Aisha watched and waited for a reply, and one didn't come straight away so she put her phone into her pocket and took in the last of the sunset.

24

MEL

It was exactly halfway through the trip, as Mel lay on a beach in Gran Canaria, that she finally felt relaxed. Every show had been a roaring success; she was now in full flow and couldn't imagine going home. Five days had felt like five months and she could get used to this life. Sophy and Aisha were with her, and she felt like it was the first time that they had all finally manged to relax together, with Sophy feeling so well. Today she seemed better.

Things had been awkward between her and Leo since their chat where they had sat outside the café and he had made his declaration of admiration towards her. They had spent the last day or so sidestepping each other and being extra polite. Leo hadn't tried to instigate anything. Being in his company had given a reminder of the thrill she experienced as a young woman, but those thrills had been short-lived, overtaken by feelings of angst and then ultimately disappointment. Mel had pushed those thoughts from her head when she had first been reunited with her ex.

'Being on land definitely helps,' Sophy had said as she lay down and soaked up the rays.

'I can't believe we get to see so many amazing places.' Aisha was busy scribbling out postcards to Martina and Jon, Otis and Jude and

Charley and hoping to get them posted before they boarded again. Tomorrow they would be in Tenerife and swimming with dolphins.

Mel lay very still. The heat was intoxicating. If no one spoke, she felt she could easily fall asleep. But Aisha and Sophy clearly didn't want to completely zone out, and this was their trip too.

Sophy was staring at her phone.

'God damn it,' she heard her mutter under her breath.

'What is it?' Mel spoke as if she were drunk. She hadn't touched a drop, but she felt like the world had a blurred edge around it today, with the sun kissing her all over and the smell of her warm skin, it was like every carefree holiday she'd had as a young woman.

'Oh, nothing,' Sophy said quickly. Mel sat up on her elbows and squinted at Sophy.

'No, what is it?' she said firmly.

Sophy looked at her wide-eyed.

'It's one of the mums at school. I said I'd do something before I left, and I forgot.'

'She knows you're on holiday, right?' Mel sat up properly and leaned in to look at Sophy's phone. Sophy jerked back slightly, and Mel instinctively reached out and grabbed Sophy's phone. Mel knew what it was like to be at the beck and call of another mother and she thought about Saskia, who had tried to lump her into an age bracket.

Mel squinted to see the phone screen in the glaring daylight and put her palm up to shelter the screen from the rays. She could hear the protests of Sophy yet, at the same time, she wasn't trying to take her phone back. Mel saw the message and realised it was part of a group chat. The group chat had a name. Reception mums.

Mel gasped.

'Oh, my days, you're in a school mums' WhatsApp group chat.' Mel began to scroll through some of the messages, all the while fully aware that she was also in a damn group chat, much to her disgust and embarrassment. She wanted to know how much more awful Sophy's group was than hers.

She looked up at Sophy. 'Some of these women are awful!'

Sophy looked crestfallen. 'I know.'

'I mean, I thought I had it bad,' Mel said and her hand shot to her mouth. Damn it. she had exposed herself.

'What do you mean?' Aisha piped up. Sophy was still looking sheepish, but Aisha, who hadn't said a word, was all over Mel's misdemeanour.

'All right, damn it. I got coerced into joining the mums' WhatsApp group. But I'm a watcher, an observer, I barely comment and quite frankly I don't have time for any of it. But it seems no one can do anything these days without a fucking WhatsApp group!'

Aisha fell about laughing and Sophy smiled, looking relieved. 'I know we had our 3 a.m. group but that was about survival. This is just nosy annoying women with too much time on their hands who want to be in our faces and all over our business. If we don't comply, they turn witchy, have you noticed?'

Sophy let out a loud laugh of relief. 'Yes, exactly, once I was folding washing and Poppy was snapping at my heels and I knew I had something in the oven—'

'A Findus crispy pancake,' Aisha said knowingly.

Sophy laughed nervously. 'No, actually, this was a proper meal.' Sophy looked like she was trying to recollect. 'A casserole, I think. But anyway.' Sophy waved her hand and Mel snorted a quiet laugh and caught Aisha's eye and they shared a look. They both knew that Sophy and Niall still ate Findus crispy pancakes from time to time and that Sophy was protective about it. What had started out as harmless flirtatious fun was now a part of their routine and that was fine.

'Anyway!' Sophy sang. 'I read the message and then I was distracted with whatever I was doing, so I thought I'd reply after I'd fed the kids. Anyway, after about three minutes there came a message from Blythe—'

'Blythe...' Mel and Aisha said in unison, with a hint of disgust. Then they both laughed. Mel knew what this Blythe woman was about, she had her very own version in the form of Saskia.

Sophy nodded. 'Yes, anyway, she sent me a message, prompting me to reply, because she needed to know and implying she knew I had seen the message.'

Mel and Aisha gasped.

'That's shocking.' Aisha's hand went to her neck. 'What was so important that you needed to reply instantly?'

'She needed to know if Max was coming to her house for the garden play date because there was a gluten-free kid coming.'

Mel and Aisha looked baffled.

'Why did she need a reply straight away and what does the kid being gluten free have to do with it?'

'Blythe knows Max always has a brioche or something as his after-school snack and he gets it everywhere and this GF mum doesn't want there being crumbs spilt at Blythe's house because the kid – Larry – picks up the crumbs and eats them.'

Mel and Aisha stared at Sophy.

'Right, no gluten. Fair enough,' Mel said.

'And she put this on the WhatsApp group?' Mel asked, she began scrolling through looking for the message.

Sophy leaned over and took the phone. 'Here.' She scrolled for a few seconds then handed the phone back to Mel. Aisha leaned in and looked over Mel's shoulder.

Both women read for a moment.

'Oh, my days, Sophy, she's shaming you on the group.'

'She totally is.' Mel handed the phone to Sophy.

Sophy looked at the messages again, then she looked up at Mel and Aisha, bewildered.

'The part where she talks about lack of consideration and contamination.'

Sophy looked at the screen, her face full of focus. Then her eyes widened.

'Oh my God!'

Mel and Aisha nodded.

'She could have messaged you separately for that. Some things don't need to be aired on a WhatsApp group. If the kid can't help himself picking up the crumbs that Max eats then this Blythe could have messaged you and asked you privately, suggest he brings a rice cake or a gluten-free muffin.'

Aisha nodded. 'They're very nice. I had one once.'

'To shame you on the WhatsApp group with all the other mums listening and watching. Rude.' Mel flicked her sunglasses down.

Aisha laid her hand on Sophy's shoulder.

'How have you managed to get away with not being in a school WhatsApp group?' Sophy asked and Mel knew that was aimed at Aisha. It was quiet for a few seconds and then Mel took her glasses off.

'Aisha?'

Aisha stayed quiet and Mel laughed.

'I knew it. You're in a group, too!'

Aisha looked sheepish and said something that neither Sophy nor Mel could hear.

'Pardon?' Sophy asked.

'I actually enjoy my group,' Aisha said, loud enough for them both to hear this time. 'Wore me down, I relented but I am now a fully fledged member of a school mums' WhatsApp group, and I am not the one that sits back and doesn't say anything, I have plenty to say. But I would never post something like that. She could have said it to you in the playground, for goodness' sake. Not everything needs to be said via an app. We actually have to have conversations as well and that's what's nice about my group, it's small and we also talk lots at the school gates, not just all over the app.'

Aisha finished the last word as though it was a full stop, then she crossed her arms.

'So you're enjoying it then?' Mel asked, intrigued.

Aisha looked thoughtful. 'I feel it's a necessary tool for mums to communicate the minor and major matters of schooling our young when we're not in the playground. But there is also plenty of time to talk face to face and your Blythe should have done the right thing.'

Mel glanced at Sophy, but Sophy's eyes were on her phone again. It was just like Aisha to take this sort of stuff seriously and fully commit and not care what Mel or Sophy thought.

'So what do I do?' Sophy's eyes were still firmly on the phone. 'I must address this. I can't allow this to just pass. I can't believe I hadn't noticed. What a knob. This was days ago as well. And there has been other stuff too.' Sophy recalled an experience to do with the fake bake and the message from Blythe about home-baked goods, which Aisha and Mel roared with laughter at and then she talked about the lack of commentary after her accidental social post about her anxiety.

'And it wasn't as if you were trying to get the likes, you couldn't have been more sincere if you tried,' Aisha said soothingly.

Mel had a large cold drink next to her, the heat had created so much condensation around the glass it almost slipped out of her hand when she picked it up but she felt she needed some more courage to say what she was about to say.

'I think we all need to quit the WhatsApp groups.'

Sophy and Aisha looked at her, horrified.

'Quit?' Sophy checked she was hearing right.

'You can't just quit the group,' Aisha said. 'It sends the wrong impression.'

'What impression? The whole thing is ridiculous. I don't need to be on constant callout to these women. I owe them nothing. I don't need to have conversations about every little thing that crops up at school from little Billy's boo boo to who is baking what for the latest bake sale. Sorry, Soph, don't go all post-traumatic stress on me.'

'It's fine. It haunts me at night occasionally, like a little tap on the shoulder just as I'm dropping off – hey, you remember when you tried to pass off a shop-bought cake as your own? That sort of thing.'

'It sounded brilliant, they could have been more supportive,' Aisha said.

'As soon as I gave my number, it was as if I signed my life away and now it's twenty messages a day. Sometimes more. Once I counted over fifty comments on one thread. Eight women. Fifty messages,' Sophy said.

'It's a joke.' Mel leaned forward conspiratorially. 'I say we cut them off.'

'Oh!' Aisha gasped. 'You can't do that.'

'We can do exactly what we want. We're grown women.'

Sophy looked at her for a few moments and then looked at her phone.

'Give me your phone, Sophy.'

Sophy reluctantly handed over her phone and Mel removed her from the group. She handed Sophy her phone and then did the same with her own.

'Aisha?' Mel said.

'No way. I'm fine. I like my little group. As I said, it's harmless. Doesn't feel anything like the toxicity that is going on in yours. But well done to you both for exiting.'

'It's easy, you just cut them off. No need to think about them any more,' Mel said, took a long drink and lay back down.

Now, thought Mel. She just needed to do the same with someone else in her life.

25

SOPHY

There had been moments when she had felt okay on the boat and so she had almost tried to push away the notion of sickness. But as they were two days from the end of the trip and she had woken not feeling well enough to go out on the dolphin swimming experience, she now found herself standing outside the cruise ship pharmacy. There were only two nights left but she couldn't keep holding off. She had been bought various types of pills and sachets and she had assured everyone that she had been taking them and that they had been doing the job and that she was doing okay. But the truth was that she hadn't been taking any of them. She was terrified of putting any of those drugs into her body for fear of what they might do to her.

Yet she was also fearful of what she was about to do. Of what she had been putting off. She stepped over the threshold of the pharmacy and took a deep breath.

She was almost 100 per cent sure that she knew what had been affecting her since she had boarded the ship. She hadn't expected it and hadn't been prepared for it. Which now she could see was silly and naive.

She walked to the counter. The lady pharmacist greeted her with a large smile, and Sophy smiled back with some uncertainty.

'Good morning, how can I help you?'

Wow, thought Sophy, you didn't get pharmacists this happy in Boots. They were stressed and overworked and harassed by hypochondriacs and endless year-round flu bugs.

'Hi there, I'm not sure if you can help me, if you even sell this.' Sophy shuffled awkwardly, then she took a deep breath and stood up straight. 'Do you sell pregnancy tests?'

* * *

Sophy sat down on the bed, holding the opened packet. It had been a few years since she had done one, but she quickly scanned the instructions just to be safe. Then she tugged out the stick and went into the bathroom. She had been holding in a mid-morning pee for over an hour especially for this, so she had the strongest chance of getting an accurate result.

Her heart pounded as she peed and when she was done, she rested the stick on the edge of the sink and waited.

A full three minutes later, she knew she need not have waited as long. In the past she had been so desperate, so excited to get the results and she was usually so sure about wanting to be pregnant and about seeing the result. But this felt so different. She and Niall hadn't planned another baby, in fact she wasn't sure she could even say when she might have fallen pregnant. Life was so busy with kids and school runs and playdates and the bloody WhatsApp group – which was no more. Sophy felt a stab of panic that she had been so rash and was surprised she hadn't seen a message from Blythe yet to ask her why she had left the group. Sophy knew she would have been deeply offended. But if this test came up positive, then Sophy knew she could use that to her advantage and explain that technology was increasing her sickness and that was why she left. But she really shouldn't worry. Blythe hadn't treated her very nicely.

Three minutes passed and it was time to turn over the stick. She was suddenly filled with panic. What if this wasn't what Niall wanted? What if they couldn't afford it? What if this was a mistake and they both ended up regretting it? But the more Sophy thought about it, the more she heard what her mind, body and soul were trying to tell her, what if it was negative? And that thought hurt her heart more than the other insignificant questions that were just logistics, really. She knew Niall was a wonderful father and he loved the bones of Max and Poppy and she knew he would want more children.

She whipped the stick over and she was flooded with relief. Relief for the last week of sickness that now had a cause and relief that she would now get to focus on the one thing she knew she was good at. Carrying a baby.

* * *

Sophy had made herself a celebratory cup of tea and drank it along with nibbling on a ginger biscuit. Sophy wondered if housekeeping had been noticing that she was favouring those over any others as there seemed to be an abundance of them. With the pregnancy test in the bin, there would be a very clear indication of the narrative behind this. Sophy wondered what other discoveries housekeeping made on ships like these.

It was coming up for lunch and Niall would be at work. Sophy wondered if it was worth chancing calling him now rather than later when the kids would be all over him, or should she just wait until she got home? It was only forty-eight hours until they would be home and she could tell him to his face.

But the temptation was too much. She dialled Niall on FaceTime – she wanted to see his face – and waited for him to pick up. It cut off after a few rings. Niall would have presumed she was on the top deck or beach and wanted to show off what a great time she was having. She was sure he would call her back when he had a spare moment. She put her phone on the bedside table and sat down on the bed. She felt a tingle in her tummy, which began to travel up into her chest as the reality set in – she was going to be a mum again. They were going to have three children. Just as Sophy began to daydream about names and how and when she would begin to break the news to her friends and family, her phone was ringing with a FaceTime from Niall.

'Babe,' he said when she answered. He looked windswept, then she spotted the garden and Max and Poppy in the background. Her heart felt so full, and she wished she was able to tell her children that they were going to have a sibling.

Suddenly she was filled with fear and panic. Was this the right thing to do, tell Niall over FaceTime, would he be able to handle it with the kids in the background?

'Hey, can you go somewhere where you're alone?'

'Okay,' he said. 'Not sure I can feel that sexy with the kids playing in the garden, but if you're quick I might be able—'

'Niall, I'm not ringing for that.' Sophy tried to think if she had ever called Niall for phone sex. She shook her head, annoyed he had distracted her so easily.

'I need to tell you something. You may want to sit down.'

'Okay.' The screen moved around a bit as Niall settled himself in the sitting room. 'What have you done, booked us an around-the-world cruise?' he joked and Sophy felt a pang of sadness that that was not something that they would be able to do for a while, that her already hard-working husband was going to have another child to be responsible for, more mess, less space.

'Erm, not quite as glamorous as that.'

She watched something flicker across Niall's face.

'Oh?' he said inquisitively.

Sophy looked around awkwardly, cleared her throat.

'It's a baby, Niall. We're having another baby.'

26

AISHA

Aisha had been trying to get through to her mum all day. They were sailing home the day after tomorrow and Aisha wanted to ask her if she needed or wanted anything. She had been picking up bits and bobs each time they docked. They were now in Lisbon, their final destination. Aisha could hardly believe the trip had come to an end. She had gotten used to waking up when her body was ready to, strolling through the ship, saying hello to people she'd begun to see each day and recognise. Getting fed each day and not needing to think about what they were all going to eat, and shopping, the preparation, and then the complaints and the moaning and then the days when they wouldn't eat what she had put in front of them.

To suddenly be thinking of only herself had felt like an out-of-body experience at first. Then she'd settled into it. The part that stood out the most for Aisha was how she was able to think. She could walk into a shop, think about what she wanted and make an accurate decision. She had been able to look at a menu and really know what it was she wanted to eat instead of rushing her choice and then regretting it, only to spend the entire meal seeing to the twins anyway. Then there were the long conversations with her friends that didn't have to end abruptly, to stay up late talking into the night knowing that all she needed to do the next day was order her breakfast and listen to a podcast. It had been absolute heaven. Aside from the underlying worry about her mum, that was.

Finally, her phone rang and 'Mum' flashed up on her screen.

Aisha answered. 'Hello, Mum.'

'Hello.'

'Are you okay? What's happening, I've barely heard a peep out of you these last few days, I need to know you're okay!'

'How are you? Been getting plenty of rest?'

'Mum,' Aisha said sternly. 'Please. What on earth is going on? I'm fine, so please stop deflecting.'

'Oh, Aisha, you were always the worrier. Always the one who was watching over me, especially when your father left.' Martina let out a huge sigh on the other end. 'I guess there is no pulling the wool over your eyes, is there?'

Aisha felt a whimper forming but managed to hold it in.

'I went to the doctor, had all the blood tests and then I went back, and they told me what is wrong with me.'

'Okay,' Aisha said encouragingly. A part of her clinging to the idea that her mother was not about to tell her terrible news.

'I got the cancer,' Martina said frankly.

The whimper that Aisha had been trying to hold in burst out of her. 'Oh God, Mum.'

'It's okay, Aisha, the doctor told me I have a good chance, I have caught it early. They can start me on treatment right away. I am not going to die, do you hear me, girl, I am going to be fine.'

Aisha felt all the energy drain out of her and she wished she could get off the boat and fly home immediately and be with her mum.

'Aisha, girl, I got myself to the doctor right away. And I knew you would worry, which was why I was keeping this to myself.'

'Mum,' Aisha wept. 'How long have you known?'

'A few days, I didn't want to ruin your holiday, but you've been messaging me non-stop, and I was going tell you when you got back. But I managed to get to the penultimate day of your trip. I did okay.' Aisha was sure she heard a smugness to her mother's voice and a hint of laugher.

'Are you happy about that, trying to keep me in the dark?'

'Don't be silly, I wanted to give you a good break, not have you worrying about me the whole time.'

'I wouldn't have gone, Mum, that is the simple answer. If you'd said you suspected something was wrong, well, I would have stayed. I would have been there for you.'

Aisha didn't hold back the tears and Martina waited for her to finish before she spoke again.

'I didn't tell you because I didn't want to ruin the holiday you have been looking forward to and, may I add, a well-deserved one too.'

'That's all irrelevant, because it's ruined now. I will never look back on this time away and think fondly, I will only think of this conversation. You should have told me.'

There was silence for a while and Aisha heard the impact of her words sink in. Her mother was telling her she had cancer and she was being unreasonable. She was being unkind. Yet this was huge and would be life changing for everyone. Aisha sensed the notion of opening a restaurant slipping away. How could she take on a restaurant when she had her mum to take care of now?

'Mum—'

'Now listen, just you get yourself back home safely and we will talk then. You can ask me all the questions you like.'

'I'll be sailing back the day after tomorrow; I get back late. I can come over first thing Saturday morning.'

'Don't rush yourself, just see them babies first.'

'I'll be over first thing Saturday, Mum.'

'Okay, Aisha. I'll have the kettle on. We'll have a nice cup of tea.'

27

MEL

'It's been quite lovely having you on board. I mean, aside from your exceptional professionalism – I will be giving you a first-class review – you, Mel, have been something else. Let's get you booked in for another.' Leo laughed but Mel knew there were splinters of sincerity in his jest. He would love nothing more than to have a class act like Mel on board any of these ships under his name. And, of course, she knew getting to spend time with her would be an extra advantage to him. But Mel knew that was the very reason she was here in the first place and neither of them could keep sidestepping the truth any more. Leo was her ex-boyfriend. They had never been friends before or after. She hadn't seen him for over fifteen years. Mel didn't feel any guilt, though, because she had been invited to do a job and she had come here and done it.

Initially when Leo had told her it was his business and he had made the choice to invite her here, she'd felt cheated. She'd felt as though the only reason she had been given this opportunity was because Leo had wanted to see her and it was nothing to do with her talent. But then she had sung to a packed theatre every night with standing ovations and there had been offers of work from proprietors of a wedding venue who were looking for a singer just like Mel to offer to their guests and a large London club which Mel was familiar with but had never before had the confidence to approach. Plus all the footage Sophy and Aisha had taken, which meant that she would be able to make her social pages and website look much better and put together a showreel.

'I am so grateful for the opportunity, Leo, it has been quite an adventure, for all of us.' She paused and looked into Leo's eyes. They were on the top deck; Southampton had just crept onto the horizon. Soon it would be time to disembark. Leo had already offered to buy her dinner at one of his favourite local haunts. A part of Mel immediately questioned how many women he had taken there before her.

'It's been lovely.'

Leo turned away and looked ahead at the horizon, where a lot of people on the deck were taking in the last bit of the view, soaking up their last hour of their holiday.

Mel caught the look in his eye, one of defeat. Leo had never been one to be defeated. Despite the endless knock-backs in his life, the wheeler dealer years, here he was the king of his domain. In another life, another time, she might have said that to him, but she wasn't his woman, and it wouldn't be right to be the one to massage his ego or inflate his hopes. Her need to be with her family again was growing stronger with every knot that they travelled closer to home.

Mel had enjoyed the holiday and she didn't feel guilty that she had done it. She knew she would return home, better and more refreshed. She had woken up this morning and shaken off any feelings of doubt or shame for being here with Leo for the last ten days. She had not instigated it and she certainly hadn't planned to be here with her ex-boyfriend. She had been flattered by his attention and admiration for her after all these years, but Mel was savvy enough to know that Leo hadn't really changed who he was. Mel had been there some fifteen years ago and whilst he could often make her feel like the most precious thing on earth, he never did the one thing she needed him to do, which was commit to her. And now it seemed as he was settling into his fifties, he was ready. Ready after Mel had gone away and created a new life, a home and a family. Now, when he chose to step back into her life, it was in an attempt to shatter all that for his own selfish reasons. Mel could have been angry if she wasn't so content with her own decisions.

She loved Daz dearly; she knew she had made the right choice back then. She had chosen Daz and left behind what could and most probably would have been several decades of disappointment and heartache. Being with Daz had meant Mel had been able to forge her career at a steady rate, with the love and support of a partner who didn't need to compete with her for his own recognition.

Mel gazed up at Leo, the two of them cruising along on the ship. She wasn't sure what this time with Leo had been; some strange glitch in the matrix, maybe. A glimpse of what her life might have been like if she hadn't married Daz. One thing Mel did know was that she wasn't confused about her life any more. Daz had been very distant recently, but she wondered if she had overlooked something, she vowed to make more effort, to be attentive and get to the source of her husband's worry and frustration. She had made some absolute bloopers along the way and car-crashed through most of her twenties, but she knew she had made the right decision when she had walked away from Leo all those years ago and into the waiting arms of Daz. And soon she would be home, and walking into those arms again, where she had always felt safe, where she had always felt loved, where she had always felt recognised.

28

SOPHY

With the news of Martina's cancer, Sophy had decided to keep the news of her pregnancy quiet until they were all back and at home again. She had almost skipped out of her cabin and had been on the way to speak to the girls, but when she arrived, she could see the fallen face of Aisha and the comforting arm of Mel around her shoulder. They had all sat together for a while, not really knowing what to say but letting Aisha speak and cry when she needed to. They had caught the cancer early, these were the words that Aisha repeated for her own reassurance and for theirs.

The trip had been extraordinary and memorable in so many ways, but when Sophy put her foot over the threshold of her house and crept into the sitting room to find her husband sitting on the sofa, watching some mindless programme on ITV, she had fallen into his arms, curled up beside him and the two of them stayed there for the rest of the evening, talking about their future.

* * *

On Monday morning Sophy was waiting for Max to be let out of school, her mind a whirring machine of thoughts. One would come at her, and she would hold it and toy with it for a while before throwing it aside to make room for the next one. She was in a full-on trance when she heard her name being called.

'Sophy?'

Sophy was catapulted back to the drizzly tarmacked primary school playground and as she came to, she saw Blythe standing in front of her, her head cocked slightly to the side as she passed her.

'Sophy,' she said more brightly this time. 'How are you? Long time no see.'

Sophy instantly felt her gut tighten.

'Blythe, hi.' It occurred to Sophy that Blythe would want to discuss her sudden departure from the WhatsApp group and that Sophy had yet to concoct a suitably believable story. What with finding out about the pregnancy, she had clean forgotten that she had ghosted the group.

Blythe was trying to smile but it looked more like a pained expression, as though she was approaching Sophy with caution.

Sophy noticed that Blythe wasn't alone. There were three other mums standing behind her, they all wore the same awkward pained expressions.

'We just thought we'd come and check in with you.' Blythe spoke slowly and softly, as though she were dealing with a small child.

Sophy put her hand to her stomach in an automatic response to the way the women were looking at her. Was it that obvious? Maybe she was further gone than she thought, and she was showing? She glanced down, checking herself out, but there was no bump to be seen. Was it so plainly obvious then? Was it written all over her sappy doe-eyed face? Or did she just look so hideously wretched from the influx of hormones the bouts of sickness that were coming in spurts throughout the day? Did she look a sickly green colour?

'Is everything okay?' Blythe asked again and looked back at the clutch of mothers she'd brought along. 'After your time away. We all saw little Max being dropped off by that other lady with the Irish accent and then I heard about your post on Instagram.' She looked around at her mum friends and Sophy felt her gut tighten in defence, in anger and frustration. She could see what Blythe was trying to do, trying to imply.

Digging around for something she could get her teeth into about Sophy so that she could own it. But Blythe hadn't been there after the fake bake incident making light of it, she had blatantly tried to make Sophy feel bad for her lack of home cookery skills, she hadn't contacted her after her accidental post where she had exposed a whole load of her anxieties and now here she was trying to out her in front of her cronies. So much for the sisterhood.

'We were worried about you.' Blythe curled her mouth into what she supposed was an empathetic expression.

Sophy blinked at Blythe and suppressed a laugh. Sophy could see it all so clearly now. She had been so keen to make mum friends and have people like her that she had been blind to the pack of vultures she had inadvertently associated herself with. These women weren't friends, they were parasites. It was just like being back at school herself and trying to fit in with a clan of kids who she thought were the most popular.

Something about being a PTA mum had intrigued her, her altruistic side had wanted to help, to give something back, but who was she kidding? She was no baker, she wasn't Kirstie Allsopp, she couldn't make things. She could stick on a nice dress and take a good photo, she could organise a great night out or market a business. Of course, to someone like Blythe the prospect of hopping on a boat and sailing around the Mediterranean for almost two weeks was unheard of. It had been unheard of to Sophy until she'd had the opportunity to go on one, and whilst her heart had hurt for her kids and husband at times, she was so glad she had done it. It was, they had all agreed, the beginning of something beautiful, an annual 3 a.m. Shattered Mums' Club holiday abroad, to recuperate and find themselves again.

'I'm actually fine, Blythe.' Sophy looked behind her at the small crowd that had gathered, were they expecting to witness a breakdown? Perhaps she should begin communicating in alternative dance, that would really throw them all. 'It was great to take some time off.'

'We all feel like just taking off sometimes.' Blythe flashed a look to her friends again with an inane grin splattered across her face and they all laughed nervously. 'It's hard work, especially with four.' Blythe rolled her eyes as if having four children was not in fact her own choice. 'But we muddle through and that's why we're here, the mums. That's why I set up the WhatsApp group, so we can share how we're feeling. A bit like your 3 a.m. Shattered Mums' group.'

Sophy frowned, the reception WhatsApp group was nothing like her cherished 3 a.m. Shattered Mums' Club group. It had made her feel sad, uncomfortable, she had questioned herself, become paranoid about checking responses, and making sure she hadn't missed anything. With Aisha and Mel, she had been able to be as frank as she liked almost from day one. She had felt a connection with two women that she had yet to experience with any other woman she had met.

Sophy felt sorry for Blythe. She wondered what good a trip around the Med would do for Blythe and all the other Blythes in the word who felt their sole purpose on this planet was to organise and care for their husbands and children then feel bitter resentment when they saw another woman doing something purely for herself. Something Sophy had managed to remind herself of whilst she was away was that she was more than just a mother. Even though ironically she had discovered she was going to be one to another living being whilst she was onboard. Sophy treasured the gift of motherhood, but even amongst the bouts of sickness and panic, she had found a little part of herself again. She had found moments of joy in just seeing her friends laughing and being at one and most of all she had realised that she needed to be more transparent and honest when it came to the posts that she put out on social media. The response that had come (and was still coming) from the post about feeling scared and out of control showed it had resonated with so many followers. Sophy was planning her next podcast around the theme and would invite Mel and Aisha on to talk about this too.

Sophy regarded her spectators with slight amusement. 'Blythe, I am perfectly well and have just enjoyed a ten-day trip around the Mediterranean with my two good friends. We had a jolly good time. The reception WhatsApp group just isn't for me. I am happy to offer my services to the PTA through any marketing or promotion, but I am not, as you have seen, a baker. You have my number, please do text me about anything you feel you'd like my help with in the areas I can offer my expertise. Have a great day.' Sophy turned and walked away from the women as she heard their muffled shocked responses and then Blythe hushing them, her voice tainted with anger. Sophy took herself to the wall where she sat down, her heart racing from adrenaline.

Then Sophy found she was smiling to herself. Not out of spite, but because she had managed to say how she was really feeling again. She understood that there were times in life when it wasn't always appropriate to say exactly how you were feeling, but Sophy felt as though something had happened to her when she had been on the cruise. It was Aisha's firm but kind words to her, to keep the post up because it was the truth that kept the followers engaged. It was Sophy's ability to express her true inner feelings to the masses, to strangers, to people she didn't know and might never meet. So when it came to speaking her mind to Blythe, a woman she had encountered enough times this year already, it just seemed to spill out. Sophy was filled with a rush of glee that she had been able to continue what had been born aboard and what she hoped would continue.

'I thought that was very admirable.'

Sophy looked to her right, where a woman wearing a baseball cap with a shock of auburn hair was standing near to her.

'Oh, what? That?' Sophy gestured to the women who were now huddled together, obviously discussing Sophy's shocking response.

The woman moved closer.

'Yes. They coerced me into joining the WhatsApp group, but after I saw you leave, I think I'll do the same. I wasn't as brave as you. But then you were so brave with your Instagram post.'

'Oh.' Sophy thought and then recollected the anonymous messenger on the WhatsApp group, the only one who had checked in with her. 'Was that you? Who sent me the message?'

'Yes,' the woman said sheepishly. 'I didn't want to contact you directly, I thought that might be a bit presumptuous. But I also figured there would have been a lot more support from them lot, especially as I know most of them follow you.'

Sophy cocked her head. 'I thought that too! But I have come to realise that people don't always act how you expect them to and that if you try to live your life with those sort of expectations then it only makes you miserable, but a lot of the time people are never who you hope them to be.'

'Wow. That is a great motto for life.'

Sophy laughed. 'Thanks. It's a bit long. I need to make it a bit shorter, a bit snappier.'

The woman laughed wholesomely and Sophy felt a warm tingle in her belly, the same sensation she'd had when she'd met Aisha and Mel and they'd all gone for their first coffee.

'I'm Sophy, by the way. Just to introduce myself officially,' Sophy said.

'I'm Misty.'

'Misty is great name!' Sophy said.

'Yeah, well, my parents were hippies back then and I can't tell you the array of names I escaped.'

Sophy laughed again. 'I can imagine.'

She took a deep breath, the stress of the conversation with Blythe was evaporating, being taken over by this lovely new woman, Misty. 'I'm not sure what has happened to me recently. This is not who I was a few weeks ago.'

Sophy felt a wave of nausea come over her. Her facial expression must have changed because Misty edged closer.

'Are you okay?' she said quietly, trying not to attract the attention of the nearby parents.

Sophy looked up and into the eyes of the woman, wishing she could tell her that she was pregnant, and it was a bout of morning sickness, but she had barely told anyone, not even Aisha and Mel, and so she righted herself.

'I haven't eaten anything yet this morning, that's all.'

'Ah, I do that but on purpose. I now don't eat until 12.30 every day. Intermittent fasting, it's called. Sounds wanky, but it works for me.'

'Oh, I like the sound of that. I host a podcast, the 3 a.m. Shattered Mums' Club. You should come on my show and talk about your fasting. I'm not always after experts, just everyday people who do cool stuff.'

'Sounds great. I'd love to.' Misty smiled. 'And hey, if you ever fancy a coffee after the drop-off, my house is a minute around the corner from here.'

'That sounds lovely.' Sophy said.

If the school playground was somewhere she needed to spend a lot of time, then it would be nice to have at least one person she could relate to. She didn't need to like everyone, and she certainly didn't need to be liked by everyone. But if she was going to be spending the next decade in and amongst these playgrounds then it would be good to have at least one friend. Sophy was sure she would get to know other mums, but everyone needed their one ally.

29

AISHA

'Do you want tea or coffee?' Martina called over her shoulder as she stood at the kitchen counter. The kitchen with its new lease of life that had felt like a fresh start, but which now felt like it belonged to a time when her mum had told her she had cancer.

'Tea or coffee, Aish?' Martina called again.

'Um... tea.' Aisha nudged a sticky stain on the kitchen table. She thought about her mum and dad sitting at the table together, eating their preferred breakfast of peanut butter, honey and bananas on toast. Martina brought a pot of tea to the table; even when she wasn't 100 per cent herself, she still maintained a certain level. Which was where Aisha got her passion for hospitality from. Watching so many people coming and going through this very kitchen when she was younger, seeing how her mother would always deal with every situation efficiently, because it was in her soul.

'Eat them biscuits too, they will fill you right up, look at the size of them.'

Aisha looked at the biscuits that her mother had put on the table. Shop-bought giant cookies. Not home-made. Aisha looked away, she couldn't face the monstrosity that sat before her, it represented so much more than just confectionery. It was a glaring sign to Aisha that Martina wasn't up to cooking or baking. And as that was the very essence of her mother, it meant that essence was missing. How much more would be taken from her if she didn't get better and how could Aisha stand by and watch?

'I know what you are thinking, and you'd be wrong.' Martina sat down with a 'humph', the air from the padded seats escaping, still not worn in. 'I ain't going nowhere. You and Charley and them boys will have me around for a long time to come yet. Now can we please just get on and drink the tea? One thing I have learned in the last few weeks is to live in the moment. Sometimes in my life I have chosen not to, I have been too busy, too wrapped up in whatever was going on or thinking about what was coming next. Now I am going to appreciate each moment, like sitting here with my daughter drinking tea and looking at giant cookies that have too many ingredients, some of which I can't pronounce, and deliberate whether I will eat one or not.'

Aisha glanced at her mother and eventually a smirk spread across her lips.

'I'll take them home for the boys.'

'Oh good. That solves that then.'

'Are you really not up to cooking or baking at all, Mum?' Aisha lifted one of the cookies and inspected the colourful smarties within its crevices.

'No, Aish, I have no desire neither. My body is telling me to rest and recuperate and that is what I am going to let it do. Also I need to start eating more raw food. We used to eat so much when you were all young.'

'Well, I can get out to the market and shops for you if you aren't feeling up to it.'

'I'll get back round to it soon.' Martina began to pour tea into a cup and pushed it in front of Aisha. Aisha added her usual splash of milk and one sugar. She took a sip; it was always exactly the right temperature when it was poured from a teapot.

Aisha broke a piece of the biscuit off, regarded it for a moment then popped it in her mouth. She looked at Martina, she felt a smile begin to spread across her face and she felt like a small child again, just her and her mum sitting at the table having a cheeky snack whilst her sisters and cousins were out of the vicinity for long enough.

Martina patted her hand. 'It's all gonna be okay.'

Aisha forced a smile, this time through the mouthful of food, and then forced herself to swallow.

* * *

When Aisha got home, Charley was nowhere to be seen. She looked in the basement, called upstairs but it was obvious she was out. Okay, Aisha thought to herself, just get a grip. It wasn't necessarily unusual for Charley to be out and about in the day inside school hours, it's just she would tend to stick to her scheduled times of recording when the boys were at school so that they could all be together for dinner and after-school activities. Aisha felt a little redundant for a while; she sat down on Otis's bed and looked around at all their little things and her heart hurt for how small they both were still, and she missed them. She knew that being at home and not having any real structure or purpose to her day had to stop.

She took out her phone from her back pocket and looked at the three missed calls from the letting agency. They were keen to get her in and for her to sign the documents. No one was mad enough to take on a catering business right now, except Aisha, who had accepted the day after, when Rachel called back. But she had yet to tell anyone except Charley, who had told her to absolutely go for it. She knew it would mean they would have less time together as a family, but the time they did have would be special and meaningful. She knew that Aisha had to do this. Aisha had already seen the business thriving in her mind's eye. She knew with her fusion of British and Jamaican she could make it into something worthwhile that people would travel to from all around and she already had the right customers at her fingertips right there in Brixton. There was such an eclectic mix in the neighbourhood and still plenty of those who had their roots firmly planted in Jamaican culture. Aisha didn't have doubts about the business succeeding, but more doubts had been planted in her mind since her mother's diagnosis and now she didn't see how she was supposed to carry on when everything was about to change, and how did Aisha know when things might begin to get better? If at all.

Her phone rang and startled her. It was the letting agent again. Her first response was to end the call. But there was that twinge, that pull, that desire that still burned within her, and she couldn't keep ignoring it. She picked up the phone.

* * *

Aisha had an hour before she needed to pick the boys up from school. Just enough time to get to the letting agent and sign the contracts. She felt a twang of doubt that she should have waited to do it with Charley, but Charley had always been supportive of the project; they had done their maths many times over, even though Aisha still hadn't put together her own proper business plan. It was more for her own sanity than for anything else. It felt right standing here in the estate agency and signing the lease on a business premises where she would soon be opening her restaurant. She felt a little sick, she hadn't even recruited any staff. Of course, she would be doing the majority of the cooking, but she would still need to hire kitchen assistants and waiting staff. Maybe even a manager of some sort if things took off. She would start with a simple old-fashioned sign in the window and see how things went from there. Aisha was pretty hot on social media, and she could ask Sophy for any tips when it came to marketing.

When Aisha put her pen down, Rachel asked her if she fancied a little celebratory drink.

'We don't do this for everyone, but I happen to have a few single bottles of Prosecco downstairs, I feel we should give the place a little toast! What do you say?'

Before Aisha had time to think about her answer – the school run was looming in her mind – Rachel was back with two miniature black bottles of Prosecco, the perfect amount for one glass.

'I only have straws.' She popped the little plastic tops and stuck a straw in each one and handed one to Aisha.

'Congratulations on your new venture, we're so thrilled. We hope it thrives.' She held her bottle to Aisha's, and they clinked. 'Now do you have a name yet?' Rachel said after a long glug of her Prosecco, disregarding the straw almost immediately. Aisha wondered if Rachel had been waiting a long time to whip out the Prosecco.

'I have a few ideas mulling around in my head.'

'Do tell!' Rachel prompted.

'Well, I was thinking that as I am half-British and half-Jamaican, it should be called Pom Jam.'

Rachel's head fell back, her mouth dropped open and her eyes rolled to the back of her head. 'Oh, my gosh, that is fantastic!'

Aisha took a sip of the Prosecco, the bubbles hit her nose. She and Rachel chatted for the time it took them both to finish their drinks, which was around two sips for Rachel. Aisha thanked her profusely and Rachel promised to be at the opening night.

Aisha walked out into the daylight, the brightness of the day hurting her eyes with the hit of alcohol in her system. She felt lighter than she had done since she had taken that phone call from Martina on the last night of the trip.

As she stood at the school gates, a few minutes earlier than she would usually be, she contemplated her life and now what her future held for her. She knew she needed to plough on with her dreams, despite what was going on around her with her mother's illness. It was all fading into the background, with the help of the alcohol she was sure, but maybe because she knew she had finally put some roots down, and she finally had done something for herself.

30

MEL

'I clean everywhere, the house sparkling.' Ksenia had just sat down, a film of sweat across her face despite the cold outside. It was Friday afternoon, the day that Ksenia always came. Mel had been lucky as that was the day that all the other clients tried to poach her. When Mel heard about this, she upped Ksenia's waged by a pound an hour, but Ksenia was adamant that Mel would always be her priority. And she had been right, four years later and she was like a family member. Skylar absolutely adored her and even though Ksenia had never shown an interest in having her own children before she announced her pregnancy, she had developed a lovely relationship with both of her daughters but especially Sky.

'You've excelled yourself. Do you fancy a little lager?' Mel was already pulling two from the fridge and popping the tops open. 'Oh, I forgot! The baby.'

'Okay, you break my arm.' Ksenia accepted the stubby. 'I have sip because I am with child,' she said, touching her stomach, and Mel laughed.

'It's twisted my arm,' Mel said and Ksenia flapped her hand and took a long sip and handed it back to Mel.

'How are you feeling about everything?'

Ksenia pulled her mouth down. 'Tristan say he manage everything, he work two, three jobs if he have to.'

'But he shouldn't have to,' Mel said, feeling a surge of sadness for Ksenia and this situation.

'I will be fine. I am always fine,' Ksenia said.

'Thanks for your work today, the place looks great. The girls are coming over tonight so that is a weight off my mind,' Mel said.

Mel had taught back-to-back yoga classes all morning, then did a food shop and then the school run. She had been cornered by Saskia, who had been absolutely fascinated by her trip away. Mel had inadvertently booked herself in for a coffee with her on Monday after the school run and already she was regretting it. Her day to relax before the full-on weekend of family stuff began. But there was something in the way Saskia had asked, it wasn't desperation exactly, but her tone had hinted that she would be crushed if Mel had declined.

There was a lamb curry bubbling on the stove, which she was going to feed the girls, and Mel offered Ksenia a portion to take home.

'No, my boyfriend cook dinner tonight. He make duck.'

'Oh, lovely. Did he get it from the deli down the road?'

'No, from the common. He find it dead on water.'

Mel almost choked on the bit of lamb she was testing to see if it was tender enough.

'Ksenia, you can't eat a dead duck.'

'We not going to eat a live duck.'

'No, I mean you can't eat a duck that is already dead. It might have been poisoned, or I don't know, anything.'

Ksenia shook her head. 'You worry too much. When I was a child, we ate the little what you call them with whiskers?' Ksenia screwed her face up and stuck her two top teeth on her bottom lip.

'Rats,' Mel said tentatively, trying not to cringe. She was almost used to Ksenia's quirks but occasionally she was still shocked by the tales she told.

Ksenia nodded. 'When I was a child in Russia, my father come home from work with two rats. We skin and roast.' Ksenia looked to her right as she recalled the memory. 'It was okay. Like chicken.'

The sound of the front door opening, and Sky's voice screeching, 'Daddy!' ended the conversation about eating roadkill or 'pondkill'. Ksenia picked up her handbag from the back of the chair.

'I see you next Friday.'

She headed to the kitchen door just as Daz arrived, carrying a wriggling Sky over his shoulder in a fireman's lift.

Ksenia took a step back to let him pass.

'Hey, Ksenia.' Daz greeted her in his usual jovial way. Her eyes could barely meet his as she mumbled a goodbye and hurried out of the front door.

Daz laughed as he put Sky down on the floor only for her to scurry back to his legs, pulling at his trousers, demanding to be lifted again.

'It never changes. Do you think one of these days I might get more than a grunt?'

'I don't think so.'

'Is it just a male employer thing?'

'I think so, it can't be men in general, can it? She has a boyfriend, they have a baby on the way. He's begun hunter-gathering for her.'

Daz frowned and Mel waved her hand, she couldn't be bothered to explain the dead duck to Daz.

'That smells amazing.' He lifted Sky up into his arms, she nuzzled into his neck. He edged closer to the oven and looked into the pot. 'Hmmm, I think it's just missing something,' Daz said.

A short sharp noise came from his shoulder, where Sky was still nuzzled, almost like a beep on a phone. Mel felt the swell of love well up inside her. This was an age-old trick that he had been doing since Leia was small. Pretending that he was going to put her in the pot. It was an act that Daz could truly immerse his full self in as it was only once or twice a month that Mel would stretch herself to a one-pot dish, the rest of the time it was salads (Mel would try to slip in the odd Ottolenghi to both of her children's horror), potatoes, corn on the cob and the odd lasagne. So when he spotted a pot on the stove, he went full fun daddy time and Sky loved it.

As Daz continued to clown around, Mel responded to her phone, which had just pinged.

5.03 p.m. – Aisha – Oh my days. I have done something mad, and I can't wait to tell you all.

5.03 p.m. – Sophy – Oh my days, so have I!

5.04 p.m. – Mel – I made a lamb curry, does that count as slightly mad? I can't believe this. Do I need to chill more wine?

Mel smiled to herself. She was really looking forward to seeing the girls after the trip away. She couldn't believe they had been back a whole week already. She clicked out of the messages and quickly went into Instagram for a quick scroll. Her heart almost stopped beating when the first picture she was greeted with was one of herself. But not on her own, she was standing next to Leo. It had been from the first night when she was wearing the red dress. Mel had been captured right at the moment she was looking up at Leo. Her eyes were sparkling, her smile was dazzling, she looked fantastic. Leo was not looking right into the camera, but slightly to the side, a wide grin on his face. The entire shot looked so casual, so in the moment. So bloody perfect.

Leo had tagged her in the image and put a short piece underneath about how it was an extreme pleasure to have Melony Fortuna aboard the *Audacious* for ten nights and what an exceptional artist she was. Mel read the words over and over and then looked again at the image, zooming in on her face and then Leo's. This was bad. She couldn't untag herself because then she would need to explain to Leo that she hadn't told her husband that she had been on the ship with him, and she couldn't just leave it there for the world and his wife to see. She knew too many people who would see it. Irene, Daz's mum, for a start. She had started a book club last year and become completely potty over social media, making TikTok videos of her current reads and posting reels of her and her gals at their book club nights. She was on it too often and would spot that immediately. She would of course be discreet and ask Mel about it, but Mel was pretty sure Irene would remember who Leo was and the role he played in the early part of her and Daz's relationship, and once her memory was jogged, that would look bad.

Mel also felt a slight swell of anger that Leo had put the image up, but then it was his business he was trying to promote, and Mel had not asked him not to. She had presumed he would fade quietly into the background after they parted ways, but alas it was not to be. Mel should have realised that everything comes back to bite you on the bum in the end.

There was no way to hide this from Daz. She should have told him already but now she knew she had no choice.

31

SOPHY

With her arms laden with the best gourmet offerings she could lay her hands on and her mind giddy with her news, Sophy arrived at Mel's. Of course, Aisha was already there, she had news too, and Sophy wondered if her news could be the arrival of a new baby too. The words 'I've done something mad' could have meant she and Charley had artificially inseminated again. Except she had never heard the two of them discuss wanting more children. Sophy was mildly perturbed. Of course, she would be happy for Aisha whatever her news because she needed the joy and support of her friends with Martina and her cancer. Yet at the same time, Sophy had already put off telling the girls her news because of Martina's diagnosis and she didn't want to put off telling them any longer. It was practically bursting out of her.

She let herself in as she always did and could hear Mel and Aisha talking in the kitchen.

'Hello,' Sophy called as she walked through the hallway into the kitchen.

She hugged and kissed both women in turn, suddenly feeling obviously pregnant as though she were showing, or they would just know that she was emitting some sort of sonic pregnancy vibe.

'Right, we're all here, good, good.' Mel had a bottle of wine open and was pouring them each a glass. Sophy decided she would accept the glass so as not to alert them to her news before she had time to say it.

'Sit.' Mel slipped into a chair at the table followed by Aisha, who Sophy now noticed was holding a folder with papers inserted inside.

Sophy took out the gourmet crackers and cordial she had sourced from the new deli in the high street earlier and handed them to Mel.

'Oh, wow, you've excelled yourself.' Mel inspected the crackers and cordial in turn. 'Thank you.' She grinned at Sophy. Out of the corner of her eye, Sophy could see a batch of gingerbread and brownies courtesy of Aisha sitting on the counter. Sophy felt a wave of nausea rise up as she thought of how hard she was finding just getting dressed in the morning, let alone cooking and baking. The smell of the food that was on the stove was also playing havoc with Sophy's senses. She had already had to ask Niall to stop wearing a certain type of deodorant because it was making her heave every morning after he had sprayed it.

'So now we're all here.' Mel raised her glass and Sophy and Aisha followed suit. 'I want to first say a huge thank you for your company aboard the *Audacious*, it was the best thing we've ever done, and I can't wait to do something similar with you both next year.' They all clinked glasses and all chorused cheers. Sophy did a quick sum in her head. Her baby would only be a few months old next summer, so she'd either be not going anywhere or taking an infant on a girls' holiday.

'Okay.' Mel put her glass down on the table and placed her hands in front of her. 'Who's going first?'

Just then, Daz walked in.

'Hi, girls.' Mel looked around and groaned. 'Daz!' she moaned. 'We're at a critical point. Both Sophy and Aisha have news.'

'Wow, news, sounds exciting. Tell me all about it later. I've just come to get some water for madam, she's declared she has a mouth drier than the Sahara Desert.'

Both Sophy and Aisha laughed.

'I can't think where she gets it from.' Daz filled up a glass from the tap and gave them all a wide-eyed comedy look before retreating back upstairs.

'Right. Where were we?'

Aisha looked at Sophy. 'Would you like to tell your news first?' Aisha looked like a child on Christmas morning, her face contorting with nerves and excitement.

'No, you go, Aish.' What could be more thrilling than a pregnancy, Sophy thought to herself, perhaps a little smugly.

'Okay, cool.' Aisha adjusted herself in her chair and pulled out the wad of paper from the folder. 'Now I know I have always harped on about this and maybe you all thought it was never going to happen, I mean at one point when the boys were tiny, I really couldn't see this ever happening. But I have finally done it.' Aisha laid the paper down on the table and lifted her hands away in a dramatic style like a conjurer. 'I've signed a lease on some premises. Pom Jam will open next month.'

Mel let out a shriek and then covered her mouth, remembering her youngest daughter was trying to sleep upstairs. 'Oh, my days, Aisha, this is epic. And I love the name too.'

Sophy let out a whoop, of course this was exactly what Aisha needed, and it was great news. But she could feel her gut tightening and her mind already whirring with tinges of regret. What had she done? How could she have been so stupid as to get pregnant again? Here was Aisha, ready to launch a business at just thirty-four, and Sophy was heading into her late thirties and pregnant again. Mel was thriving with her singing, burlesque and yoga and jobs were pouring in after the cruise stint and Sophy was heading back to the world of babies again. It was just about bearable when she had Poppy as Sky, Otis and Jude were all still toddling about. But now their firstborns were all at school and Aisha clearly had no intention of starting over with a new baby and was intent on having her own business baby, and there was no way in a million years Mel was going to be a mum again in her late forties. So that meant that Sophy would be all alone, in no man's land again. What would she do, could she start another 3 a.m. Shattered Mums' group? She had the social media and the podcast but the support of the girls that first time round was the only thing that kept her sane. Sophy hadn't realised she was crying until Aisha had her arm around her and Mel was pushing tissues her way.

'Hey, what is it?' Aisha soothed.

Sophy wiped her eyes. 'I'm happy for you, of course.' Sophy's voice broke and she held her head in her hands.

Mel was up and across the room, so both her friends were next to her. Then Sophy heard the quiet tones of Mel speaking to someone else in the room. She grabbed the tissues and dabbed her eyes and there was Leia in the kitchen, looking like the exact replica of her mother, massive hair tied in a bun on the top of her head. She was wearing jogging bottoms and a tight crop top, gold jewellery and big hooped earrings. She looked a little tired and pale, as though she had just come round from a snooze and was now in the kitchen looking for food. Sophy saw herself in Leia at almost sixteen, only she would have been scrambling past several other siblings to get to the fridge for the last biscuit in the tin.

'I can bring you some food through, if you like,' Mel was saying to Leia and Sophy felt bad that she was being forced out of her own kitchen because her mum's friend was clearly having some sort of breakdown.

'It's fine,' Sophy said brightly. She blew her nose. 'I'm fine. I feel better.' She looked at Aisha, who was bending down by her side, and Mel and Leia over the other side of the kitchen; they were all looking at her expectantly.

'I am really happy for you, Aisha, I really am, it's the best news ever,' Sophy began and not one woman spoke. 'It just makes my news feel so redundant because the thing I have been meaning to tell you all for days now is that I am pregnant.'

Collective gasps resonated around the room. Aisha squeezed Sophy's arm, again slightly too hard. Christ, did this girl not know her own strength?

'That is amazing, Sophy.' Mel's arms were around her, as were Aisha's. Through the bundle, she could see Leia tentatively approaching. Mel reached out her arm and pulled her daughter into the scrum.

Once she had been released, Mel loaded a plate of the curry and rice for Leia, who sat down at the end of the table and quietly listened. She was almost an adult – she certainly resembled one physically – and she was often present at these get-togethers or would at least make an appearance once during the night, always eager to feel like a grown-up and catch up with the goss. When things got too fruity or when Mel felt she no longer wanted her daughter to overhear or participate in the conversations, Leia would solemnly retreat back to her bedroom or head out with friends.

'I found out on the ship. This was why I was sick.'

'Oh!' Aisha said. 'This makes sense.'

'I had an inkling,' Mel said, 'but the sickness came on the second you boarded.'

'I know, it was weird, but it was purely coincidence. I've done the test and worked out my dates and it all adds up.'

'So how far gone are you?'

'About seven weeks now, I think.'

'Until you go for your first check-up and they try and tell you you're further on.' Mel rolled her eyes.

'Yeah, they did that with Max and Poppy, and I was like, were you there when the act happened? I know when I got pregnant.'

'It's annoying because then that's where all the complications begin when they think you're further on and they start offering inductions when you know you have at least another week to go,' Mel said and Sophy nodded in agreement. Sophy cast her memory back to before Poppy was delivered and the final midwife telling her that she should be induced and Sophy almost telling her to F off; Niall had to step in and managed to defuse the situation with a mug of Horlicks and a custard cream. Poppy was born at home nine days later, as she was supposed to be.

'How is Niall?' Aisha asked, always conscious of the partner's phenomenological experience in life-changing matters like new humans entering the world.

'He's happy. I think he has always wanted a big family, and we discussed having more kids, but this was a bit of surprise, if we're being honest.'

'But a good surprise?' Aisha looked at Sophy, wide-eyed.

'Absolutely. I'm only upset because I am starting over again and that takes me right back to who we all were four years ago, up at all times of the night and barely able to speak or function in the day for months on end. You will have your new business and Mel, you're always doing so well and keeping busy. We might end up, you know, drifting. Well, I will. I feel your lives will move on without me.'

Aisha was already shaking her head fiercely. 'Absolutely no way, not a chance on earth. I need your help with Pom Jam – you're coming on board, Sophy, whether you like it or not. You're my marketing guru.' She took her hand. 'And I don't expect anything for free, I'll pay full rates.'

'Mates' rates,' Sophy said through teary eyes as they began to fill up again.

'And the holiday thing can wait until you're ready. We won't go away without you, Soph. It's all or nothing.' Mel grinned. She took herself over to the stove. Leia had moved forward in her place.

'Congratulations, Sophy. It's really good news,' she said sweetly. Sophy held out her hand and they had a half-awkward hug as Sophy remained seated.

'I'm serving up, okay?' Mel returned to the stove, Leia returned to her food and Aisha stayed put, clinging to Sophy.

'We're here for you, okay?' she said quietly as though the words didn't need to be heard by anyone else.

Sophy nodded.

'Now it's lamb curry, as you know, but I'm putting on a slice of toast for you, Soph. Okay? Marmite and toast and a cup of tea,' Mel called over authoritatively and without question and Sophy felt herself welling up again.

32

AISHA

The unit was in good shape and Aisha wasted no time in getting inside and seeing what was what. There were a few good pieces of kitchen equipment that she could use and she had joined a used catering supplies group on Facebook and was picking up a few more bits this week. She had put an advert in the window and five people had already contacted her. One of them had worked as a waiter at the place when it had been an Italian restaurant and one was a qualified chef, which was a bonus. The other three seemed a bit hit and miss. But it was early days yet.

Charley had been overjoyed and said she would be there this morning to help her with whatever she needed. But so far it was 10.30 and she was nowhere to be seen. The door opened and Aisha looked up, surprised to see her mum and dad standing in the doorway. Martina was surveying her surroundings and Jon looked awkward and a little out of place as he did in most situations that required him to be away from his home comforts.

'Now, what is it you would like us to do?' Martina announced. Aisha stood dumbstruck for a moment. She considered telling her mum to get home and put her feet up, but she was also in a mind to tell Jon that he shouldn't have brought her mum here and that he needed to get her home immediately. But something stopped her in that moment. Looking at the two of them standing there, Martina ready to participate as she always was and Jon, well, just being Jon, she realised this was how it was supposed to be. Her mum and dad here to help her with her first business venture. So she pushed all thoughts of sending them on their way to the back of her mind.

'Right, well, Dad, if you could get that brush over there and start sweeping out all the nooks and crannies.'

'Right, love, which brush?' Jon looked around and Aisha pointed to the corner. 'Right you are.'

'Mum, I've bought paint and I'm going to give the loos a fresh coat, do you fancy that?'

'Sounds good to me, that's why I wore my overalls.' She pulled off her coat and underneath she was in a faded blue boiler suit covered in specks of white paint from when they had decorated the house. Aisha was impressed, her mum was always one to be organised and it seemed the cancer wasn't going to stop her either.

Aisha was just about to go into the back room with Martina to get her started on the paint when the door opened again and she heard a whole load of noise, laughter and general commotion. Coming through the door were Mel, Sophy, Niall and Daz.

'I told you to just bring the biscuits,' Mel said.

'But I'm good at gourmet snacks now, see, the new deli has changed me.' Sophy said.

'I gave up an afternoon of golf for this.' Daz pushed forward. 'So let's get cracking.' He moved into the building. 'Oh, hi, Aisha, Martina.'

'I brought tools and sandpaper and stuff like that.' Niall pushed to the front. 'Whatever you need, I have loads more in me van, so just shout.'

'I'll go and get the coffees; don't suppose you have a decent kettle yet?' Mel piped up from the back.

'Why are you all here?' Aisha asked and then instantly felt silly for saying so.

'To help, you,' Mel said. 'Back in a bit.'

'You said you were doing stuff here today, so all the kids are with

Irene and Mike.' Sophy walked over and planted a kiss on Aisha's cheek. She looked radiant but ready for action. Aisha knew she probably felt rough, but she was here and that meant so much. Aisha could barely believe her luck that she had landed such an amazing bunch of friends.

Niall was already off surveying the interiors and Daz followed behind him, looking for all the world like someone who knew exactly what he was doing. Maybe Aisha could badger him to crunch some numbers for her later, that would make him feel a little more at home.

'Well, that is friendship right there, isn't it?' Martina said in her daughter's ear.

It is, Aisha thought and even though her two best friends were here with their husbands, ready to get stuck in and help, Aisha couldn't help but think about Charley and her whereabouts. Charley knew that today was the day she was making progress on the unit and getting it ship-shape, ready for some of the new equipment to arrive and to put a lick of paint over a few bits. Charley had said she had a few errands to run and then she would be there, but it was getting on and there was still no sign of her anywhere and she wasn't sure what was keeping her away.

The day drew on and Aisha immersed herself in the cleaning and scrubbing and painting until five o'clock rolled around and everyone looked as though they wanted to leave.

'I'll just stay on for a little bit longer,' Aisha said, even though she was exhausted, but there was an uneasy feeling creeping through her body as she thought of returning home to the twins, who were with the babysitter, not knowing where Charley was and having not heard from her all day either.

'Okay, well, you take it easy tonight; you've done enough today, girl.' Martina patted her daughter's arm. Jon came and gave her an awkward hug.

'Well done, Aisha, we're really proud of you, both me and your mum, aren't we, Martina?'

'That's right, very proud.' Martina looked at Aisha.

'And you're going home to rest, aren't you?' she asked her mum. She had made sure Martina had taken it easy all day, only doing things that required no lifting or heavy exertion.

'I'm cooking a chilli,' Jon piped up. 'It was one of the recipes I perfected when I was... away.'

Aisha smiled at her dad; it pained her when he struggled to put into words the two decades he'd spent away from his family due to his mental health. It wasn't something you could just drop into conversation. Her father had been on a massive journey and in the four or so years he had been back in their lives, Aisha still felt there were massive gaps during the time he was away that they hadn't covered, but there was never enough time to just sit down and talk to Jon about it all. But one thing she was sure about was that she didn't hold any resentment towards him. She was old enough to understand and she had been through depression after she had the twins. If she ever felt any twinges of sadness for time lost, she simply recollected her own feelings during those early months of motherhood and then tried to multiply that by ten, or some level where she felt it was too much and her own family would be better off without her.

'We love you, you're amazing, you're going to be fabulous, this place is going to fly. We're so proud.' Mel wrapped her arms around Aisha and held her there for a moment. Sophy stepped up next but only hugged her lightly.

'I'm feeling pretty rough so going to get off.' Aisha noted she had lost all the radiance and the tone of her skin was now almost translucent.

'Oh, Sophy, I'm really sorry, you should have left earlier.' Aisha was pained by her friend's appearance.

'You didn't hold me captive. I wanted to be here; besides, this is me for the next few months now, I have always been a sickly pregnant woman. Not fun.'

'Okay, well, get home, everyone, and thanks so much for coming. I can't wait for the soft opening, it's going to be awesome.'

Aisha waved everyone off at the door and they all left in the same unapologetically lairy way they arrived, Niall almost carrying his wife down the road to their van. Aisha stood in the doorway for a moment and was taking in the buzz of the street, imagining what it would be like to be here as proprietor in a few weeks' time, seeing off guests at the end of the night, when she spotted Charley on the other side, further down the street. Aisha lifted her hand to wave. Charley was hurriedly walking away from what would soon become Aisha's restaurant and Aisha worked out that she could have just come from any one of the alleyways, because why would she walk past the restaurant and not come in? Charley knew this was where Aisha was going to be all day, yet there she was, hurrying away in the opposite direction.

Without hesitation, Aisha pulled the shop door to, there was nothing of any value in there and she was only popping over the road. She saw a slight gap in the traffic and raced across the road. Once safely on the other side, she realised there was no sign of Charley anyway. She stood and looked up and down the path, which was busy with pedestrians. She turned back to the way she had seen her coming and there, she spotted the top of her head bobbing in between the heads of others. She raced after her, almost ready to shout out, to ask where she was going and in a such a hurry. But the words wouldn't come. Then Charley ducked into an arcade. Aisha slowed, ready to make the same exit. She walked through the vibrant mall and scanned the area for Charley. She wondered what she could possibly want to be doing in here specifically so close to dinner time. Shouldn't she be back at home by now, relieving the babysitter and getting the boys their tea?

Suddenly Aisha felt her stomach tighten like it was in a vice as her eyes landed on Charley. But Charley was no longer alone. She was with a woman. Aisha watched them for a moment, taking in their every action and trying to work out their body language. They seemed pleased to see one other. Aisha quickly assessed the woman, who was petite with long dark wavy hair, wearing wide-legged trousers and a floaty white blouse, there was a ton of jewellery on her, ethnic stuff, not the sort that either Charley or Aisha was into. The woman took something out of her bag and handed it to Charley. Someone nudged into Aisha as they walked past and she turned to see an old lady pulling a shopping trolley behind her.

'Sorry,' Aisha mumbled, looking back at Charley and the mystery woman and not being nearly as polite as she would have been when she was in someone's way. But there was something about this interaction that was capturing Aisha yet at the same time preventing her from walking over and making her presence known. The two women seemed to know one another, and Aisha was adamant that she knew all of Charley's friends, they had been together that long. Which meant this was someone she had met recently. Then the pair of them leaned into one another and embraced and Aisha felt her eyes prickle with tears. She began to step backwards, immersing herself with the crowds, she didn't want either of the women to turn and see her staring and encroaching on what seemed quite a private moment. Aisha felt as though she shouldn't be here. But she had only run after her girlfriend because... well, because she was her girlfriend and that was perfectly normal. Now Aisha felt as though she were doing something wrong.

The two women began to part, and Aisha took a few steps back, ready to move away but holding on for a few last seconds in case she missed anything more. The woman headed off, leaving Charley standing still, looking down at the package in her hand. Aisha turned and ran all the way back onto the high street. She made it back to the unit and let herself in. Suddenly all she wanted to do was get home and be with her boys. She was so confused about what she had just seen but it all seemed to add up to the same thing. That Charley was hiding things from her and that spelled trouble.

33

MEL

'I'm so glad we bought this house when we did, it's perfect for what we wanted,' Saskia droned, and whilst living next to a primary school was convenient when your children were indeed at primary school, how would Saskia feel when the screaming kids could be heard from their sitting room when Fin wasn't a child any more?

Mel was usually very sociable, but she had been holding back from making eye contact with many of the mums in the playground, she didn't need the drama or the politics in her life. She enjoyed having people at her house and enjoyed dropping in on others and so she had agreed to break that barrier with Saskia. Mel still contemplated that initial comment she had made when they had first officially met, where Saskia made a link between them because of their ages, although Mel was pretty sure Saskia was a teeny bit older than her. And Mel was getting flashbacks now of the mornings or afternoons she had raced into pre-school to drop off or pick up Sky and had glanced at Saskia. Her face now did seem that much more familiar.

Now, inside Saskia's home, Mel scanned the gleaming kitchen for any signs that it might have been lived in by two adults and a young boy, but she could see none. Did this woman have a cleaner in every day? Mel could not fathom why there wasn't one toy scattered about the place or a pile of unopened letters. The house was absolutely immaculate.

'It's a beautiful home, Saskia.'

Saskia cleared her throat and looked for a moment as though she were struggling to swallow. For someone who had just boasted about her house, she didn't take compliments very well.

'Thank you. Now what tea would you like?' Saskia strode over to a huge white cupboard and flung it open to reveal inside an array of teas and coffees. Some were in clear jars, which were marked with home-made labels; others were still in their original packaging. They were tucked in neatly and were all facing forward, as though they were still on a shelf in the supermarket. Mel thought about the film *Sleeping with the Enemy* when Julia Roberts returns home to find her ex-husband has been in the house and arranged all of her cupboards to suit his own psychopathic OCD.

Mel shuddered and Saskia cocked her head.

'Are you cold? The house should be at the optimum temperature, Stuart paid an absolute fortune for the heating. I tell you it's been an absolute game changer.'

Mel shook her head and shifted on the island seat. 'Nope, not cold, just someone must have walked over my grave.'

'Oh.' Saskia snorted. 'What an absolutely hideous thought. You don't believe in all that, do you?'

Mel shook her head. 'I don't know what I believe in, really.' She pointed to the cupboard. 'I'll take a camomile.'

Saskia slipped a teabag out of the box and then Mel watched as she arranged it, so it was exactly where it had been before she'd touched it. How utterly exhausting.

'I have to say I am mighty impressed with how you handled the WhatsApp group thing.' Saskia flicked on the kettle.

'Handled it?' Mel asked.

'Yes, I'm sure some of the mums were a bit put out.' Saskia leaned against the kitchen counter as the kettle gently whirred to life, a very delicate sound if ever she heard one. Probably something else that Stuart paid a fortune for.

'I just left the group, Saskia; I was abroad at the time, and I had just had enough. I know it was short-lived, but I am not very good at multiple people in a group. When I say multiple, I mean more than three. How do you cope with running this house and being a mum and being on the PTA? A WhatsApp group is just one more thing to have to worry about.'

'Oh, I don't know; I just find it fits around me.' She turned back to the kettle, which had already boiled. Mel wished her own life were so easy. She also began to secretly wish that her house could be this clean as Saskia placed a white teacup and saucer on the squeaky-clean surface in front of her. She began to feel a sense of calm. There was something to be said for a tidy house creating a calm mind. Mel had Ksenia and she did a great job of putting things back in their rightful order and really getting to the nooks of the dirt and grime, but the second she walked out of the door, the hallway was already littered with shoes – always an extra three or four pairs of trainers in the hallway which belonged to lanky teenagers who had somehow bypassed Mel and gone up into Leia's room. Then there was Sky's mess and Daz was always running out of the door and Mel, who worked later in the morning, was often the one left to tidy things away and a lot of the time she just didn't have the will to do it, she usually had classes to teach and then the dinner and shopping and then the school run again. There was no way a normal human could live the way Saskia was.

'What did you say Stuart did again?' Mel enquired as she lifted her teabag from her cup and placed it on the saucer. A droplet of yellow-brownish tea landed on the counter and Mel saw Saskia's eyes dart to the offending liquid. She rubbed the back of her neck and Mel wondered if this was to prevent herself from reaching for some kitchen towel and wiping it up. When Saskia removed her hand, there was an angry red blotch appearing in the spot where she had just been rubbing.

'He works in the financial market. He's a stockbroker.' She smoothed her hair on one side. 'He's away a lot. How's that tea? Can I offer you a biscuit?'

'I won't. I like to fast in the mornings, I finish eating at six in the evening and I won't eat now until midday.'

'Oh, wow!' Saskia relaxed a little and leaned her weight against the counter. 'That is very admirable. I'm afraid I'm an evening snacker.' Saskia gestured to the fridge. 'And the wine. Hate myself in the morning for it.' Saskia's eyes pooled with tears. 'I get over it pretty quickly,' Saskia added when she made eye contact with Mel again. 'That's what we girls do, isn't it?' she said, trying to sound jolly, but there was jaggedness to her voice and Mel was starting to think differently about Saskia. She had never seen this Stuart and the house did not resemble one that a man came home to, one who worked in the city, one who would throw his briefcase in the hallway and kick his shoes off in the dining room.

'Could I just use your loo?' Mel asked.

She stood up and began walking away as Saskia called after her, 'Yes, it's just down the hall.'

But once outside the kitchen, Mel went to the end of the hall, past the washroom and straight upstairs. As she had thought, upstairs was even more immaculate than downstairs. She peeked into a room that must have been Fin's. Beige and blue. A shelf with a few token books on it, a single bed with a tightly stretched duvet, a fluffy rug next to the bed and a bean bag in the corner next to another bookshelf. There were some wooden toys in a basket in the corner, but other than that it looked pretty sparse. She scooted past another two bedrooms, made up for guests like hotel rooms, and then the main bathroom and then finally the master suite. She paused for a few moments unsure whether what she was about to do was totally wrong. She barely knew Saskia, but alarm bells were ringing. Saskia was downstairs implying that she was still happily married. Mel felt Saskia needed help and clearly wanted to be friends. If Mel was going to give anything of herself to this woman, she needed to know the truth. She poked her head around the door and then swiftly entered. She went straight to the wardrobes and opened door after door that revealed women's shirts, dresses, drawers that homed stockings and lingerie. She headed into the en suite, a tranquil uncluttered space with thick white fluffy towels folded just so next to a gleaming marble-floored shower big enough for three.

She pulled open cabinets and drawers uncovering all of Saskia's products but nothing that suggested a man shared this space. Not one tie, not one aerosol. It was clear to Mel that Saskia's husband did not live here at all.

Once back downstairs, Mel slipped back into her seat at the counter and immediately noted that Saskia had cleaned up the spillage from her tea. Mel had begun mulling over why someone as attractive and confident as Saskia would want to lie about her relationship with her husband. The ring was still there, so they may or may not be married. Perhaps it was short-term. But who removes every item from their house if they're on a trial separation? Mel knew she had done wrong by snooping, but she wasn't sure why Saskia wasn't being completely honest with her. Mel was a busy woman; she didn't have time for the PTA or the mums in the playground, but there was something about Saskia that was intriguing Mel. And now she wanted to know more. Saskia seemed lost, but Mel imagined there was a side to her that she would be able to bring back to life. Maybe it was all about the challenge, but at the end of the day, there was room in Mel's life for one more friend.

She drank down the rest of her tea as Saskia stood there, trying not to snatch the cup away the second Mel had finished.

'Saskia.' Saskia's eyes brightened at her name. 'What are you doing on Saturday night?'

* * *

6.07 p.m. – Mel – I'm about to get Sky in the bath, the filthy mutt, what a state they get in at school, but I wanted to throw it out there about this Saturday. I know it's short notice and I know you've all had enough of hearing me warbling on, but I'm bringing a new mum to my gig on Saturday, and I could do with your support. She seems a bit lost, and I think she could do with a night out. Only I don't want to leave her sitting alone whilst I'm doing my set, so I thought, you know... you lot.

6.13 p.m. – Aisha – I'll be at the restaurant all day Saturday, few more things to do and some equipment to install, but I can get out in the evening. Sophy? Are you free at all?

6.20 p.m. – Sophy – I just had my head in the toilet. I don't know where that bout of sickness came from, but I will try my hardest. You know I will be there if I feel up to it.

6.24 p.m. – Mel – Of course, I know, and I appreciate it massively. You're both superstars. Her name is Saskia. I'm going to help her.

6.26 p.m. – Sophy – I thought you were steering clear of the mums at the school?

6.28 p.m. – Mel – All of them, except this one. The school playground is a cruel mistress, I need at least one ally, don't I?

6.31 p.m. – Aisha – I agree. Good on you Mel. We'll help won't we, Soph?

6.32 p.m. – Sophy – (Sick face emoji)

34

SOPHY

The thought of facing the autumn and winter feeling this nauseous was not ideal. Sophy's bedside table was scattered with ginger biscuits, and she was lying in bed thinking about getting up to get the children ready for school when the bedroom door opened, and Niall walked in carrying a sleepy-looking Poppy and a cup of tea. He put the tea down next to the bed, nice and weak the way she had been taking it these last few weeks, and then Poppy crawled from his arms and snuggled in next to Sophy.

'Are you sure I can't take them to school?'

Sophy lifted her head off the pillow and looked at her husband. 'Niall, you did it twice last week, I need to just crack on.'

'Right you are. I'll be off then. Bye, Pops.' He ruffled his daughter's hair. 'Max is downstairs.'

'Oh.' Sophy sat up and jumped out of bed. 'I forgot about him.'

'What will we do when we have three?' Niall said, monotone, but Sophy knew he meant no harm.

'I will leave one somewhere for sure.'

'Me ma did with me. Traumatised, I was. Lost me in the aisles of a supermarket for what felt like hours, the shelves looming down at me.'

'Oh, Christ, Niall, you never said. That must have been terrible for you, akin to unaccompanied refugee children crossing the Mediterranean,' Sophy teased as she pulled on a pair of joggers, sprayed some deodorant, put on a blue and pink T-shirt, her two favourite colours, and scraped her hair back into a ponytail. Niall came and kissed her.

'Right, have good day, I'll see ya later.'

Sophy half waved as she hunted for a pair of trainer socks. She scoured her drawer, only finding one of each pair. She gazed at the pile of laundry next to her drawers where it had been sitting for three days, waiting to be folded and put away. She thought of her life with three kids, one of which would be a baby for a long time, hunting for trainer socks and other objects to get her through the day.

'For the love of... is it so unreasonable to get a pair of socks in this house, I mean, is it really?' Sophy muttered to herself.

Downstairs she found Max at the kitchen table, a small Hulk figure in his hands.

'Oh, sweetie.' She kissed him on his still-warm-from-bed cheek and put Poppy in her highchair.

She began putting waffles in the toaster and then began slicing a banana. Once both Poppy and Max had breakfast in front of them, she picked up her phone. There were seven missed calls and fourteen messages from Jeff. What on earth could Jeff want all last night and this morning?

She was about to listen to her answerphone messages when the doorbell rang. Sophy hadn't even applied make-up yet and it was getting on for 8 a.m. She had to leave in half an hour. Who on earth was that holding their finger on the doorbell?

She raced to the front door and swung it open. Jeff was standing on the doorstep. He looked haggard, as though he hadn't slept all night.

Sophy was still holding her phone and could hear Jeff's voice coming through on the message.

'Call me straight away, please.' He sounded so desperate, the sort of desperation that she could now see in his eyes.

'Jeff, what is it?' Jeff half collapsed against the doorframe.

'I've been up all night calling you. It's Mum. She's had a heart attack.'

* * *

It felt strange doing the school run with her ex-boyfriend, especially taking Poppy with her as well. They pulled up at the school and adjoining nursery in Jeff's Jaguar and Sophy was reminded about how she used to love being driven around in Jeff's car, how it made her feel at the time as though she were really worth something. She was so not that person any more, she felt that just walking along the road holding Niall's hand. But today no amount of flash cars could make up for the way the driver and passenger both looked. Jeff was weeping intermittently and Sophy, who had yet to eat a thing and hadn't applied any make-up, looked hideous. As Jeff pulled up outside the school in the area marked 'No stopping at any time', it was just her luck that the first person Sophy saw was Blythe and her crew. There was first the look of horror that someone should dare to pull into that spot and then looks of confusion as Sophy exited the car with both children, looking as though she had been on an all-night bender, whilst Jeff sat with the window wound down, trying to wave to Max, but looking more and more red-eyed and shivering as though he were on some massive come-down.

Sophy grunted a greeting to Blythe, who tried to look as though she were sorting bags and lunchboxes for her four children but was really looking between Jeff and Sophy.

She hurried both her children to their drop-off points, kissed them fiercely, more so than she had ever done in their short lives, and hurried back to Jeff.

Back inside the car, Jeff pulled away, now openly weeping.

'I don't know what I'll do if she dies.' Jeff choked out the words.

Sophy sucked in a deep breath and looked out of the window, just catching Blythe pointing Sophy out to another mum.

'She won't die,' Sophy said, more as a matter of fact than as a way to soothe Jeff. Years ago, Sophy might even have felt a little flicker of something like relief if this had happened when she and Jeff were still together. But the emotional distance that their split had created between her and Wendy meant that she no longer had her in her life and didn't need to worry about what she thought of her. Sophy now just regarded Wendy the way she would any other human. She wished her health and happiness and right now Wendy didn't have either. She wasn't healthy and Sophy could bet she was pretty unhappy too.

They arrived at the hospital and Jeff clung to Sophy's arm as they navigated their way to the department where Wendy was.

Why had he called her? Where was his current girlfriend? Sophy wasn't entirely sure he had one at the moment. Why did he feel he needed her here with him? These were all the questions that were flying through Sophy's mind, but she couldn't articulate any of them, partly because she felt if she spoke, she might be sick, and secondly because it didn't seem appropriate to start quizzing Jeff.

Outside the room Wendy was in, Sophy finally spoke.

'Should I come in?'

Jeff looked dumbfounded. 'Yes, of course,' he whispered.

Again, Sophy didn't question anything, she just followed Jeff through into a room with three beds. There was a curtain all the way around one and Jeff nodded towards it. Suddenly Sophy felt her stomach tighten and her mouth fill with saliva. What would Wendy look like, and would she be able to bear it? She had some sort of relationship with Wendy now, and even though there was no love lost, Wendy was still Max's grandmother and despite how Sophy now felt about her only son, she didn't wish Wendy any harm and certainly did not want her to die.

Jeff opened the curtain and there sat Al, clutching his wife's hand as though he might not ever let go.

Wendy lay there with her eyes closed, a drip coming from her arm, looking pale and extremely frail for a woman in her seventies who had always been pretty fit and healthy.

Whether it was the hormones or just feeling overwhelmed by it, Sophy felt she couldn't stop the tears that came and then she felt Jeff's hand in hers and he gave it a quick squeeze before going to his mother.

As they left the hospital and headed back to the car, after an hour of sitting very quietly with Wendy during which she only made occasional noises and the odd jolt, Sophy finally asked the question.

'Just out of interest, why did you come to me first?'

Jeff took a moment before he spoke.

'Because despite where we are in our own lives, you're my family. You and Max.'

Sophy felt a surge of tears threaten to erupt and took a deep breath and swallowed them down. She would save them for a private cry when she got home.

35

AISHA

She had been holding onto what she had seen on the high street for days now and all she wanted to do was blurt it out to Charley every time they spoke to one another.

Who was that woman and why are you being so shady, what are you hiding? But Aisha couldn't say any of those words because she was scared of what the answer might be. Had Aisha made the wrong decision taking on a restaurant, maybe that wasn't what Charley wanted, or maybe she was encouraging it because she was seeing another woman? The words that Sophy had spoken back on the ship in her cabin about there being many 'the ones' came back to her. Just because she and Charley had Jude and Otis did not mean that they were bound together for eternity.

In the playground Aisha waved to the boys as they trundled off into school. She stood and repeated the same mantra she had been saying for weeks now. *Keep them safe, keep them well.* And she turned and headed for the tube station. She got out at Brixton and headed straight for the restaurant. It was really beginning to resemble one now and today was the day the chairs would arrive. She had bought several pieces of industrial catering equipment, which would be installed on Saturday, and now the tables and chairs were in she could start to arrange them how she wanted them. All in all, she would probably get thirty covers seated and maybe five or six at the bar, but that was enough for her. She didn't want to be run ragged and besides, she anticipated a steady turnover of customers all day and evening. She only planned to open Thursday, Friday and Saturday to start, just to see how trade went, and the staff she had employed were happy to oblige and grow their hours with the business.

Charley had promised that she would come today and oversee a few things with her, make sure that she wasn't making the wrong decisions on anything. Not that Charley had any experience in hospitality, but it was good to have a second pair of eyes.

The door opened and Charley bundled through, clutching her mobile. She was also clutching takeaway coffees and pastries, which Aisha was thankful for as she hadn't eaten yet.

'Right, I'll put these here and then you can tell me what you need me to do. I'm here for you.'

Are you? were the words that crept into Aisha's head, and she parted her lips to speak but instead swallowed them down.

'I just wanted to rearrange the tables and chairs a little bit and then we see where we're at.'

'They look fine where they are.' Charley sat down in one and slurped her coffee.

'Yes, but I want to experiment, get them right, try all the options.'

'Fine.' Charley stood up and took off her coat and placed it on the back of the chair.

Aisha heard something in Charley's tone that she didn't like. Why was it all such an effort? It wasn't as if she were asking a lot of her. It was just moving a few damn tables and chairs. One thing Aisha was striving for from the outset was continuity. She didn't want to set the restaurant one way only to discover it didn't work at all.

'Once we're set up, we need to do some role play, you pretend you're a customer coming and going, see how it all fits.'

'Role play?' Charley raised an eyebrow suggestively. 'I didn't think that was your bag?'

Aisha ignored the comment and began moving the chairs to the side of the room.

'Oh, so I get the silent treatment.' Charley stood by the table. 'Where do you want this?'

'Are you having an affair?' Aisha heard herself say. She hadn't meant to address the matter today but somehow it just slipped out. Charley looked dumbstruck. Maybe a little too dumbstruck.

'I am shocked,' Charley said.

'Clearly.' Aisha continued to drag the table without making eye contact with her girlfriend.

Aisha only heard the sound of the door closing so she knew that Charley had left. She felt some relief, it had not been on her agenda to argue with Charley today, she had too much to do, too much to think about, and Martina had her first meeting with the specialist today to start her on her recovery programme. There wasn't going to be any chemo, which was what was keeping Aisha sane for now, and Martina had said they had already had great results from this treatment.

Aisha couldn't fathom why Charley had just walked out. Was she really shocked or had Aisha caught her out? The one thing that had always bothered Aisha was that they had never got married. They had never made that official public commitment to one another. They had been happy enough as they were and then they decided to have a baby, which turned out to be two babies, and things had been non-stop ever since. Maybe if Aisha had shown more interest in being married... She shoved the table hard. This was going to take longer with just one so she needed to focus and stop stressing about what could have been. She would find time to talk to Charley because what she didn't say was, 'No, I am not having an affair.'

36

MEL

The table was set, the house was immaculate as Ksenia had just left and Mel was cooking Daz's favourite, lamb shank with broad beans and pommes anna and a red wine jus. It had taken her over an hour to prepare the meal and now it was ready, she felt sick with nerves. She was going to explain to Daz what she should have told him from the start, the minute she knew she was going to be on a ship cruising around the Mediterranean thousands of miles away from her husband and children with her old flame. What had she thought would happen? Did she think that Daz would have forbidden her to go? Or was it that Mel herself had been set on going and being there because she wanted to see Leo? But she had only found out it was Leo after she had agreed to do the gig. In hindsight, should she have cancelled? She knew what the answer was, it had been staring her in the face for weeks in the form of her husband. He deserved to know then and he deserved to know now.

Leia was giving Sky a long bath, then having a little movie night with her. Mel knew she would be paying for Leia's time in some form in the next week, whether it be lifts or having several of her friends over at once for pizza and movies. When they had bought the house, they had always known that the little snug just opposite the sitting room would get used by a teenager plus a handful of friends on a regular basis like it was a youth club. Mel resented it and loved it in equal measure. A dichotomy of parenting that she found herself in regularly.

Daz walked through the door just after six and came into the kitchen.

'Whatever that is, it smells like home, and I want to eat it immediately,' Daz announced. He opened the fridge and took out a beer.

'Are we having wine?' He opened the beer and took a long glug, almost finishing half of it.

'I think so.' Mel lifted herself out of her seat where she had been waiting. Everything was as it should be.

'You sit, I'll get it.' Daz pulled out a bottle from the rack. 'I've been wanting to drink this one since Christmas, it's the one my brother got us.'

'Oh, yes. I'd forgotten about that,' Mel said and got up anyway to bring the food to the table as Daz scoured the drawer for the wine opener.

'Where are the girls?'

'Sky wanted a movie night with Leia, so they are both upstairs.'

'Well, that's a turn-up for the books, isn't it?' Daz said, referring to the endless times Leia would try to get out of her big sister duties. As much as she loved Sky, Leia had a social life that could rival a Kardashian. And it was just as documented as one, based on the number of posts she put on Instagram. But they were tasteful and arty and that made Mel happy.

'It is. Gives us a bit of time alone.' Mel tried to sound casual but realised that was never something she would say, she and Daz rarely planned time together, it would always happen one way or another.

Daz turned and eyed her suspiciously but said nothing. He popped the cork on the wine and brought two glasses to the table. Mel wanted Daz to enjoy his food and so she said nothing more for the remainder of the meal.

'I could do with a cognac and a cigar now,' Daz said as he pushed his chair back and pushed his feet out to the side; he was a tall man and even though their table was large enough, he always looked for more leg room. 'That was incredible.'

Mel drained her wine and began to form the words she wanted to say. But before she could speak, Daz was already speaking.

'So, are you going to tell me what's going on or do I get best out of three?'

Mel tried to look shocked and offended. She hadn't wanted this to be one of those meals where it was obvious she was buttering her husband up for something.

'Oh, come on, Mel. You've cooked me lamb shank three times in the last five years. Once after we found out you were pregnant with Sky, once when you wanted to talk about mortgaging the house for the extension and now. So what's the special occasion? If you tell me it's another baby then I am moving to Mexico.'

Mel laughed nervously.

'No, no baby.'

'But there is something.'

Mel cleared her throat and leaned forward. She had thought about this for too long, she needed to just let the words out.

'A few weeks before we went on the cruise, I found out that Leo Monroe was the one who was in charge of the entertainment. It turns out it was his business. He was on board the ship the whole time we were there.'

She heard Daz exhale as he took the information in, but Mel continued.

'I didn't tell you because I was worried how you would be about it; I didn't want you stressing about it the whole time I was away.'

Daz took another deep breath again and let it out the way he did when he was working on some big numbers.

'I'm just trying to take this in. You didn't tell me because you were worried about how I might react?'

'Yes, because it's Leo and we had that thing, and although it's ancient history, I know how you feel about him, how you felt about him then.'

'Exactly. You know and I know it's ancient history, but you still chose to not tell me.'

Mel was quiet as she thought over how it must seem from Daz's perspective.

'Well, I guess I was being selfish. I thought there might be a small chance you'd kick off in some way and I didn't want my time away with the girls to have been marred by anything.'

Daz sighed again; Mel wondered if there was even any oxygen left in the room now.

He stood up, hesitated for a second and then walked out of the room. That was the extent of what Daz had to say on the matter. There wasn't going to be some mumbled refence to it during a heated debate, there wouldn't be any more conversations unless Mel wished to. Daz had summed it all up in one sentence. Leo was ancient history, Mel knew that when she received that first text from him, when she ran into his arms to greet him, when he told her how he still felt about her.

Mel had been there for the gig first and foremost. She loved to perform, and it was a fantastic opportunity that had turned out to be a wonderful adventure for them all. She would have been there with or without Leo. She shouldn't feel bad about that. There had been moments when she had felt giddy with nostalgia, but her heart was with Daz and her children. It had been nice to remember that another man had once had feelings for her and maybe still did. But Mel was never going to be Leo's consolation prize and Daz had won hands down.

37

SOPHY

Three ginger biscuits later and a large cup of peppermint tea, dressed in the comfiest smartest clothes she owned, Sophy was ready for Mel's gig. She was so intrigued to meet Saskia. The venue was a dinner and dance place, Sophy was hoping she would be able to keep some dinner down.

As soon as she arrived, she could see she was the first person there. She ordered a soda and lime, with lots of ice, the only thing she could seem to keep down, and waited.

A woman dressed in flared white trousers and heels with hair swooping behind her arrived and Sophy immediately knew this was Saskia. She felt a surge of adrenaline as she prepared herself for the next few hours and she knew that was all she would need to keep the sickness at bay for that time.

Sophy held her hand up and waved as Saskia stood and searched the room with her eyes. When her gaze landed on Sophy, she looked confused, then embarrassed, and finally she walked over to the table.

'Hi. I'm Sophy.' Sophy went to stand but Saskia reached down and shook her hand.

'It's so nice to meet you and for Mel to invite me here tonight.'

'Well, she puts on a cracker of a performance so I'm sure you will love it. Oh, look, here's Aisha.' Sophy waved over at Aisha, who came trundling over.

'You look great.' She stood to kiss her friend. Saskia flicked her hair over her shoulder and looked around the room uncomfortably. Aisha was in a floating black skirt and shimmery blue top with matching shimmer on her eyes. 'This is Saskia, Mel's friend.'

'Hi, Saskia.' Aisha went for the handshake. 'Now we're acquainted, let's get settled. Who's drinking what?'

Saskia sat down and pushed her hair behind her ear. 'Well, I'll drink whatever you girls are having. Is it a champagne sort of night?' Saskia blinked her eyes wide. Aisha glanced at Sophy, and Sophy knew what the glance meant. Were they revealing the pregnancy to this stranger? Sophy decided to take the lead.

'Lemonade for me, I'm on a detox after the cruise,' Sophy said and Aisha almost winked at her.

'How about Prosecco?' Aisha said to Saskia.

Saskia nodded. 'Sounds good to me.'

* * *

When Mel joined them after the first set, the room was buzzing. Sophy felt as though she was letting go of all the stress of the last few days. Wendy was doing okay and was now stable. There had been nothing more from Jeff after his heartfelt words. They had impacted Sophy so much at the time, mainly because they were so unexpected, but she realised that when faced with the end of a life, whether their own or of someone they loved, people changed. She had seen a new side to Jeff, a side she had never seen before. It had made her sad because seeing his mother so close to death had brought his barriers down and he had shown a piece of himself that he had kept hidden all the time she had been with him. But the barrier went back up almost immediately and whilst Wendy may not have died that day, for that fleeting moment, Jeff's ego had.

'I hope you've been keeping Saskia well oiled.' Mel sat down and took a sip from a glass of Prosecco that Sophy had poured out for her just minutes earlier.

'We certainly have!' Aisha raised her glass a little overenthusiastically and spilt some of the liquid over the side.

'Oh, I say, someone is having a good time tonight.' Mel smiled knowingly at Sophy, who giggled, as they both now knew how easily Aisha got drunk and what a great drunk she was as well.

'Sophy hasn't touched a drop. She's on a detox.' Saskia swished her hair around, this time with a lot more confidence. Sophy had liked Saskia from the moment she had met her. She had an air of superiority about her, but Sophy saw straight through that and to the heart of the woman underneath. Mel had informed her about the absence of her husband and Sophy was keen to do all she could to make Saskia feel welcome. Aisha certainly seemed to be enjoying her company.

Saskia shouted something across the table which Sophy or Mel didn't hear.

'What's that?' Sophy sipped her lemonade through a straw.

'I said,' Saskia shouted louder this time, 'I've never been friends with any lesbians before.'

Sophy nearly choked and Mel sat back, trying not to laugh.

'I mean there were girls at my school who obviously wanted to try it on with me, it was all jolly hockey sticks where I went to school but I was never that way inclined. I've always loved men. I love the really beefy ones, all brawn and no brains.' Saskia swigged back her Prosecco and then called the attention of a passing waiter and began talking to him.

Mel took a moment to catch Sophy's eye as if to say 'see'. Sophy nodded.

'She must have been living under a rock not to have integrated with the LGBTQ... hang on, did I miss a letter... community,' Mel whispered. And Sophy and Aisha nodded.

'I've barely integrated with the LGBTQ community.' Aisha scoffed.

'No labels, just live, I say.' Sophy was always about letting everyone be who they wanted to be.

'Hear, hear!' Mel chorused.

'Who's here?' Saskia swung her head left and right as the waiter walked away with her order.

'No one.' Mel laughed.

'Is it a hunky man? Where are all the hunky men?' Saskia whined and Sophy realised that without actually having the discussion about her marital status, Saskia was beginning to open up a little and Sophy wondered if by the end of the evening, Saskia would reveal exactly what was going on.

'You must know a few hunky men in your profession, Mel?' Saskia had shuffled her chair closer.

'Oh, I know one or two, all brawn and no brain.'

'Oh, fantastic, exactly what I'm looking for. Do tell me more.'

Mel thought for a moment. 'Well, there is this bouncer, Matt, he would be right up your alley.'

Saskia hooted out a laugh so loud it made three tables turn and stare.

'Excuse the pun, I meant he is fit and not that intelligent. I was doing this gig one night and I referred to the owner of the pub as someone who couldn't organise a piss-up in a brewery. And I kid you not, a few minutes later Matt was on his phone, and he was typing into Google – how to organise a piss-up in a brewery.'

Saskia looked at Mel and for a second Sophy thought she might not get the joke, but then she howled with a laugh so infectious no one could keep a straight face.

The night wound up with Mel finishing her second set, Aisha and Saskia hanging onto one another for dear life and Saskia telling Aisha to promise to introduce her to all her gay friends. Mel hugged Sophy tightly.

'Urgh, not too tight.' Sophy was exhausted and had stayed way later than she had meant to.

'Sorry!' Mel released her. 'I'm just glad you're here and thanks for being so sweet to Saskia, I couldn't ask for a better bunch of friends.'

'You're welcome.'

'Shall we walk you to your car?' Mel helped Sophy on with her coat.

'No, I'll be fine.'

'Well, text when you get home.'

Sophy had never been so glad to be going home and so, after receiving an incredibly long hug from Saskia where she had to check she hadn't actually fallen asleep on her shoulder, she then moved on to Aisha. She gave her a quick kiss on the cheek, knowing full well she would text tomorrow morning asking when Sophy had left, as she didn't remember.

* * *

Sophy crept into bed, trying not to wake Niall.

'How was your evening?' he whispered to the wall.

'Oh, I thought you were sleeping.'

'I was.' Niall flipped over and wrapped an arm around her. 'I heard you come in. I wasn't fully asleep. I don't like to think of you driving home late at night.'

'Ah, I'm a big girl.' Sophy plumped her pillows up so she could fall asleep in one comfortable position and not feel too sick.

Niall propped himself up on one arm.

'I'm serious, Soph. I worry about you, I worried when you just had Max, now we have Pops too and now there's another one on the way.'

'Do you think we are taking on too much?' Sophy whispered.

'No, no, I don't, but I just feel us more, you know. We're really becoming something, aren't we? It's not just you, me and Max, we're a proper family. I just want us all to be happy and healthy. That's all I want, Soph. Nothing more.' He dropped his hand and rolled over and began softly snoring.

Sophy felt the tears welling up again. This was all she had ever wanted. She promised herself that once the sickness had passed and she no longer wanted to permanently lie down, she would appreciate just how lucky she was.

38

AISHA

Aisha laid three dresses on the bed and assessed them all one by one. Which would she be the most comfortable in? Which one truly spoke to her and said *I'm the one you should be wearing on the opening night of your very own restaurant*? It was a tough call made even tougher by the fact that she and Charley had barely spoken over the last week. It had made it a little more bearable for Aisha because she had scarcely been in the house all week. She had been conducting interviews, setting up wage apps on her phone, and having a meeting with the food hygiene lady. Hopefully a five-star rating would be coming her way soon.

The twins burst into the bedroom, fighting over a tiny toy, followed swiftly by Charley.

'Leave Mama alone, she needs to get ready.' Charley scooped up Otis with one arm.

'Can weeee come?' the boys chorused.

Aisha couldn't help but smile and looked in the reflection in the mirror and caught Charley smiling too. It didn't happen all the time, but when Otis and Jude both said the same thing at the same time completely unconsciously it was the most magical thing ever. One of the joys of having twins was being mesmerised by this incredible phenomenon.

'I've booked an Uber,' Charley said.

'An Uber? I was happy to get the tube.' Aisha picked up one dress and held it against herself.

'It's your big night, you don't want to be on a tube on an occasion like this.'

Aisha eyed Charley through the mirror again and said nothing. She liked what was coming out of her mouth, but she was still mad with her for not saying anything else since she had asked her if she was having an affair. Aisha presumed Charley was mad with her for asking it in the first place. But what could she do? Charley had been acting a little off for weeks and Aisha had no idea why.

The doorbell rang and the boys whooped.

'Tiannon, Tiannon,' they both sang, out of synch this time.

'I'll let Tiannon in and get them all settled with a film.' Charley followed the boys out of the room and closed the door. Aisha abandoned the dresses and went to her wardrobe, where she picked out a pair of faux leather trousers and a hot pink shirt.

* * *

Her trousers squeaked on the surface of the car seat each time the Uber took a corner. Neither Aisha nor Charley mentioned it, even though under normal circumstances it would have been exactly the talking point for them, and Aisha was sure Charley was dying to say something. But too much time had lapsed since they last properly spoke and to suddenly launch into a conversation about something so juvenile would put both of them out of sorts. There was a lot to be said and all the time in the world to say it but neither of them were willing to be the first to smash the ice and speak. Sometimes Aisha wished she was back at school when you could send a note to your intended via a school friend, *Aisha wants to meet you at the back of the bike sheds at break*. But Aisha wasn't a child any more and if there were things that needed to be said then she needed to say them. But tonight was not the night, tonight was about the opening of her new restaurant.

Her new chef Lucy was hard at work in the kitchen when they

arrived. Aisha set to work nudging chairs into place, touching up the sprays of purple flowers on the tables.

'Shall I pop the sparkling wine?' Charley asked and Aisha flinched at the words. She hadn't been able to afford to stretch to champagne, and so a Prosecco of sorts was the best she could offer. She had gone over her budget as it was and needed to watch what she was spending. She had stretched to good chairs and funky tables, invested in a second-hand pizza oven, a hot plate and a pass. With the help of Lucy, she had nailed a simple but gastronomic menu of Jamaican- and British-infused small plates with some classic Jamaican dishes. It was a real-life fully functioning business.

It wasn't long before the guests began to arrive. Friends of both her and Charley and her sisters had all made the journey from their home-towns and her cousins were there too. Martina was the last family member to arrive with Jon.

'Mum, Dad!' Aisha kissed them both on their cheeks. 'You look spec-tacular, both of you.' Aisha held her arms out to look at them both. Martina was wearing a black sequin top and black trousers, and Jon was in a smart blue shirt and jacket.

'Well, if we can't make an effort for the opening of our daughter's first business venture then when can we?' Martina clasped her hands in front of her and looked around. 'My, my, you got it looking mighty fancy, girl.'

'It looks amazing, Aisha; you must be really proud of yourself.'

Aisha felt her eyes well with tears. Was this how it was going to be for the rest of the evening? She was going to be a bloody wreck by the time the toast came around.

'I hope you love the food, Dad.'

'If it was inspired by your mum's cooking then it's all I'm used to.' Jon looked around nervously and Aisha's heart hurt for him. This was going to be difficult for him, trying to socialise with this many people could spike his anxiety. She wanted to make sure that the evening didn't become too much for either of her parents, especially Martina, as she was just beginning her treatment. Aisha heard a whoop from the other side of the room and saw her cousins Ruben and Marcel, up to their usual tomfoolery.

'Let me clip the ears of them boys, I'll be back.' Aisha watched as Martina strode over to her two adult cousins and saw them shrink with whatever Martina was saying to them. Aisha could imagine it was something about this being Aisha's night and the two of them had better behave themselves as they weren't still too old for a proper dressing down.

Niall and Sophy arrived next, and Aisha hugged them both, trying not to squeeze Sophy too hard as the pregnancy sickness seemed to come on worse in the early evening as well as the morning.

Aisha handed her a drink.

'It's a ginger mojito mocktail. I made it for the non-drinkers and thought it would be perfect for your sickness too!' Aisha said happily. 'There's pina coladas for everyone else.' Aisha pointed to the small bar area.

'Oh, right you are.' Niall lifted one with his large hands and almost downed it in one.

'Careful, Niall, save some for the rest of the guests.' Sophy laughed and Niall apologised.

'Don't, it's fine. There's plenty to go around and there's sparkling wine for the toast. Sophy, you'll have fizzy elderflower.'

'Ooo!' Sophy looked and sounded excited.

There was a bit of a commotion at the door and Aisha turned to see Mel and Daz and Saskia all arriving together.

Saskia threw her arms around Aisha, coating her with perfume. She looked around. 'My goodness, what a beautiful little restaurant and I love the name!' Saskia hooted.

'It's good to see you, Saskia, I am so glad you could come.'

'How could I not, I had such a lovely time the other night. You girls are just the best.'

Mel threw her arms around Aisha. 'My God, this is gorgeous, look at the place. It's an actual restaurant. Aisha, you have an actual restaurant!' Mel held onto Aisha's hands and Aisha tried to feel the moment, the way her friends were, the way they saw the fairy lights and heard the low bass of the reggae music and the scent of plantain caramelising and chilli and garlic all wafting from the kitchen through the open door. She tried to feel it and live in the moment just for a few seconds, because soon it would all be over, and she would have missed it.

'Where should we put these?' Mel held up a large box and a card.

'Oh, my gosh, presents? I didn't expect those.' Aisha put her hand over her mouth. 'I hadn't thought about that.'

Sophy stepped forward and Aisha noticed Niall was clutching a bottle bag and a card as well.

'Don't worry, I've got this.' Sophy wandered over to the other side of the room with Mel's gift and her own. She pulled away two chairs from a small table and pushed them into the corner of the room and then nudged the table forward, so it was a bit more central and obvious to the eye when guests arrived. Sophy then arranged the gifts she had been holding in the middle of the table with their cards on top.

'I have one too!' Saskia waved a box in Aisha's face and trotted off to the table.

'I can't believe this.' She turned to Jon. 'Can you believe this? All these people here to see me and they bring me presents. This was my gift to everyone, not the other way around.'

'Don't knock it, lass,' her dad said. 'They are giving you them gifts 'cos they love you and wish you well.'

'I know,' Aisha said, a little taken back. 'I just can't get my head around it.'

Jon gently touched her arm and Aisha looked at his hand there and then patted it with her own.

More guests arrived, until Pom Jam was bursting at the seams, it seemed. Aisha had barely spoken to Charley all night and had watched her from a distance, doing her thing with her friends, occasionally she would move around and speak to a few people. She saw her interacting with Sophy and Niall and someone must have introduced her to Saskia at some point because she was now practically on top of Charley and her friends, looking like an excited child in a sweet shop as she experienced her first close-up contact with some of the LGBTQ crew. It was very entertaining.

It was getting on for 10 p.m. and most of the food had gone out, tiny bowls of rice n' peas, jerk chicken wings and so many other wonderful dishes that she was so happy that her friends and family had got to try.

Aisha knew now was the time for a quick speech, so she went to the front of the room, gave the nod to the staff to begin walking around with glasses of fizz and got up on a chair. She clinked a fork on her glass a few times and everyone slowly began to take notice of her, the noise finally died down until Mel let out a giant whoop and everyone looked at her and laughed.

'Thank you,' Aisha said, 'to my personal cheerleader, I take her everywhere with me.'

There was a flurry of laughter.

'Seriously, though, every single one of you who is here tonight has played a significant role in my life.' Aisha's voice broke and Mel whooped again.

'We love you, Aish!' came a voice from the crowd, probably Mel's' again.

There was movement to her left and Aisha looked down to see Charley had arrived next to her. Aisha felt herself fizz up with warmth inside. Charley held out her hand and Aisha looked at it for a second and took it.

'You've all always believed in me and my ability to do things with food.'

'Great things!' someone shouted.

'And I want to thank you all for being here today, for being there then. For loving me and supporting me.'

Aisha raised her glass.

'To Pom Jam!'

'To Pom Jam!' everyone shouted and cheered and clinked their glasses and then the music began pumping out again.

Aisha stepped down and Charley was still there by her side. 'I got something for you, it's on the gift table,' Charley said. 'Do you want to open it now or later?'

Aisha looked at Charley. She had been eyeing the table getting more and more packed as the night went on and she was dying to see what was on there, maybe give a few of the gifts a quick squeeze.

They arrived at the table and Charley located her gift out of the tens that were stacked up.

'Open it.'

Aisha took a deep breath and ripped open the gold paper on the rectangular package, which was about the size of a shoebox.

She was confused when she saw the packaging, what looked like candle holders in the half-light.

'Oh, thanks,' Aisha said.

'You don't know what they are, do you?' Charley took the box out of Aisha's hand and opened it. She pulled out a purple intricately designed glass tumbler. She put it on the table. Then she took out another one, this time an orange one, then a green one until it finally clicked.

'The glasses.' Aisha gasped.

'The glasses. The ones you were looking at on your phone all those years ago. Well, I went on your phone, copied the link and held onto it all these years, hoping they would still be in stock when you finally decided you wanted to open your own restaurant.'

'Yes.' Aisha could hardly speak. She looked at the glasses and counted six altogether. She remembered the moment she had been searching for them on her phone all those years ago as though it were yesterday. Charley had seen her checking them out and had made a comment about the cost of them. But Aisha had always had them in her mind as the ones she had wanted for her restaurant one day.

'Oh, and there are another nine boxes out the back in your storeroom. Sixty glasses all together. They'd look great as water glasses, or with a special gin in them.'

Aisha was crying, proper hot tears this time, ones that she felt she had been saving up for months.

'But you've been acting so weird, I saw you with that girl in the arcade, and you've been on your phone a lot. You changed your passcode. That's why I asked if you were having an affair...' Aisha blurted.

She looked at Charley through teary eyes. 'Are you?'

Charley looked down, scuffed her feet about.

'Ah, Aish, don't make me do this here.'

Aisha thought her heart was about to stop. Here it was then. Charley was going to finish with her on the opening night of her restaurant. Keep calm, keep calm, Aisha thought to herself. You'll get through this. The glasses were a token parting gift. Charley was about to split up with her.

But then Aisha realised Charley wasn't next to her any more, she was standing on the chair that Aisha had just got down from. Oh God, was she about to announce their break-up to the room? Who the hell would do that? She tugged at Charley's arm, but Charley yanked her hand upwards and put her fingers in her mouth and whistled loudly. The room came to a complete standstill right away. Aisha wished she'd had that response with her tinkling glass.

'Hello, everyone, I'm so sorry for interrupting your evening again, I know you all just want to get on and drink and keep the celebrations going, but I felt there was one more thing I needed to share with you all.' The chair wobbled and Charley looked as though she might lose her balance and fall off.

'What the hell are you doing?' Aisha tugged at Charley's trousers, looking around at the confused faces in the room. Everyone who knew her and Charley well enough was here in this room and they all knew that she was not the sort of person to stand on a chair and make announcements to a room full of people.

'I hadn't planned for this, but as it's Aisha's special night, I thought why not. Fuck it!' Charley wobbled again, there was a collective intake of breath. Aisha wanted the floor to open up and swallow her. At least everyone here loved her, there would be support for her after this.

Charley jumped down from the chair and Aisha thought she had been spared the humiliation. She looked around for someone to come and rescue her, to soothe her. To get her a goddamn drink.

Then she noticed that Charley wasn't standing any more. She was still next to Aisha, but she was now crouched down low. When Aisha looked closer, she saw that she was not on both knees. But on one knee.

The room erupted. Clapping, cheering, whistles, everything. It was so loud that Aisha couldn't actually hear what Charley was saying and mainly because she was so far away and also because the noise level had gone through the roof.

Charley turned into the room and put her fingers in her mouth and whistled again. The room went silent.

Charley turned back to Aisha, still on one knee.

'I was going to save this for another day. I had it all planned out, rings, a whole special occasion. But you sussed me out, because I'm not good at being subtle. So fuck it, I'm asking you now. Aisha, you, Jude and Otis are my world. I love you so much. Will you marry me?'

The room went wild. Aisha thought her eardrums would burst. She tried to speak but the words were lost in the chaos. But somehow Charley had read her lips and understood that what she was trying to say was yes.

Yes.

Yes.

Yes.

39

MEL

'Oh my God. I can't actually believe that night actually happened, can you?' Mel said to Daz in the taxi. She felt as though she might have drunk all the sparkling wine, all the pina coladas.

'It was a pretty amazing night all round. Charley's proposal was epic.'

'That just shows you how mad life is that she had been preparing all that time for this grand proposal, thinking that was what Aisha needed, because she wanted to make it special and memorable, but actually it was all too much in the end and Aisha will remember that night just as well if not more than whatever Charley had planned.'

'What did she have planned, did you know?'

'Don't have a clue.'

Mel leaned her head back, closed her eyes and sighed.

'Do you remember when I proposed to you?' she heard Daz say after a few moments. She tried to open one eye, but her head was beginning to hurt.

'Of course I do,' she said softly.

Daz took hold of Mel's hand and gripped it.

'I knew then and I know now, you're the woman I want to spend the rest of my life with.' Daz squeezed her hand. 'I felt like the luckiest man on earth, and I never thought for a moment that I was not going to be with you. Despite things that appeared to be obstacles.'

Mel admired the way Daz could say what he meant without needing to go into all the messy details. Leo's name did not grace Daz's lips. 'I got you, Mel. And you got me. I don't need to ever go back to the past, this is us. Here, now.'

Daz was slurring now. He was often a man of very few words and certainly not ones that involved what he referred to as mushy stuff, and he could become heartfelt and usually after a few drinks.

Mel squeezed Daz's hand back and then felt herself nodding off as the gentle bump of the car ride lulled her into a light slumber. The car jolted to a halt and woke her and she sat forward. 'What?' she called out, unsure where she was.

'Home, babe,' Daz mumbled and the two then toppled out of the car and headed into the house.

* * *

'I need to text Aisha, check on her.' Mel held her head in her hands as Daz placed a coffee in front of her the next day. 'I can't lift my phone, everything hurts.'

'I guess that's the result of drinking all the champagne then all the cocktails then insisting Aisha cracked open the spirits behind the bar.'

'It wasn't champagne, Daz.'

'Well, I wouldn't know. I was drinking beer.'

The doorbell rang loudly and Mel held her hands over her ears. 'No, whoever it is, we're not in.'

'It's my mum and dad. We're cooking Sunday lunch, remember.'

Mel sat up and almost spilled her coffee. 'Oh, fuck!'

In the end, it was a group effort, it couldn't have happened any other way. Mel was in no shape to peel potatoes and carrots and baste the chickens. Mike was on gravy duty, occasionally adding juices from the pans, and Irene made sure no one forgot the Yorkshire puddings, even though Mel reminded her that traditionally Yorkshires went with beef.

'So it was a good night then?' Mike asked.

'It was,' Mel said. 'A nice prelude to the soft opening on Thursday.'

'Why do they call it a soft opening?' Daz said, refilling his glass. 'It sounds rather saucy.'

Irene tapped her son on the arm. 'Now we'll have none of that.' Irene looked at Mel. 'This was how he would always get with his brother at the table, even before they were old enough to drink alcohol.'

'Some things never change then.' Mel sat back and sipped her wine. Sky slipped out of her own chair and climbed into her lap. Mel pulled her in, holding her close, sniffing her hair and head.

'You know exactly what it means, Daz.' Irene looked at Mel. 'It's a gentle easing into the opening of the restaurant with a reduced menu, isn't that right, love?'

Mel snorted a laugh. 'Someone's been doing their research.'

'I googled it after you said that was what was happening. I like to keep abreast of what you girls get up to. I think it's wonderful that Aisha has her own restaurant. We will come, won't we, Mike? I'll have to have something mild, though, will she be doing anything mild, or will it all be spicy?' Irene asked.

'It's a mix of British and Jamaican. I'm sure there will be some things that aren't too spicy.'

'Ahh, that's good.' Irene put her knife and fork together neatly on the plate in front of her. 'I do love my food, but I can't take the spice. Mike's the same, aren't you, Mike?'

Mike looked at Mel. 'I wish I could say different, Mel, but you know me, I only have to look at an onion bhaji and I come out in a hot sweat. I like them but they don't like me, I'm afraid.'

Mel squirmed in her seat at that statement. As though Sky could sense she was uncomfortable, she looked up at Mel. Mel kissed her on the lips and Sky smiled and snuggled back into her arms.

After dinner, Mel and Daz insisted they wash up whilst Irene and Mike had some quality time with their grandchildren.

Daz dutifully stacked the dishwasher and Mel washed the pans and wiped the surfaces. Once everything was finished, Daz asked Mel to sit down.

'Okay,' she said suspiciously as she pulled out a chair at the table.

Daz went to his briefcase and took out a bunch of paperwork, which he placed on the table in front of him.

Mel didn't say a word. She let him speak.

'I know I've not been my best self these last few months. The truth is, I am probably having some sort of mid-life crisis. There must be a better word for that by now. Anyway, I have always loved my job, but just recently, I have begun to see accounting for what it is. Boring and predictable. It has been getting me down. I have been keeping it in and not talking about it, which has manifested itself as mood swings and feeling frustrated. I am sorry if that has taken its toll on you, but that's how it is. I'm ready for a new challenge and I just couldn't see what it was I needed to do to make myself happy. Then you told me about Ksenia's predicament and so I got to thinking.'

He pushed the paperwork towards Mel.

'This is a business plan for a cleaning company. All the figures are here...' he pointed to a paragraph in the centre of the page, 'the forecast and overview and on the next page...' he turned the page, 'is a more detailed plan.'

'Oh my God.' Mel's hand shot to her mouth and she felt her face go hot.

'When you told me that Ksenia couldn't afford to keep her baby, I thought of this. Well, I've been thinking for a while of something that I can do that isn't accounting, but still uses my skills as a financial expert and I thought what better than a cleaning company? I would be the CEO and Ksenia would manage it. She can have a team of cleaners that she manages and so when she has her baby, she can take the right amount of time off with maternity pay and then go back to work flexibly, she can work from home, around the baby, however it needs to be.'

Daz scratched the ridge of his nose and continued looking at the paperwork from upside down. Mel was on her feet and around the other side of the table. She threw her arms around him.

'I love you so much, Darren Fortuna.'

40

NINE MONTHS LATER

Sophy

Sophy was over the moon that the weather had held out. The sky had
been blazing blue since she opened her eyes at 5 a.m. She'd heard the
birds tweeting at 3 a.m. when she was awake feeding Fionn. She had
been transported back to the days when she had been awake at that
hour feeding Max and had yet to meet Aisha and Mel, her 3 a.m. gals.
Now she had another son, and he had been here for almost two months,
but it felt like forever. It was racing past at a rate that Sophy was not
familiar with. Everyone told her it was because she was enjoying it. If it
felt like a drag, like it had a little with Max and a lot with Poppy for the
first few dark months, then there was probably something wrong. But
for the first time in a long time, Sophy felt as though everything was
right.

She had Niall, three amazing, beautiful children, gorgeous friends
and now she was about to see one of them wed.

'Ready?' Niall was next to her, where she had chosen a shady spot outside the old factory to give Fionn a massive feed before the ceremony so he would sleep through the whole thing.'

'I think so.' Sophy handed their son to Niall so she could adjust her dress and straighten herself out before they went in.

'Most people are going through now.'

Sophy took Fionn again, and Niall looked crestfallen for a moment – he was besotted with his son. His first biological son, even though he was still an amazing dad to Max, Sophy could feel the pride radiating from him and he wanted to hold Fionn all the time, something he hadn't got to do with Max when he was a tiny baby.

'Sorry,' Sophy said as Niall reluctantly handed him over, she would give him back to him as soon as the service was over so he could show him off to everyone.

Max and Poppy had been playing on a stretch of grass in front of the venue and when Niall called them over they came running.

'Remember, kids, nice and quiet when Aisha and Charley are saying their vows.'

'What are vows?' Max asked. Sophy noted a smudge of grass on his trousers, but she said nothing.

'It's words you say when you promise someone something,' Niall said.

'What will they promise?' Max asked, scrunching his face up. Sophy could hardly believe he was five years old.

'Well, I guess we'll have to wait and see, won't we?'

'So they will tell us now?'

'They will say them to each other in a minute, in the ceremony,' Niall said.

'Which is why we need to be very quiet so we can hear what they are saying to one another.'

'Okay,' Max said then turned to Poppy, who was wearing a bright yellow dress. 'We have to be quiet, Pops, so Aisha and Charley can say their...' Max looked up at Sophy questioningly.

'Vows.' Sophy smiled.

Max nodded and whispered, 'Vows,' to Poppy. Poppy nodded earnestly and the five of them headed into the venue.

* * *

The brides walked down the aisle together with Jon in between them, wearing white dresses. Charley's was lace with long sleeves and off the shoulder, pinched in the middle with a hint of train, her hair was loose and curled. Aisha's was a little sleeker, lace sleeves to the shoulders, the rest of the material was plain white, scooped under the bust and straight down to her feet. Both carried a modest bunch of purple flowers. They both looked lovely.

As the music started up, Niall took Sophy's hand and clutched it. Tears had already sprung to Sophy's eyes and now she had no hands to wipe them away with, her make-up was going to be ruined.

Poppy and Max were standing just in front of Sophy and Niall, leaning on the chairs in front of them, which were reserved for Martina, Jon, the sisters and the cousins. There was no family of Charley's, but the venue was packed with all of Charley's friends, who over the years had become Aisha's friends.

Poppy turned and looked at Sophy and then nudged her brother. Max spun around and began rooting in the pocket of his trousers. He pulled out one singular folded tissue and held it out to Sophy. Sophy slipped her hand out of Niall's and looked up at him. He grinned. Sophy knew that had been a little touch he had prepared earlier, giving Max a special role which he was able to fulfil. She dabbed her eyes, thankful she had been able to save her make-up in time, and watched as the couple reached the front.

Charley had written a jingle and it played out over the speakers and had everyone in tears of laughter and joy. They exchanged some simple vows then kissed. At which point Max turned and looked at Sophy and Niall with a look of amusement and embarrassment.

After signing the marriage documents, the couple then danced back up the aisle to 'I'm Yours' by Jason Mraz.

Everyone gathered outside, where there were buses waiting to take them back to Pom Jam for the wedding breakfast.

'Oh, my goodness, I couldn't stop crying.' Saskia had joined the queue just behind Sophy and Niall. 'That ceremony was something else.

I mean, come on, you don't see weddings like that these days. Nothing like my wedding, anyway, it was all stuffy church and hymns, and Stuart barely kissed me when the vicar said, "You may now kiss the bride." I should have known then that he wasn't in love with me,' Saskia said without a hint of sadness. She had finally been able to open up to Mel about her situation. It turned out that he had left her six months after they moved into that house. Saskia had been on her own for all that time.

It made all three of the women sad and they had begun to include Saskia in their group activities a lot more. It was as though that little lifeline was all she needed, just to know there were three women at the end of a line. They even had their own WhatsApp group.

'How's the internet dating going, Saskia?' Niall asked as the queue moved forward.

She looked at him confidently. 'It's going okay, Niall, thanks for asking. I have swiped left a few times; I think I feel ready to get out there.'

'So you should, you're a lovely-looking lady, any man would be lucky to have you.'

'Aww, thank you, Niall.' Saskia turned her head on an angle at Sophy and mouthed, 'I love him,' as Niall bent down to pick up an already tired Poppy. Sophy laughed, a tired happy exhausted laugh. The world felt a little fuzzy again being a mum to a newborn, as though she were underwater, but things were different this time. She had Niall, and she had the most amazing friends.

41

AISHA

'Are there too many people in here, do you think we crammed too many in?' Aisha was trying to sit down at the top table but kept standing up to look at what was going on in Pom Jam. There were around forty adults and children in total in her restaurant and Aisha had known it would be just right, but now she was here, she was panicking.

'Sit down,' Charley said through a smile. 'We have enough staff here to tend to everyone's needs, please, sit down and enjoy our wedding.'

Aisha sat back down and looked around the buzzing room. Jude and Otis were currently sitting, still snacking on bread and juice with some colouring, but she knew that within the next twenty minutes they would be up and making their way around the venue, entertaining the guests. Although the star of the show, aside from her and Charley, was little Fionn. Aisha thought back to the days when the twins were that small and how hard it had been for her. The dark places she had been to in her head. Sophy had suffered post-natal depression with Poppy but with Fionn she seemed to be thriving. But he was still, as Aisha remembered the phase well, in the fourth trimester. Any week now, he could wake up and realise he wasn't in the womb any more and Aisha was on standby for that. She had already told Sophy to text or call any time of the night and day, and even if she didn't pick it up immediately, she would respond and Sophy would know that she would be there, eventually.

Charley stood up and clinked her glass and everyone settled down.

'Hi, everyone, erm, it seems I like to make a habit of public speaking in this place, let's hope this is the last of the speeches. As you all know, I spend most of my time in a windowless basement writing and recording silly little songs and reading audiobooks, so I am very much out of my comfort zone, and I have not had nearly enough of this stuff yet.' Charley raised her champagne glass. They had been able to fork out for the real stuff on this occasion what with how well Pom Jam had done in the last nine months and the savings they had made by catering the wedding breakfast themselves.

There was a smattering of laughter and Charley waited for it to die down again before she spoke.

'We want you all to relax and have a good time for the next few hours. We have lots of delicious food for you to eat and then we'll push the chairs back and have some dancing.'

There was a collective whoop and then laughter and Aisha spotted Mel and Saskia as the culprits.

'So without further ado, I want to say...' Charley turned to Aisha. 'Thank you for making me happy and for giving us two beautiful boys and for building this life with me. I love you very much.'

Charley raised her glass. 'To Aisha.'

'To Aisha,' the crowd roared, and Jude and Otis flung their hands over their ears.

Charley sat down and Aisha slowly and tentatively stood up.

'I'm not much of a public speaker either...' Aisha began, and the room settled. 'So all I will say is...' Aisha choked up again, for the twentieth time already today. Charley reached up and took her hand.

'You lot are the best. And I love my wife.' She raised her glass and the crowd erupted. 'To Charley!' Aisha screamed.

'To Charley!' the crowd called back.

42

MEL

Ksenia sat down next to Mel at Pom Jam after the wedding breakfast and handed Daz a small bundle. Ivan had been born not long after Fionn and was still a small mewling infant. Ksenia had taken to motherhood so much better than Mel could ever have imagined. She was caring and attentive to her baby boy and Tristan doted on them both.

Daz was taken aback when he received the baby, he and Ksenia had never exactly been close but since the launch of Fortuna Premier Cleaning Services, and becoming a mother, Ksenia seemed a little softer on Daz. What Daz had done setting up the business was nothing short of amazing in Mel's eyes. They had been trading for six months and had already racked up fifteen contracts of all sizes. Ksenia was now on maternity leave but was already eager to return to work and begin her role as operations manager. Daz had told her she needed to hold off and go back when she was ready. Time with baby Ivan was more important and the business wasn't going anywhere. Ksenia was set for life. She would never need to worry about finding clients again. Daz was instrumental in bringing in business, Mel had never seen this side to him before. It was highly attractive and had brought a whole new element to their relationship. She had the hots for her new wheeler-dealer husband who landed massive deals in his home office by day and sent his wife weak at the knees by night. It was exactly what he needed at this stage of his life, to be in charge, which made him feel alive.

'We have question for you and Mel,' Ksenia said as she stroked Ivan's head, letting him know his mummy hadn't gone too far away. Tristan was bending down next to her, grinning at them both.

'We like to ask you to be godparents.'

Mel gasped. 'Oh, my days!' She looked at Daz. 'Daz!' she squealed.

Daz's eyes widened but Mel could see a slight smile forming at the edge of his lips.

'I mean, yes! I'm in!' Mel said and leaned over and kissed Ivan's head.

'Daz?' Ksenia asked.

Daz sucked in a breath. 'Does this mean I'm the godfather?'

Mel laughed. 'Yes, you're the godfather.'

'Then yes, I'm in.'

Suddenly Sophy and Niall were behind them, cooing over baby Ivan, and Mel called, 'Daz is the godfather!' Aisha and Charley, who were just a few tables away, joined them to hear the news.

They all clinked glasses and shouted, 'Cheers!' as the photographer arrived just in time to snap a photo of them all, their glasses raised with huge smiles across their faces.

EPILOGUE
ONE MONTH LATER

3.13 a.m. – Sophy – Hi, girls. Fionn has been awake for a full-on hour now. I could cry if I hadn't been here twice over. And I know you won't see these messages for a few more hours. But here I am, thinking of you both. Remembering when we were doing it together. I miss you all, I miss our 3 a.m. Shattered Mums' Club. It's just me, but I'm so glad I had you both the first time around. I wouldn't have been able to have done it without you. I love you both. X

6.31 a.m. – Aisha – Hey, Soph. The boys decided to wake at the crack of dawn, that's the summer mornings for you. I miss our 3 a.m. chats. You're doing a great job, never forget that. Fionn is so lucky to have you as his mummy. Love you too.

8.45 a.m. – Mel – Let me in on this mush fest. Love you too, Soph. We're always here for you. No matter what time of the day x

ACKNOWLEDGMENTS

Thanks to Boldwood Books for publishing this sequel to *The 3am Shattered Mums' Club*. Writing Aisha, Mel and Sophy has been so much fun and I have loved bringing them back after four fictional years.

Thank you Sarah Bennett for all of your cruise knowledge!

Thanks to Emily Ruston for all your advice on the edits on this one. I couldn't have done it without you, again!

Writing this book has posed a few challenges as I have been writing a thriller at the same time and as a family we have made a huge move to Scotland. It's been a blast so far and I cannot wait to get cracking, plotting my next book now I am here and settled.

Thanks to all you readers for your love, support and messages.

A huge thank you to my three children for giving me all the fodder to be able create the little world that these three mums inhabit.

ABOUT THE AUTHOR

Nina Manning studied psychology and was a restaurant-owner and private chef (including to members of the royal family). She is the founder and co-host of Sniffing The Pages, a book review podcast.

Sign up to Nina Manning's mailing list here for news, competitions and updates on future books.

Visit Nina's website: https://www.ninamanningauthor.com/

Follow Nina on social media:

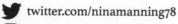 twitter.com/ninamanning78

instagram.com/ninamanning_author

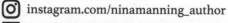 facebook.com/ninamanningauthor1

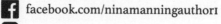 bookbub.com/authors/nina-manning

ALSO BY NINA MANNING

Women's Fiction

The 3am Shattered Mums' Club

The 6pm Frazzled Mums' Club

Psychological Thrillers

The Daughter In Law

The Guilty Wife

The House Mate

The Bridesmaid

Queen Bee

The Waitress

The Beach House

Boldwood

Boldwood Books is an award-winning fiction publishing company seeking out the best stories from around the world.

Find out more at www.boldwoodbooks.com

Join our reader community for brilliant books, competitions and offers!

Follow us
@BoldwoodBooks
@TheBoldBookClub

Sign up to our weekly
deals newsletter

https://bit.ly/BoldwoodBNewsletter

Milton Keynes UK
Ingram Content Group UK Ltd.
UKHW041548300923
429668UK00002B/19